"A writer of immense gifts, with a voice—s
unsparing—unlike anyone else's. *Sugarless* is a cold-eyed accounting that
refuses to blame, and an act of deep forgiveness that refuses to forget anything—an important, funny, heartbreaking, and beautiful book."
—TONY KUSHNER

"*Sugarless* is a boy's life. It is the rough chutes and ladders of adolescence
against a realistic and hilarious evocation of the 70s and if you ever wondered what makes boys tick, or you've been in danger of forgetting,
Sugarless—compassionate, funny, wrenching and real—is the book you've
been looking for."   —AMY BLOOM, AUTHOR OF *LUCKY US*

"*Sugarless*, James Magruder's juicy, fruity new novel, combines the heady
flavor of adolescent hormones with original cast albums and high school
speech competitions. The result is a tart rite of passage into gay adulthood
that's not at all saccharine but packs a surprising emotional punch...The
astringent ending of Magruder's impressive and highly entertaining first
novel leaves us eager for his next work of fiction."
—JOHN DENNIS ANDERSON, *GAY AND LESBIAN REVIEW*

"This fascinating coming-of-age story...may be about a homosexual relationship in the 1970s, [but] the story captures the struggles of teenagers,
straight and gay, of every generation."   —*PUBLISHERS WEEKLY*

"Magruder's best feat here, though, is the way he steers these characters
through decisions reactionary and ill-fated without ever passing judgment
on them. Richard occasionally passes judgment on people, but it's the
impudent, churlish action of a teenage boy who is rapidly losing his place
in a house that no longer feels like home, if it ever did. And in that hu-
manity, he makes lanky, awkward Richard Lahrem—Stephen Sondheim
fan, wearer of bikini underwear with brightly colored piping, *speech club*
team member—into an accessibly familiar American teenager, trapped
between being his parents' son and being himself."
—BRET MCCABE, *BALTIMORE CITY PAPER*

"Rarely have I read a coming-of-age story as compelling as *Sugarless*.... It carries all the angst of *Catcher in the Rye* without feeling forced.... Magruder has created what I believe will become a classic of gay literature."
—WARD HOLZ, AUTHOR OF *OUR LIVES*

"Teens who come across it will of course find its coming-of-age, coming-out storyline enormously supportive, particularly if they're contending with parents prone to a fervent belief in the power of Jesus. But this is a grown-up read, focusing as much on young Rick's boorish stepfather and hapless mother as on the travails of the sexually questioning—and desperately horny—youngster." —RICHARD LABONTÉ, *BOOK MARKS*

PRAISE FOR *LET ME SEE IT* (2014)

"In this witty, elegiac collection of linked stories, Magruder (*Sugarless*) traces the paths of two gay cousins, Tom Amelio and Elliott Biddler, as they grow up in the Midwest and eventually become wised-up, crisis-addled adults. Spanning 1971 to 1992, and set in cities ranging from Madison, Wis., to Paris, the collection captures a critical chapter in gay history."
—*PUBLISHERS WEEKLY (STARRED REVIEW)*

"Be prepared to laugh out loud and get misty-eyed. Magruder has written that rare, wonderful beast: a comic gem with an emotional punch."
—BOB SMITH, AUTHOR OF *REMEMBRANCE OF THINGS I FORGOT*

"Each entry is a world unto itself, told variously in third and first person and offering deeper insight into a disjointed family whose whole saga remains a mystery to the final pages. *Let Me See It* offers a vivid snapshot of love and loss during the initial AIDS era, as well as its overlooked legacy today." —*AUSTIN CHRONICLE*

"Much of the poignant beauty of Magruder's book hinges on the very different ways the two young men confront their sexuality and the crises and consequences that await them in adulthood.... Elliott Biddler's 1980s are almost unbearably harrowing for reflecting the blitheness with which so many entered into a decade that would snuff out those lights that burned brightest for beauty and for love. And Tom's devotion to him reminds us of how family (chosen, un-chosen, or both) can sustain us through our worst sufferings." —*Lambda Literary*

"By turns comic and melancholy in tone yet always razor-sharp in its insights." —*Kirkus*

"*Let Me See It* is psychologically rich, erotic, disturbing, subversive, irreverent, and witty as hell." —Gina Frangello, author of *A Life in Men*

"I loved being in the grasp of stories so alight with lust and danger and longing and loss, just as I loved Elliott and Tom—two remarkably complex and empathetic protagonists. From the first page, I fell headlong into their world and by the last, I was so very sad to leave it." —Laura van den Berg, author of *Find Me*

"There are few authors who write with as much sensitivity and tenderness as James Magruder; he has a way of finding something beautiful in the most heartbreaking moments. Like the fate of the model of the Great Pyramid of Tenochtitlan, made out of sugar cubes, which appears in the opening chapter, you fear the characters' lives will be swept away by some great unhappiness, but you cannot help but marvel at the gleaming beauty of the moments that lead you to it. With sharp touches of humor, this is a marvel of a story." —Kevin Wilson, author of *The Family Fang*

Also by James Magruder

FICTION

Sugarless
Let Me See It
Worth Our Breath (a chapbook)

THEATER

Three French Comedies

Love Slaves of Helen Hadley Hall

JAMES MAGRUDER

Queen's Ferry Press
8622 Naomi Street
Plano, TX 75024
www.queensferrypress.com

Published 2016 by Queen's Ferry Press

Cover art and design by Lori Larusso

Interior design by Steven Seighman

First edition May 2016

ISBN 978-1-938466-91-5

Printed in the United States of America

for David Nolta,
the boy in 332,
then
now
and always

PART ONE

Rugburns

"O, nothing is more alluring than a levee from a couch in some confusion: it shows the foot to advantage, and furnishes with blushes, and recomposing airs beyond comparison."

—LADY WISHFORT

Chapter One

Yale University, that robust institution of the Nutmeg State, maintains two residence halls for its graduate students, a caste within the greater academic community that ranks above food service staff and below faculty nephews. The first, completed in 1932, is the Hall of Graduate Studies, a Gothic Revival edifice replete with interior courts, vaulted ceilings, loggias, a clock tower, witty gargoyles, and its own dining hall; HGS for short, the building closely resembles some of the fabled colleges that shelter the apex of the Yale pyramid, the undergraduates.

Several blocks east of HGS, at 420 Temple Street, stands Helen Hadley Hall, a somewhat different entertainment. Yale College did not admit undergraduate women until 1970; Hadley opened in 1958 as a residence for female graduate students resisting the reproductive imperatives of the Eisenhower Era. A five-story, pink-bricked, tar-topped rectangle bordered by a cement wall, Helen Hadley Hall expresses in its architecture the then-prevalent conviction that women of scholarship are a source of contagion.

Who the real Helen Hadley had been was of little concern to those I gathered within my skirts, but my full portrait in oils in the first-floor lounge did incite occasional acts of speculation. Socialite? Bluestocking? Gertrude Stein's first wife? My material legacy, a dozen Sèvres plates depicting shepherdesses with crooks and lambs, was locked in a vitrine standing next to my portrait. The key to this cabinet was as lost as the riddle of my identity. The "Hadley China" was all that remained of a broken engagement in my youth. Though not a multimillion-dollar endowment such as many of the undergraduate colleges enjoy, the plates are nonetheless a graceful touch in this otherwise cheerless vault that bears my name. I admit to a flutter of vanity when every once in a while, a great while, a resident pauses to ponder their porcelain luster through the dusty glass.

The layout of Helen Hadley Hall was none of my doing. Each floor contains thirty-six cubicles. Each cubicle is equipped with a wooden desk and chair, a twin bed, a freestanding metal bookcase, a built-in dresser with a mirrored medicine cabinet, a leatherette easy chair, and a closet. The variable in the room is the student, who might be anyone from anywhere studying anything at all. Each floor has a kitchen with two refrigerators and a dining pen, a phone booth, and two gender-specific bathrooms. On the first floor, in addition to the common lounge and the TV room, there is a coin-operated laundry, a piano, a foosball table, and three vending machines. In the late seventies, a computer room with two mainframes and a printer replaced a row of overhead hair dryers original to the building. Facing the front desk, which is generally manned by foreign students practicing their diphthongs, is a dovecote of mailboxes.

Cultural tensions, if they surface, center around the kitchens and their uses. It is no one's business, really, that the Chinese leave viands to ripen on the counters. Or that Australians aren't vigilant about cleaning up after themselves. Or that Southerners borrow staples. By the end of every month, the Hadley refrigerators are a goulash of odd tubers, strange cuts of meat, weepy fruits, and dairy cartons heavy with curds. The cooking oil spills pooling on the cabinet shelves are as attractive to roaches as the unsecured bags of rice are to rodents. Little wonder then that the campus exterminators, on scheduled visits with their traps and mists, refer to 420 Temple Street as "Smellin' Badly Hall." I take no personal offense. Strong smells mean strong living.

I was born in 1895, and I passed from solid to vapor in 1951. You might imagine that a human organism whose spirit began before the flight at Kitty Hawk to have seen and heard it all. To that I counter that Love and its many permutations still quickens my blood. The emotion keeps me, if not young certainly, then passably evergreen. The earliest Hadley years, what I call the bebop and petting-party years, were placid, yes, but a tremendous shift occurred after the launch of Professor Djerassi's contraceptive pill in 1960. Thirteen years later, Roe v. Wade provided a way out for a traditional breeding crisis; Yale and Hadley Hall had gone coed; President Nixon had breached the Great Wall of China; foreigners began matriculating in increasing numbers; and gays and lesbians—what my Suffragette circle at Oberlin termed "nethersexers" in 1912—began conducting their attractions more openly.

Every September a fresh batch of residents arrives at 420 Temple Street. Every year I select my favorites, follow their adventures, cheer on their shifts and stratagems, and pick up their lingo. When it comes to love, there is nothing new under the sun, yet I find it equally true that—and here I borrow the title of a song popular during my salad days—"Every Little Movement Has a Meaning All Its Own." Based upon my decades of observation, I find that getting some is one thing. Getting there is even better.

Today, some fifteen years into the third millennium, Yale threatens to bulldoze my home, and this is why I write. Before I see my Sèvres shepherdesses stacked on the sale table at the New Haven Historical Society and my portrait consigned to a climate-controlled basement in the British Art Center, I have decided to chronicle my favorite year. This would be the nine months in 1983–84 during which Silas Huth, Becky Engelking, Nixie Bolger, Carolann Chudek, and Randall Flinn took up the manacles of erotic attachment and parsed meaning from every little movement of their rapacious, beating hearts. Theirs is a communal tale of love surprised, love confessed, betrayed, renounced, repelled, of suspect leanings and trembling declarations, of hymens under siege and innumerable searching looks in the mirror.

I trained as a chemist, not as an author of creative nonfiction, but I can promise you carnal congress, a near-homicide, and a wedding finale. If things at first seem thick on the ground, or overly populated in my laboratory, I pray that a higher power grant you patience, or that your upbringing prepared you to listen to a maiden aunt holding forth in the side parlor before a holiday feast. If neither applies to you, then my advice is to hold fast to Silas Huth, who as our tale begins, on a muggy Friday night in the middle of September 1983, is in Room 303 tucking a white button-down Oxford shirt into a pair of his scantiest cutoff shorts, a mixed fashion message quite in keeping with his character.

The first facts about Silas Huth lent him instant appeal for me. He had been left as a foundling in the baptistery of the Mission San Xaiver del Bac, south of Tucson. The state of Arizona named him for reasons lost to time. His powerful bond with Nancy "Nana" Eagle Eye, his final foster parent, convinced Silas that his birth mother had also been a Yaqui, when she might just as easily have been Pueblo, Navajo, Cajun, Mexican, Maltese, Sicilian, Polynesian, or a mongrel mix. No one could prove that Silas wasn't Native American. He checked that box when it suited him, or when it paid. In 1983 the Yale French Department was paying him very well indeed, fellowship plus stipend.

Silas was a slender man of twenty-two, with green eyes, sharp planes in his face, a cleft chin, skin the color of mustard seed, and glossy black hair cropped short. An underdog by any American standard, he had nonetheless grown up as spoiled as a dauphin or pasha. Every trailer in Fruitland Acres had been open to the smart aleck who checked volumes of *The World Book Encyclopedia* out of the bookmobile and read them end to end. Women especially could refuse him nothing—trinkets, quarters, jujubes, nips of whiskey. A neighbor, Cécile Tanner, who had married an American liberator in 1944, began teaching him French when he was nine. Five years later, when presented with his astronomical test scores, the Jesuits at Brophy College Prep in Phoenix airlifted him out of the trailer park and his real education began. After Brophy, he received a four-year scholarship to Arizona State University, where he finished fifth in a class of six thousand and twelve.

"Whoever gets Silas gets the prize," ran the close of one of his Yale recommendation letters. He had slept with this professor, and other junior faculty, and the Dean of Student Life, but it was his ability to tweeze apart Symbolist poems and absorb vast quantities of literary theory that astounded mentors of both genders and sent him to Connecticut.

He traced an arrow of Dior's *Eau Sauvage* behind each earlobe, then lengthened his face in the mirror, one of his dependable come-hither looks. Silas was arrogant about his appearance and his intelligence, but insecure about the rest. This was *Yale* after all. In some lights (as well as in his own worst moments) he might be classified as half-breed trailer trash. He was whip-smart, strategically sincere, a brilliant reader of text, and most to the point this September night, he hadn't had sex, a fail-safe remedy for his seesawing ego, in fourteen days, practically a record.

Just before ten, Silas paused on the first floor of the dorm to check his hair in the window and scoff at the hoopla in the lounge. His enemy,

Peter Facciafinta, a lithe charmer who supervised the dorm desk staff, was hosting a "Climb Ev'ry Mountain" sing-off. Dressed in a habit and wimple, Peter was presently spinning an enormous wooden rosary around his waist for a clutch of dazzled Koreans.

Silas strong-armed the outer glass door and went into the night. The air was thick with the smell of blown tiger lilies and the echoing calls of tipsy undergraduates. As he threaded his way through the Georgian quadrangles, the fringe of his cutoffs tickling his thighs, Silas fumed anew at the thought of how Scott Jencks, the blue-eyed Princeton paragon, should belong to *him* and not to Peter Facciafinta. He and Scott were in the same department. They both claimed to understand the writings of Jacques Derrida. They were nearly the same height.

Before flying to Connecticut, Silas had paid a visit to Nana Eagle Eye. Over a bottle of Old Times, he promised to go straight in graduate school—well, not straight, more like *clean*; he would study hard but he would also stop being a heedless slut and use his head to find, have, hold, and love one very smart, very WASPy, man. The father he had never had, or would ever know, but age-appropriate. A butch, moneyed Pilgrim named Archibald or Pearce or Schuyler.

Once he had settled into Room 303, Silas chose not to cruise the campus; undergrads were off-mission. Given the late-summer humidity, the uncloseted Hadley men eyed one another listlessly, but none came close to matching Silas's criteria until Registration Day, when he was browsing the French section of the Yale Co-Op.

Shelves of books had stimulated him since childhood days inside the Fruitland Acres bookmobile. Wishing to share his delight in a superbly annotated *Chanson de Roland*, Silas turned and suddenly faced a man with blond, wavy hair and cornflower eyes. A patrician beak. A protagonist's jaw. A tufted throat. Pectorals pushing against the combed cotton of a lime-colored polo. A finely muscled forearm leading to a thick wrist leading to a Princeton ring and two fingers pinching a copy of Stendhal's treatise *On Love*.

Yale has been the queerest of the Ivies since the Louisiana Purchase, so there was no need for subterfuge. The young men understood one another perfectly, and then—kismet! Not only was this Scott Jencks with the bit-able fingers starting his first year in the French Department, he too lived at Hadley, on the second floor, in room 204. Silas was way past smitten when out of the blue Scott apologized for acting spacey.

"Spacey?" said Silas.

"It's just that I met a guy last night, at Partners. We had sex for eight hours straight. It was like jumping off a cliff, and I still haven't hit bottom."

Silas's lips formed a reply, but were they syllables?

"What's most incredible is that he works at the front desk of the dorm. You must have seen him, a hot little Italian thing."

"Peter?"

"Peter. Peter Facciafinta," said Scott, moaning out the vowels.

Bested by Dago town trash! Within a week, Peter was living in Scott's room and had begun tending the desk in pajama bottoms and a Princeton T-shirt, leaving Silas to believe, with tears before the mirror, that he had lost Scott Jencks to Peter Facciafinta by one day. And so it came to be that, after another week of unthinkable celibacy, Silas skipped the Hadley sing-off to try his own luck at Partners.

In the early eighties, Yale was Out and Proud, but New Haven's home-grown nethersexers were, I regret to say, Still a Little Ashamed. Partners Café, at the corner of Park and High Streets, drooped accordingly. Outside, the club was surrounded by scabby triple-deckers with trash nests under the stoops and spent bottles in the tree boxes. Inside it was a template of the times, starting with the Betty Boop hand stamp and the two-dollar cover, continuing with the faux-Tiffany lamps over the bar, the glass brick windows, the Broadway partisans yodeling Jerry Herman around a piano below, Donna Summers and Blondie caterwauling above, and everywhere a tangy miasma of smoke, desire, sweat, poppers, and urinal pucks.

Upstairs, men in gold jewelry and Cuban heels were lined up around the dance floor. In this sea of acetate and terry cloth, Silas's all-cotton shirt gleamed like the flag of a yacht, but he could find no kissing cousins of Scott Jencks. He slipped into the back row and watched the dancers gyrate under the mirrored disco ball. Before he knew it, a man had approached him and was holding out a glass.

"Rum and Cokes are two-for-one."

Silas accepted the drink.

"Bombs away. I'm Luca Lucchese."

A townie. Silas bent stiffly from the waist. "A pleasure to meet you, Luca."

Luca smiled, and Silas felt a flutter in his stomach. Then Luca turned to set his drink on the rail. A first glimpse of his meaty hindquarters made Silas gulp half his cocktail. Here was the most callipygous stud Silas had ever met. "Callipygous" and its variant "callipygian" are Classical Greek for "bootylicious." (As I hinted earlier, I cover the waterfront, lexically speaking.)

"What do you do?" asked Silas, absolutely not caring what Luca did.

"Odd and ends."

"Where did you go to school?"

Luca's shrug was so surly that Silas felt weak at the knees. "I started a business degree, but lost interest," he said. "Things sort of…*sprang up*, if you know what I mean."

"I do know," said Silas, shifting a leg to give breathing room to his penis. He held out his hand. "I'm Silas Huth. I go to Yale."

"You sure had me fooled," said Luca, with another grin.

For the time being, we shall leave this town-gown encounter and return to the dorm. In cinema, this is known as a crosscut. I promise not to overuse the technique.

In Room 315, Becky Engelking, a trained soprano and former pitch pipe for the Iowa State Swingletuners, couldn't decide how casual to dress for the sing-off. The posters said "Come As You Are"—scant help, really, since Becky had left Ottumwa to become someone else. She asked her mirror, "With barrettes, or without?"

No one at Yale had heard Becky's way with a song, but there was evidence that her vocalese had already brightened dorm life. "You make life better with your trills. I hear you through the wall and am happy, yes." That nice Indian girl next door—Indian Indian, not American Indian, like that Silas person down the hall—had said that to Becky only the day before. She had been filling a row of plastic cups with a steaming pea mash while Becky cut up frankfurters into her mac and cheese, and they had gotten to talking. Of course a foreigner needed to put her better foot forward, but Becky, who was all for international exchange, wouldn't dream of being standoffish with this lively nut-brown maiden.

"And what is it that you are studying, Lakmé?" she had carefully enunciated.

"Lakshmi. Lakshmi Dawat."

"What a unique name."

"I am reading Blake."

"That's so interesting, Lakshmi. Blake was a poet, right?"

"He was, yes."

"'Stopping by Woods on a Snowy Evening' is my favorite poem. Have you ever seen snow, Lakshmi?"

"I was a fellow at Oxford University for two years."

"Well, isn't that wonderful! India and England. I love to travel myself," said Becky, who had first crossed the Mississippi only three weeks ago. "Trains, planes, boats, doesn't matter. California, here I come!"

After another flattering pout in the mirror, Becky decided against the barrettes. Better to go caszh. She tucked a lace handkerchief into the heart-shaped cleft of her sateen bodice and went over her text. Truth to tell, she would have preferred to compete with a more operatic selection than "Climb Ev'ry Mountain." The Yale School of Music was her big chance, and Becky, bent on wiping every trace of the family farm from her patent leathers, was saving herself for Donizetti. But now what about her pumps? Surely her appearance could support the glitter of rhinestone clips. They brought her luck, but no, she mustn't appear too grand at her New England début. Let *la voce* speak for her, and tell all that it knew. She ran a brush through her corn-silk curls, humming, *"a dream that will need all the love you can give—"*

The key change touched something inside. Becky swiftly pulled her lingerie bag from the back of a dresser drawer and drew out two sparkling crescents. She would jewel her feet for luck, and for Brent Fladmo.

It was Brent Fladmo who had talked her into entering the sing-off. He was an organist—from Iowa too!—and already he was saying nice things. On a recent stroll on the town green, the talk flowed, and when the white spire of the First Congregational Church drew them to a bench for contemplation, Brent said that he had always yearned to play Bach in just such a house of God. The steeple bell chose to toll the hour at that moment, giving Becky, who was full-gospel Baptist, a thrill not completely divine. Later, a wino passed a remark, and Brent drew his arm through hers to shield her from scandal. He was a gentleman and, she had to admit, a cutie.

It was time to go. Before turning out the light, Becky arranged a gauze capelet around her firm, pink shoulders and checked the mirror for any trace of dinner in her smile.

Downstairs, piano chords and laughter eclipsed the pleasing sound of her swishing taffeta skirts. She paused at the portal to the lounge and, with an endearing sense of occasion, nodded to my portrait, as if to thank me for inviting her to the ball. Then she stepped forward into the light.

There was no mistaking one of her competitors. Becky found Peter Facciafinta's habit and wimple an instant affront to Julie Andrews and the remaining von Trapps, who were said to be in Vermont. Come as you are indeed! No one would appreciate her purity of tone with this kind of showboating going on. Looking around, Becky didn't recognize anyone besides Brent Fladmo, and goodness, was he intending to accompany her in shorts? His legs were whiter than she had permitted herself to imagine in her nighttime reveries, but this she pushed from her mind. Come to think of it, *who* were the judges and were they even *musical*? She turned to flee, but it was too late.

"Becky!" squealed Peter. "You look like Beverly Sills at dress rehearsal. All you need is a pocketbook."

All right, thought Becky, love the sinner, hate the sin, you couldn't be a Swingletuner without knowing some picklebiters. She drew a finger to her dimple and smiled like an Iowa sunrise. "And you, Peter," she replied. "You look like—like—like—a hotdogging cornholer! All you need is some mustard."

No one who heard could make sense of her retort, including Becky.

Nearby, behind a card table fronting the fireplace, a tall woman with chestnut hair was pouring wine and spreading crackers with pimento cheese. This was love slave number three, Ms. Nixie Bolger, in her own words a Kentucky-born straight shooter who took her bourbon neat.

Twenty-five, with a master's degree from the University of Toulouse, where she had studied Voltaire's correspondence, Nixie was already queen of the third floor, because, clearly, she had Lived. Her room was strewn with articles of experience: unguents in glass jars, a set of silver julep cups, a bottle of crème de cassis, Spanish toothpaste, and a taupe carousel of birth control pills. No one held such glamour against her. Since Nixie served spirits and potted meats along with rib-sticking portions of her life story every afternoon at four-thirty, it didn't matter that she had a full-length coyote coat in her closet and a Greek lover across the Atlantic.

Even the teetotalers knew that Nixie had left Stavrolakis Heliotis sobbing in a train station on August 6th, the Feast of St. Clare. Everyone had passed around the snapshots of their *vie de bohème*: the inverted triangle of Stavi's torso tapering into a mesh bikini, his mane of raven ringlets, the buckets of mussels they'd shucked and savored in the sun, their motorcycle rides to Marseilles. For those who had never been to Europe, an afternoon in Nixie's orbit was The Grand Tour in one woozy package deal.

Once she was asked about the bad times. Nixie's outsized hazel eyes narrowed as she pulled hard on a Gauloise. "Well," she replied in that thrillingly forceful way she had, "Stavi's feet stunk so bad I had to lower his socks out the window in a pail every night." For some in Nixie's new circle, Stavi's socks were the most intimate romantic detail they had ever heard. Others thought they provided too much local color and would rather she didn't mention them again. (Nixie had a tendency to repeat.)

Tonight Louisville's bourbon-neat straight shooter was keeping her own counsel. The previous weekend she'd gone to the Price Chopper with some floormates. Nixie was aware that a man named Walt Stehlik was in the back of the station wagon. But she wasn't *aware* of him until, turning around in aisle three, she caught him dropping a box of Pampers into her shopping cart. It was all in fun, but when their laughter trailed away, he had held her gaze with a pleading expression.

For six days she thought of little else. She lured new neighbors to her booze hours, but no one knew the first thing about Walt Stehlik. Wednesday morning she had caught the back of him, six-feet-four of sleepy maleness with richly knotted calves, heading into the men's bathroom. Suppressing an impulse to tail him into the shower, Nixie had one of her *determinations* right then and there: one day she would call him Burly. That would be her pet name for him, to whisper in the night, and then in the morning, over pancakes.

Nixie would have come to the sing-off in any case, with a sleeve of Saltines and a jug of four-dollar red, that was her way, but while Brent Fladmo warmed up the crowd with a Rodgers and Hammerstein medley, she was praying, with the fervor of the situational Catholic, for Burly Stehlik to show up and strafe her again with that bone-melting look in his eyes.

She felt a tap on her shoulder.

"That's a cute dress, Nixie," said Becky Engelking.

"Thanks. I love your cape. Some wine?"

"Gracious no," said Becky, patting her throat. "*La voce.*"

The lights flickered, and Brent Fladmo segued into a rollicking "Lonely Goatherd." At three minutes to curtain, Walt Stehlik strode up to Nixie's refreshment stand and downed a cup of wine for courage. Resisting the impulse to pluck the pencil from his mop of auburn hair, Nixie offered more wine. "To celebrate your victory," she said, forgetting the touchy soprano standing beside her.

"Could be," he said with a smile. "Now—it's Nixie, isn't it?—I have to warm up."

Walt Stehlik remembered her name. Nixie took a hit straight from the jug, then remembered to thank God *and* St. Cecilia for answering her prayers.

On a whistle from Peter Facciafinta, the sing-off began.

Back at Partners Café, the din was louder now, the dancing more abandoned, the bathroom cloudy with cocaine and related revelry, and the elbows and knees of Silas Huth and Luca Lucchese were making intentional contact.

Every college town has a stock of Luca Luccheses: cunning, dark-eyed pistols, good with their hands, and up for anything. Eventually all the improvising and angle-playing wears them out and they settle into union jobs and fertile wives, but until then, watch out. Luca Lucchese, twenty-eight years old at the time of our narrative, was at his peak of insolence and availability.

"What are you?" Luca asked Silas apropos of nothing.

The question had many answers. "What am I what?"

"What is your heritage?"

"I'm half Yaqui, probably," said Silas. "The other half I don't know. I'm a mongrel. A mongrel Native American foundling boy."

Luca, generous with his smiles, asked whether Silas ever wondered which parent had given him his gorgeous green eyes. All Silas knew in that moment was that an explosion was imminent. Luca knew it too and detached Silas from the wall. They took the stairs two at a time. Out on High Street Luca stopped, drew Silas to him by the nape of his neck, and said, "All I want is for someone to sit and watch TV with. And lots of amazing sex."

"I don't have a TV," Silas stammered.

"We'll buy one."

A choir of angels singing "*We'll*" circled Silas's heart and flew into the stars. Getting into Luca's panel truck, he forgot all about his promise to Nana Eagle Eye. He didn't need a Scott Jencks. He needed what Scott had, a townie goombah to call his own.

Inside Yale territory, as they drove past the green-shuttered colleges, Luca pulled Silas's hand to his face and began sucking his fingers. Such tenderness from Luca, whom Silas expected to be a rutter, made him nearly cream his shorts. Finger baths and the like were, he felt, his special talent, instilled and refined in him by certain priests, lay brothers, and coaches at Brophy Prep.

You might wonder here at my position on the sexual exploitation of minors. Trust that I find it the worst crime in the calendar. And yet, while "sexual" means what it says, "exploitation" is a term with linguistic slip-page and the word "minor" is a legal abstraction. My cousin Olivia was sent off at fourteen to a man twice her age, and the marriage was long and happy. My cousin Hetty wasn't so lucky. I should be the first to help dig a mass grave for pedophile priests and child pornographers, but I am also a woman who has observed over time how twelve differs from fifteen. Silas Huth, who had needed a leg up, began at fifteen. By the time he reached Arizona State, his Jesuit training—sex conducted as a prolonged and sensitive piece of music—was part and parcel of what made him "the prize." Silas would take twenty minutes to remove a shortstop's jockstrap with his teeth, or a professor's boxers, if he thought it would work to his advantage, and what was sex for, except as a place where men might stop time in tandem?

He and Luca enjoyed nearly an hour of chamber sex in his room, languid yet capable of combustive measures, before Luca was released from his briefs. An unseen oboe held a count of eight as Maestro Huth dealt with a surprise in *m* major, *m* as in *massive.*

Where was that thing going to fit?

Silas vamped with his hands as he reread the signs. Luca was shorter than Silas, with average extremities, regular ears, and no perceptible Adam's apple. But wait, of course, the back end of things, the callipygian coronet, the poetic pistons, the *culo magnifico,* the giant scoops of vanilla spumoni—in cultivating the aft, Silas had neglected the fore and forgot that you can't drive in a spike with a tack hammer.

Luca whispered that it was okay if he didn't climax. The moment Silas realized that he pitied Luca—an eel that size was too big to envy—was the moment he got busy. With pity came tenderness. With tenderness came eventual intercrural release. Undoing a man was like breaking the code of a poem.

Later, draped against Silas's flank, Luca murmured, "Read me something, baby."

Silas, drowsy and rosy with a job well done, was confused by this call for additional stimulation. "Read you what?"

"Read me something you're reading." Luca's breath tickled the fringe of hair around Silas's left nipple. "Read me something *French.*"

And the angels sang again. From where he lay, Silas could just reach the Baudelaire on his desk. His heart swelling against the weight of his horse-hung wiseguy, he began to read aloud by the knife of light slanting from a streetlamp through the side of his window shade.

Now, before every lamp at Helen Hadley is extinguished, let me place a final period on that far-off Friday night. Becky Engelking won the sing-off in a rowdy voice vote that failed to satisfy. She would have preferred a panel of judges, and if not a gold cup for her efforts, then a silver medal or a bronze plaque. Nor did it escape her notice that Brent Fladmo had clapped hardest for Walt Stehlik, despite Walt's crack on the final F-sharp.

Chapter Two

Rhinestone shoe clips? Pancake breakfasts? Bitable fingers? Should not these highly developed minds have hewed to higher promptings than the mossy maneuvers of paperback romance?

Recall their youth, and despite all efforts at camouflage, their lack of sophistication. The tenants in my cinderblock settlement house weren't Daughters of the American Revolution or Sons of Cincinnatus, the trust-fund Muffys, Tuffys, Taylors, and Treys. 420 Temple Street took in the great-great grandchildren of the men and women who had flooded Ellis Island and Locust Point, Maryland, before going off to break the plains and fire up the factories.

I shall now risk eye-rolling on your part when I aver that, yes, life was simpler then. Do hear me out. Thirty-some years ago, beneath the shoulder pads of The Great Communicator and his crystal-gazing, gargantuan-headed First Lady, there were no personal computers or cell phones or cash machines in Connecticut, which meant that the money one withdrew before the banks closed on Friday had to last all the way to Monday. There was no Internet, only the card catalogue and the Yellow Pages. The Soviet Union was into its fourth decade as global bugbear. A mysterious disease had begun destroying the immune systems of urban male homosexuals, but had not yet been identified as a virus. Quiche had peaked, fresh pasta had begun its ascent, and in this world before the West discovered sushi, the seas were filled with fish.

Before paging and texting and Tweeting and whatever gerund of communicaton is next in store for us, there existed an agony called waiting by the phone. The drama of it—the calories consumed, the tears expelled, the hygiene delayed, the distracted vacuuming, the bargains struck with God and Lucifer—was considerable. I refer disbelievers to Vikki Carr's "It Must Be Him." Those with more patience might read Dorothy Parker's "A Telephone Call."

In 1983, Nixie Bolger and Silas Huth were among the few Hadleyites with private phone lines. Everyone else pitched their ears for a ring in the floor booths next to the elevator, or relied on messages taken by the desk staff. I have digressed to this extent because Luca Lucchese had "left" his black jean jacket in Silas's room on Saturday morning, a positive sign that had become a positive catastrophe by Tuesday afternoon. Silas Huth wasn't someone you didn't call, but there he sat, obsessively checking for a dial tone and wondering whether a white panel truck might have crashed on the Merritt Parkway.

Around five, Silas went down for his mail. A message slip in his pigeonhole made his heart race, but it was from UPS, not Ma Bell. Nana Eagle Eye had sent a care package. Silas rarely wept, but the dusty bag of candy corn, the pack of athletic socks, and the tin of crushed oatmeal cookies that he unwrapped in his room made his eyes sting. The tears threatened to fall outright when he found a rumpled five-dollar bill inside a repurposed valentine. Too old now to take in more children, Nana lived on next to nothing a year.

Dry it up, he thought. For starters, you hate candy corn. He wrote Nana an upbeat reply and enclosed a check for sixty dollars. One day he would have a full stationery wardrobe, MA, MPhil, PhD trailing his name, and he would get Nana out of Fruitland Acres and into a house with insulation. And a *color* television, *with* remote.

 Silas left his room to rustle up a stamp, bringing the candy corn as wampum. A young man with a narrow, freckled face and a strong nose sat alone at a table in the dining pen, a volume of Tennyson on a tilt between his water glass and soup bowl. Silas sighed. In his experience, the odds of a man having a stamp on his person were next to nil. But this was Randall Flinn, a history of art student who wrote one of his siblings every day of the week.

"Excuse me."

Randall looked up. Silas couldn't see his eyes through the glare cast on his spectacles.

"Do you have an extra postage stamp I could have?"

"Brooklyn Bridge or Martin Luther?"

"Excuse me?"

Randall took out a wallet bulging with Mass cards and scraps of paper. "I have both."

"You're shitting me."

Randall winced at the vulgarity, then fished out three Brooklyn Bridges and five Martin Luthers. He accepted candy corn in lieu of the twenty cents, and the young men got to talking.

And that is how Silas Huth, prodigy of competition and copulation, first ran up against Randall Flinn, prodigy of art and faith. Their friendship will evolve and complicate, but their initial dynamic was Silas doing his best to shock Randall and Randall doing his best to appear unshocked. Their first conversation in the over-bright dining pen was a performative magpie vaunt through Ophuls and Altman, and Vatican II and the Indian Removal Act and the destruction of the ancient library at Alexandria, Balzac and Bronzino and Shostakovitch and The Cars and Roxy Music and Cap'n Crunch and Count Chocula and Wallace Stevens and Thomas Aquinas and Mother Teresa and where they had been for the moon landing and Nixon's resignation and Elvis's death, Freud and Pater and Lacan and Lukácz and the instability of meaning. I couldn't follow the half of it, but their enthusiasm was captivating. Watching bright young things come to know one another is an eternal delight for me.

On they went, finishing the candy corn and drying Randall's dishes. They made halting plans—Randall at first too reticent to suggest it, Silas at first too proud to ask—to see *Picnic at Hanging Rock* at the Law School Film Society that Friday.

Silas escorted Randall to his room. Through the open door he saw a portable television, its antennae surmounted by a pair of tinfoil drupes that Randall had fashioned to improve his poor reception. The sorrows of Silas's phone vigil, forgotten in the fizzy kitchen parley, returned tenfold. Thoughts of another night pinned between a mute phone and *Ella Fitzgerald Sings the Blues* made him lash out at the young man from Livonia, Michigan.

"Maybe you'd like to fuck Luca too!" he cried. "You've got what he wants, Randall. Five channels. Five channels for ten inches!"

Randall's expression brought Silas instantly to heel.

Untangling what lay behind this outburst took another two hours and all of Nana's oatmeal cookies. As midnight approached and the plangent Hadley symphony of foreign tongues, horns, strings, sopranos, deductive reasoning, and cribbage circulated through the corridors, Randall learned more than the etymology of *callipygous*. He learned about amyl nitrate, the cremaster muscle, tops and bottoms and versatiles, the handkerchief code, butt plugs and the gag reflex, and that the Luca Lucchese Sex Solution—intercrural—is the practice whereby a man reaches orgasm by rubbing his penis between the thighs of his partner. That it was Oscar Wilde's preferred method of intercourse when he went "feasting with panthers" didn't lessen Randall's unvoiced dismay to hear it.

Silas liked to shock, but he wasn't insensitive. He wanted Randall to like him and surmised from the articles of faith in his room that there were limits to what he ought to disclose. He thereby skipped certain Jesuit teachings and began with his college *beaux*. Lest Randall think he had screwed his way into Yale, Silas halved the number of faculty hits and moved on to the older pick-ups at the bars in Phoenix and Sedona, and his standing invitation from a married fullback who played for the San Diego Chargers. Before they said goodnight for a second time, Silas brought over Luca Lucchese's black denim jacket. Sharing his hopes for a town-gown romance made them plausible once more.

Their only awkward passage went something like this:

"What about the cancer?" asked Randall, looking everywhere but at his green-eyed guest.

"Cancer?"

"The gay cancer. Aren't you scared?"

Silas smirked. "I'm too young to get it. And when I find the right guy to settle down with, we'll only have sex with each other."

"But until then?"

"I haven't slept with *hundreds* of men. Luca makes forty-eight. (Here Randall dug his teeth into his lower lip.) I don't do drugs, and there have been no reported cases in Arizona. Herpes is more frightening."

"You said you did cocaine."

"That's not an injectable."

"Why does that not reassure me?"

Silas laughed. "Hey Randall."

"What?"

"What's the hardest part about having AIDS?"

"What?"

"Telling your parents you're Haitian."

This prehistoric jest, typical of its time, fell flat, but Silas left with a lighter heart. Randall, for his part, devoted a decade of his nightly rosary to continued health for this sarcastic imp from Arizona. Reaching over to turn out his desk lamp, he rubbed his fingertips together. Had they really run along the collar of Luca Lucchese's jacket as if it were the Veil of Veronica? In an effort to make Silas Huth like him, had he really offered the opinion that Luca was playing hard to get? This worked with his sisters, but a man who had lain with forty-eight different bodies? This last was inconceivable. No one had seen Randall Flinn naked since the locker room at Livonia High.

Silas's telephone with cord has gone the way of the typewriter ribbon, but something that will always be true is the Amazon Queen with a strung bow and a man in her sights. After his manly rendition of "Climb Ev'ry Mountain," Walt Stehlik had accepted more wine from Nixie Bolger's jug but his answers to her questions had been too terse for comfort. He was a stage management student at the drama school. He was from Arkansas. He was Lithuanian on both sides. After five days of silence, Nixie, needing allies, revealed the fresh vector of her heart to Becky Engelking and Randall Flinn at one of her booze hours.

"Was it a king-size box?" asked Becky, after Nixie had narrated her adventure at the Price Chopper.

"Was what *what?*" said Nixie, scraping pâté from a tin, a task made more difficult by the five large rings on her right hand.

"Was the box of Pampers king-size or regular?"

"What difference does it make?" Honestly, Nixie thought, American women fixated on the strangest things. Her girlfriends in France would have grilled her about Walt's *forme.*

"Details matter," said Becky, separating a piece of salami from its rind with her teeth. "I have a minor in psychology. If Walt put a king-size box in your cart, that means he is king, and he wants to make you his queen."

"Huh," said Nixie. "Pâté?" she offered.

"Goose fat coats the voice," said Becky, whisking splayed fingers across her throat, a gesture borrowed from a Renata Scotto album cover. "Practice later."

"Randall?"

"Oh no, no thank you," said Randall quickly. It was his first time *chez* Nixie; pâté on top of her wine selection was chancy. He reached for a saltine to settle the burgundy burn in his esophagus.

Becky sighed. "It must be lovely for you, Nixie, a fellow and all..."

Three times she toured Nixie's chamber with her glance; three times she took in the bust of Voltaire on the bookshelf, the peacock feather fan, the hat tree, and the mannequin hand draped with a pirate's ransom of necklaces. Randall, whose life with six full-strength Irish sisters had given him intuitive powers, asked Becky if something was wrong.

"Let me run and get my Triscuits," she answered, but, fingering a ridge of chenille in the bedspread, Becky made no effort to move.

"Something *is* wrong," he said. "You're in love too."

"Gracious no, Randall—I'm here to make music."

That feint put off neither listener. "Who is it?" barked Nixie. "Does he live on this floor?" Becky cast her eyes to the linoleum. "Is he foreign?"

"Certainly *not*, Nixie!"

"Don't tell me! Let me guess."

Nixie mentally roamed the floor and knocked on every door, just as she did to find boon companions for her at-homes. But cute and native-born and not Walt Stehlik? Who could it be? Randall, running the same race, had the complicating thought that Becky might be interested in Silas Huth. Although he had been open about his sexuality with Randall, telling Becky that Silas was gay could be breaking a confidence. Not telling her was a sin of omission. Or at the least, it wasn't kind. What was the protocol here?

Finally Nixie broke a tense silence with "How about Canada?"

Becky whooped. "Oh Nixie, you couldn't mean Pierre Humay!"

"I just thought, since he loves opera—"

Pierre Humay's sabbatical year from McGill University in Quebec was designed to bring him up to speed on the latest critical methods, but from what his Hadley neighbors and French cohort observed, most of his time was devoted to soothing the red-tinted whorls of his hair into presentable formation on the top of his skull. Silas Huth had already dubbed him "Lady Henna Comb-Over."

"Ewww!" said Becky. "He has to be forty-five! Have you seen his gums? What is that orange crud around his teeth?"

"I try not to look," said Randall.

"He has boils on his neck!"

Their laughter eased the tension, but they were no closer to solving the mystery. Nixie and Randall faced the music at last and looked to Becky with eager smiles.

"Gosh you guys," Becky said. "It's Brent."

"Brent? I don't know a Brent," said Randall.

"Brent *Fladmo.* Room 312."

Becky sounded so hurt that Nixie threw her arms around her and breathed "I'm so happy for you" into her ear. She connected the name to the face. Brent Fladmo—not a lot of chin, bowl haircut, played the organ—"Oh Becky, it's too perfect, you're both musicians!"

"From Iowa!"

"No," said Randall.

"Clear Lake!" shouted Becky.

Soon the women were weeping like half-sisters in a Russian play. Becky retraced every step of her walk with Brent, and Nixie retold her Price Chopper story. This time, and for all time, the Pampers box was king-size.

Before leaving for practice, Becky generously wondered whether Randall might also be in love. Randall's snort was definitive, and his answer rapid-fire. "Oh my dear dear Lord, no. No no no. I want to be a Ken doll down there."

The vague sweeping motion Randall made south of his abdomen got a laugh, but he was in earnest. His heart was temperate, stirred for God, family, and the paintings of the Italian Baroque. He had lived at home as an undergraduate, hadn't needed a curfew, and never missed a day in the Catholic calendar. Bossy older women found him irresistible, but he had withstood several sieges at the University of Michigan, the most persistent being that of Judy Ellis, a poet twice his size with the dangerous hunger of a wolverine.

Forged in the fires of a large Irish family, what Randall yearned for was a flight into silence. The happiest time in his life had been two weeks spent at the monastery of San Pietro in Perugia during his junior year. The diurnal order of the chants and prayers, the connection to centuries of reflection, the chance to disappear into vast spaces of thought, the renewal of self through the abnegation of self, the supernal via the simple… Randall felt he was inhabiting, and helping to sustain in the tiniest way, a living work of art.

No one, not Judy Ellis or any Flinn, was privy to Randall's correspondence with the office of the Abbott of San Pietro during his last year in Ann Arbor. The Abbott had insisted Randall wait to enter the monastery until after he took his master's degree. Randall, who would never question a man of God, left for Yale secure in the knowledge that he would be made a novitiate in a year's time.

Randall revealed nothing of this to Nixie and Becky; he let them laugh at his Ken quip and thanked his hostess. Next time, she must let him bring the wine.

Nixie put away her wares, and as she finished her tin of meat with an index finger, she tried to work through what had happened that morning in French 678: Versions of Oedipus. Out of the blue, it seemed, Professor Gidwitz had said to Carolann Chudek, a mother of two teenage boys, "So you want to fugg your mudder." And instead of an "Excuse me?" or "You take that back!" Carolann had said, "I guess I do. I guess I do want to fuck my mother" like she had just leaped to safety from a burning building. Nixie was appalled, but her colleagues were nodding their heads as if they all wanted to fugg their mudders too. What version of Oedipus was *this?*

Carolann Chudek's release was a textbook example of the Gidwitz Effect (c. 1978–1996). Runteleh Gidwitz had been a pupil of psychiatrist-philosopher Jacques Lacan. Her beauty and her brilliance served as a terrifying projection screen for hundreds of Yale votaries. With her alabaster skin and cropped, wavy black hair departing from a widow's peak, Professor Gidwitz looked like an Italian film star of the fifties. Lecturing without notes, her untraceable accent echoed that of a vanished civilization, Etruria perhaps, or Carthage. She positioned her hands in

Sphinx-like symmetry at the edge of a long, polished seminar table, and like the Sphinx, her paws never moved. All agreed that her eyes, without any perceptible turning of the head, seemed always to bore directly into *you*, curious but cool, surgical but veiled. Gidwitz's sincerest tribute may have been the number of undergraduates who "went" as her for Halloween.

Nixie couldn't make heads or tails of what was going on in seminar, and Gidwitz's assigned readings in Freud and Lacan passed through her undigested. After years of straight-up literary history in Toulouse, Nixie had fallen down the rabbit hole of *text*. Or to put a finer point on it, she was lost in the modish lack thereof. "There is no text," the Post-Structuralists trumpeted, only *readings* of text, or readings of readings of text. Skeptics like Silas Huth took to this methodology like a duck to a junebug, but Nixie had been trained in the verifiable. Her Oedipus course would have begun with a pull-down map of Greece, not a discussion of *the mirror stage, the displacement of desire, the leaving of the breast,* and today, *mudder fugging.*

Nixie Bolger, you see, was an improbably, charmingly pre-Freudian throwback of a woman. A Gibson girl for the Reagan Era, she resisted interpretation with a charismatic lack of self-doubt and would never guess, for example, that her instant turn toward Walt Stehlik at the Price Chopper was in reaction to her own mother, Pauline Bolger. With no ocean to separate them now, Pauline's lyre thrummed loud and clear. The footling days in France were over. Cakes fell when the eggs were stale. It was time for Nixie to find a mate.

Nixie put her luxuriant mass of chestnut hair behind her ears, lit a cigarette, and reached for a campus map. Although she and Becky had devised a tag-team Amazon manhunt for Walt and Brent for Friday, it wouldn't hurt to locate the drama school in the meantime.

On Chapel Street that very same Wednesday, Silas Huth and Scott Jencks and Carolann Chudek were processing their Gidwitz Effects at Atticus Books & Café. Founded in 1981, Atticus was among the first of its kind to sell scones and books together. Back then a coffee didn't trail Italian suffixes like a servant role in a comic opera—it came caf or decaf, small, medium, or large.

Carolann Vass had married Lou Chudek right out of high school and had had her boys by the age of twenty-two. After sixteen years serving the Carpet King of Waunakee and Crown Princes Ricky and Ronnie, she had enrolled at the University of Wisconsin. She took on a French major with the same intensity she'd brought to homemaking, graduating Phi Beta Kappa at thirty-nine. The Mellon Foundation, selecting an inaugural class of graduate fellows, had awarded her a full ride to Yale, and now, sitting over coffee with two handsome bachelors, luxuriating in the knowledge that she wanted to fuck her mother, other new thoughts began to twist like wisteria over the arms of her little purple chair—for example, who else might she want to fuck? Lou had been her first and only. She had never been unfaithful to him, nor, she supposed, he to her. A wave of tenderness passed over her as she thought of how understanding he had been about her educational journey. A cloud of steam rose from her refill. Life was wonderful.

"Did you check to make sure after class?" Scott was saying.

"Are you kidding?" said Silas. "I checked them twice *during* class."

"Your what?" asked Carolann.

"Our testicles," said Scott.

"Why would you have to check them?" Carolann had never discussed male urogenitary matters outside the home. She hoped her tone was just as saucy.

"To make sure that Gidwitz doesn't have them in her mouth," said Silas.

In the midst of Carolann's store-rattling burst of laughter, Silas and Scott thought they heard her gasp out, "But Lou has really big balls!" and then scream all the harder, her hands clutching and freeing the air around her. The Gidwitz Effect.

After she'd wiped her eyes and adjusted her jewelry, Carolann said, "You guys should come over to my apartment for some homemade cinnamon rolls. Ooh, better yet, we can have a make-your-own-pizza party."

"What's that?" asked Silas.

"Well goosie, everybody takes a pie plate with some of my good yeast dough and homemade tomato sauce. And then you put on your own toppings. I set out bowls of olives and peppers and pepperoni and sausage and lots and lots of cheese. How about next Friday?"

"I might have plans," said Scott.

"Doesn't Peter work the desk on Friday nights?" asked Silas. Acting as Facciafinta's Boswell was a way for Silas to manage his loss. Scott's molten Norsk resplendence, generous nature, and faultless French had made a gash in Silas that refused to scab over. Luca Lucchese, by contrast—well, Silas would pay to watch Gidwitz shred that phallus like a mortadella in a lawnmower.

"Who is Peter?" asked Carolann.

"My boyfriend," said Scott.

"Bring him along! The more the merrier! Pizza pizza pizza! I love gay guys!"

Each declaration was higher in pitch and louder in volume, making it clear to Silas and Scott that Carolann had never met a homosexual, a state of affairs unthinkable today outside deep space. She began laughing and clenching the air again, but this time her laughter had a staccato repeat, like she was stuck between gears.

Her gaze suddenly fixed on Silas. "Are you a homosexual?"

"I'm getting a doctorate in the humanities. Of course I am."

"Of course you are," she repeated wildly. "What do the humanities have to do with it?"

"It's been the gay province since before the monks," said Silas.

"Studying a foreign literature is a guaranteed signifier," said Scott.

Ricky took metal shop and thank God, she thought, Ronnie got C's in Spanish. "And are you going to bring a Peter with you on Friday?" she asked Silas.

"I wish I had a Peter," said Silas, "but I don't."

"Did Professor Gidwitz put that in her mouth too?"

"No."

"No? Isn't your peter big enough for a woman?"

A clerk dropped a stack of books on Carolann's next laugh-ratchet. A livid Silas was ready to reveal just how many inches he was working with, but Scott rallied for both of them. "Hardly," he said. "Gidwitz is a lesbian."

In a pause as quick and violent as a thunderclap, Carolann's lips drew away from her teeth. "Then she can come to my party too—it can be the theme! Gay gay pizza party!" She freed her hair band from her scalp. Holding it high above her, she whirled her head back and forth as if called by an inner demon. Her handsome bachelors scootched back in their little purple chairs. Hadn't Oedipus put out his eyes with Jocasta's hairpin?

"She is *not* a lesbian," she hissed. "You're just saying that because I was the star in class today. You want to spoil my breakthrough."

"No, we loved your breakthrough," said Silas, who, truth to tell, was jealous of the glow *mudder fugging* had cast upon this hausfrau. "We're saying Gidwitz is a lesbian because she is. Do you have some kind of problem with that?"

"NO!" Slam went the hair band onto the head. "I just had some hair in my mouth."

The waiter returned. Carolann trumped the check with a credit card, but she wasn't finished. She asked them who else was gay.

Atticus Books & Café had grown as silent as a tomb.

"Michelangelo."

"Tchaikovsky."

"André Gide."

"Richard Simmons."

"Oh no, goosies, I mean in the department. C'mon. You can tell me."

The young men looked at each other. Scott took a breath, then listed eighty percent of the male students and six faculty members. Carolann fussed with her purse and murmured an occasional "I always thought so" or "Of course *he* is" until Silas, seething still over her slur to his equipment, threw out the name of Carolann's academic idol, department chair Nathaniel Gates. At that, she let fire with her fists on the tabletop. The milk sloshed out of the creamer in rhythm to her shrieks of "NO no NO no NO NO NO!"

It wasn't true, and Silas knew it. Nathaniel Gates was known for his liaisons with a series of *Parisiennes* from the École Normale, the lipstick traces of which were embedded in the acknowledgment pages of their dissertations. This piece of mischief wasn't fair to Carolann, or to the waiter who had to wipe down the furniture after they left.

Two nights later Becky Engelking was sitting with Walt Stehlik near the fireplace in the Hadley lounge. She had clicked the lamps down a notch for atmosphere, but there wasn't anything she could do—so far—to dislodge the Chinese man in flip-flops reading a newspaper nearby.

Becky had knocked on Walt's door and asked for help with her character in opera scene study. "Is it because he's 'a blackamoor,'" she was presently wondering aloud, "or is it because he's a general that Desdemona falls in love with Otello?"

"In Shakespeare," Walt replied, "Desdemona falls for Othello while she's doing her chores. He tells her about the dangers he's lived through on his military campaigns."

Walt was pleased to be heard. No one at the drama school sought his opinions. It was his misfortune to be stage-managing a new, avant-garde play set in post-apocalyptic Las Vegas. Its hero was a man with pods for fingers who loved a radioactive showgirl. A chorus of three sisters, all named Helga, did a cootch dance wearing giant fake breasts. It was his job to make these things happen. It kept him up nights.

The Chinese man spat a pistachio shell over his newspaper. There were other couches to light upon, but none so near the piano, and Becky was hoping to be coaxed into performing light opera favorites later.

"What kind of chores would she be doing, Walt? My teacher, Estrella Cincha, wants our work to be as specific as possible."

Walt leaned in to emphasize his importance. "Shakespeare doesn't say. The choice of props is usually left to the stage manager."

Becky gave a little yip. "What are those things in your beard?"

Walt freed a rice puff and popped it into his mouth. "Cereal," he said. "I get so busy, I have to eat on the run."

"Men with beards," she sniffed.

"It's all a matter of taste. There's lots of ladies who like a good thigh scratcher."

Becky bridled at the indelicacy, but recovered quickly. "Some ladies," she replied, "but I'll never tell."

Your lady from Louisville for starters, she thought, recalling the upsetting afternoon Nixie had revealed too much about her *vie intime* with Stavi Heliotis. Brent Fladmo didn't harvest rice puffs from his chin; he breakfasted on white toast with marmalade. Becky felt vaguely ashamed that she knew where Brent kept his foodstuffs, guiltier still that she sometimes found herself staring at them. One sleepless night she discovered that his bread bag had come undone in the refrigerator. Its twist tie lay trapped in a puddle of oyster sauce on top of the crisper. She furtively ate her last English muffin in the dark, holding it close to her mouth with both hands, like a raccoon. Then she transferred her twist tie to his bread bag to make things right. Before creeping back to bed, she moved her jar of apple butter next to his yellow mustard on one of the shelves in the door.

Walt stood with his paperback *Othello.* "I guess I should be going. Miles to read before I sleep," he said, overheartedly.

"No, Walt. You mustn't until I find out how you got to be so brilliant. You are going to be famous one day."

"I just hope to have a job when I graduate," he answered. "My student loans are humongous."

Becky clasped her hands together and slid to the floor, ready to strangle Nixie for dawdling so long. "*Vergogna, Otello, vergogna...*"

"What's wrong, Becky?"

Walt checked his watch, and she wanted to die. Her bold segue into Desdemona was another of her gestures that fell like a muskmelon down a grain silo. Back home Becky had despaired of becoming the diva she knew she was meant to be. How could she be a diva when everyone laughed at her smallest attempts at temperament, when she couldn't summon up the imperiousness necessary to return a sweater in a department store, when in her darkest moments she saw herself as they all saw her: the big needy girl? Her voice was rich in *portamento*, the technique required to bridge and sustain the intervals between musical notes. What Becky lacked, what she yearned for, was *portamento* for the chutes and ladders in her emotional score—such a tool for threading the needles of her impulses lay beyond her grasp. Until she had it, borrowed it, copied it, *stole* it, she knew she might as well chuck Yale and go back to Ottumwa to teach the third grade.

"Why are you on the floor, Becky?" said Nixie, cutting through like ammonia with lemon. She set a box of Sociables and a jug onto the coffee table.

"I'm being coached."

Becky stood and saw Brent holding out a wedge of Brie. "Cheese, Brent, how thoughtful," she said, accepting the gift. He had a new part in his hair.

"How have you been, Becky? I haven't seen you in ages," said Brent.

"I could say the same for you, Walt," said Nixie.

"Is this a private party?" said Walt.

Nixie and Becky looked at each other, falsely bewildered by male obtuseness.

"Brent and I just came down to see the sights," said Nixie. "There's loads here for everyone."

And that was true. There was world enough and time, and much to remember after: Brent measuring Becky's hand against his own and declaring that only a spinet could provide the setting for her delicate fingers. Becky tugging Brent's forelock to assess the difference in his part. Brent shortening Becky to *Beck*. At one point, when the mirth had tapered off, Nixie decided that she and Walt should read out the accusation scene from *Othello*. Walt's Desdemona was marked by a rather generic wringing of hands, but Nixie's Moorish fire astonished one and all when she grabbed the back of Walt's head and said, "I took you for that cunning whore of Venice that married with Othello."

Desdemona looked up. Othello's eyes were adamant.

There they were then, tangled in pentameter, all according to plan.

"More of this anon, milady," said Nixie, breathlessly snapping a cracker against the husk of the Brie. Walt's beard was close enough to rake with her fingers.

"Strong stuff," drawled Brent. "I know I could never forgive a cheating heart."

"I couldn't agree with you more," said Becky.

"There's worse things than cheating," said Nixie, with strange emphasis. "I remember one time in Montpellier..."

"Goodness, look at the time," Becky broke in. Nixie, when warmed by wine, dug through the loose change of her romantic past, and Becky didn't want to spoil the fun with even a nickel's worth of indiscretion.

After cleaning up their area, they walked two by two to the elevator. Everything was falling into place: Walt was going to give Nixie a tour of the drama school and Brent had promised to come help reorganize Becky's records. Some time later, they would blush to spot one another trundling to their respective bathrooms with sand pails of cleansing agents. Perhaps their robes and nightgowns, giving clearer form to the undercurrent of their hours together, were an overstimulation.

In my time as presiding spirit of the dormitory, I had known several Nixies and a great many Beckys. I had witnessed dozens of double-play combinations on the couches, but a mother of two making a fresh start at thirty-nine was a novel variation, so it was with a sense of adventure that I followed Silas and Scott and Peter and Pierre Humay over to Carolann Chudek's apartment on lower Mansfield Street.

In Waunakee, Carolann's luaus, brat and keggers, Easter brunches, and Christmas wassails were coveted invitations, but that night she bombed in New Haven. Expecting an overflow crowd and an hour of post-pizza charades, Carolann was heartsick to have entertained seven guests for ninety minutes. "Why did I go to all this trouble?" she moaned to Roberta "Bobbie" Sproull, who was helping with the clean-up.

"Because you're a nice person," said Bobbie, pausing in her transfer of mounds of grated mozzarella into Ziploc bags. "Because you wanted people in the department to get to know one another in a relaxed atmosphere with lots of fun and good food."

"No, it's because I was lonely," snapped Carolann.

"Okay, that's a reason too," said Bobbie. Cheerful and sensible, a straight-ticket Republican from Indiana—that was Bobbie Sproull, Lord love her, first to last.

Who among her new circle could have warned Carolann that homosexuals don't eat in front of one another? Or that faculty *never* mixed with students off-site? None of her guests had spoken French either, and Carolann, who had gotten a late start with the language, needed the practice. She wiped her eyes on her apron and moved to collect wineglasses in the next room.

"I never did hear of putting chickpeas on a pizza," Bobbie called out.

Carolann heard them dropping into a bag, beige hailstones on her heart. "For God's sake, Bobbie, throw them out. I bought them special for Jasmina, but she didn't eat the least little thing."

Bobbie came and stood in the doorway. "Funny—I thought I'd read somewhere that cocaine made people hungry."

"Shush, Bobbie! Someone might hear you!"

Second-year student Jasmina Wha-Sab was the daughter of a Lebanese banker. The civil war in her homeland (1975–1991) had forced the family to flee Beirut for Paris. After a B.A. at Wellesley, Jasmina had come to Yale to be punished at close range by Runteleh Gidwitz. An ever-shifting number of incompletes on her transcript added to her Eurotrash mystique.

As a hostess gift, Jasmina had brought Carolann three ounces of cocaine. By far the strangest reaction to the stimulant had been Peter Facciafinta's topless belly dance on the coffee table. Carolann had been running down *"Scott's little boyfriend"* all week, so now, hoping to lift her mood, Bobbie mildly disparaged his vulgar display.

Carolann squirted some dish soap into the sink. "Bet you could bounce a quarter on Peter's stomach. Yowsah."

The compliment surprised Bobbie. "I thought you disliked him. Sight unseen."

"I don't know about that," said Carolann. "Silas is a pill, but Peter made me laugh."

"How is Silas a pill?"

"All those snooty questions he asked about my Mellon. As if he thought I didn't deserve one." It pleased Carolann to think she could like some gay guys and not others, just as she did with normal people.

"Silas has his own fellowship, Carolann."

"From the Bureau of Indian Affairs," said Carolann. "Affirmative action in action."

"You don't know that," said Bobbie, who privately thought if anyone filled a quota, it was a Midwestern housewife who had trouble conjugating the future tense.

"He doesn't look so Indian to me," said Carolann.

"Native American," said Bobbie.

"Then his name should be Squanto Huth. Squanto Running Mouth? Squanto Little Pickle?"

"That isn't very kind."

Bobbie's disapproval made Carolann giggle all the harder.

After Bobbie had zipped up her poncho and gone home, Carolann sat down to consider her change of heart about Peter Facciafinta. Mood swings made her feel young. As the wife of a short-tempered merchant, as a mother keeping track of children two rooms or three yards away, she had spent literally half of her life jumping to conclusions, sealing off channels and blinding herself to chance. A room of her own for the first time in decades, not to mention Runteleh Gidwitz's permission to articulate the unspeakable, had begun to unblock every eddy in her brain. Thinking was no longer a spigot to turn on and off. Thinking was becoming a delta of associations.

Peter had disarmed Carolann straightaway with a "That smells *faaaaab*ulous!" He'd made a pepperoni happy face on the pizza he'd had two bites of. He inspected the Chudek family portrait on the mantel and said the boys were cute, but not in a way that made her nervous. He made everyone laugh except sourpuss Silas, and wove the halting filaments of speech into something approaching conversation. After that, he did snort four lines of coke and almost broke the coffee table with his belly dance, but her boys did that too. (Not cocaine, but rutty smudgy boyish things.)

That was it! Peter was a *boy*! Carolann knew how to manage boys. And what were screaming faggots but boys who *didn't* want to fugg their mudders?

Carolann ran into the bedroom to record her findings. She snatched a notebook from the nightstand, and for a split second glimpsed an intoxicating goddess in the floor-to-ceiling mirror. She sat down on the bed to wonder about her too. Peter Facciafinta, her changeling boy, the fruit of queered thinking, knew who that goddess was, knew her power. Who could she have to sire him with? Who would be the Peter Daddy Daddy Peter?

To assist the declaration of her unconscious, Carolann drew up her hair, parted it in the center, and made of it two heavy plaits. She stood, Aphrodite with a spiral notebook. From a mighty river made up of a thousand pulsing tributaries gushed forth an answer as obvious as sin. A book called *Plots and Pleasures* had pushed her toward this doctorate. She must give herself to its author, Department Chair Nathaniel Gates.

The phone began to ring. Carolann knew it was her husband. Insights roiled about her in neon squiggles. If she was able to accept Peter, adopt him as the boy of her gates, the boy from her Gates, then she could be unfaithful to Lou. She *must* be unfaithful to Lou.

Carolann took a step. She would adulter. Moreover, she had come to Yale *to* adulter. She unbuttoned her shirtwaist, let it gather at her hips, unhooked the hasp of her brassiere and let it fly. The phone kept ringing. Moving to the mirror, she whispered, "This is who I am," until her nipples touched, then stiffened against the cool of the glass.

It was at this moment that, transfixed as Carolann was by her tableau of self-discovery, I decided to relax my house rules and admit a mother of two as my first-ever off-site love slave.

Two hours later, Randall Flinn had finished Ruskin's *Seven Lamps of Architecture* and was getting ready to watch his MTV. Music videos were a guilty pleasure, and his sister Kathleen, whose business it was to be up on everything, had pointed him to a catchy dance tune, "Holiday," by a brand new singer with a blasphemous, one-word name.

There was a loud plonk against his door, then a second, then furious knocking.

Randall opened his door. Silas Huth stood there, barefoot and red-eyed, sloshing a fifth of Bacardi held in his hand and asked, "Do you want to help me kill Peter Facciafinta?" What wasn't in the bottle was on his breath.

"What?"

"I need a funnel. I can kill Peter in twenty minutes with a funnel."

"Shush, somebody will hear you."

"If you had postage stamps, Randall, you have a funnel. They go hand in hand."

Silas stumbled in. His jaw went slack, as if he were shocked to find Randall's walls bare of kitchen equipment. With the over-precision of the very drunk, he set the rum on Randall's desk blotter. That went well enough, but when he tried to cross his legs in the easy chair, his right ankle veered off his left knee three times before he gave up the effort.

"Do you think Nixie will help me kill Peter?"

"No one is killing anybody tonight," said Randall. "What happened?"

After Silas, Scott, Peter, and Pierre Humay had fled Carolann's apartment, Peter suggested a nightcap at Partners, but in a gratifying first moment of public friction, Scott had forbidden Peter to add liquor to the cocaine already in his system. There was to be no repeat of Wednesday's shenanigans, when Peter had nearly slipped into a diabetic coma after forgetting his insulin shot and getting drunk. Belligerence had magnified the danger; though his temperature was dropping a mile a minute and he'd started slurring his speech, Peter kept insisting he'd taken his insulin and punching Scott. Scott had finally had to pin Peter's shoulders to the bed with his knees and force-feed him marshmallow circus peanuts until he stabilized. Otherwise he might have died in twenty minutes.

"Diabetes is a terrible illness to have," said Randall, in an effort to dampen Silas's sinister enthusiasm.

"Whose side are you on?" said Silas. "I'm the prize, not Peter. Never forget I'm the prize."

"You're the prize, Silas. And you lost Scott by one day."

"One single solitary day."

"So the coma was Wednesday?"

"*Near*-coma," said Silas, shucking his loafers. "Dammit."

"While we were at *Picnic at Hanging Rock*?"

"I guess so. Or after."

"Wow."

"Wow what?"

"Life and death are happening around us all the time," said Randall. He had loved the Australian film and enjoyed hashing out its mysteries with his new friend. To have, if one were to believe Silas, Peter Facciafinta struggling for life one floor below their spirited late-night discussion was a juxtaposition worthy of a quattrocento altarpiece.

Silas ducked the metaphysics. "Do you remember circus peanuts?"

"I do," said Randall. "They're those nasty orange things from when we were kids."

"Worse than candy corn."

"Or spicy gumdrops."

"Or malted milk balls."

Silas seemed to have settled down, so Randall, who had never wanted to kill anyone, not even in fun, motioned for the Bacardi cap. He sealed the bottle and changed the subject. "How was make-your-own pizza?"

"Grotesque."

Silas kept Randall laughing with imitations of Carolann's deranged *Gemütlichkeit* and her heinous French, and malicious speculations about the orange impasto along Pierre Humay's gum line. Needing something to do with his hands, Randall took out a deck of cards. They were both too punchy to play anything more challenging than crazy eights, but play it they did, until their eyes were tired and happy little slits.

Chapter Three

Carolann Chudek took a week to act upon the declaration of her unconscious. Her initial obstacle was access. Nathaniel Gates wasn't teaching fall semester. His office hours coincided with *Versions of Oedipus*, and no one would dare skip Gidwitz. The when and where of the meetings he chaired were state secrets held by Diane Bluder, the department secretary who guarded the door to his office with cheerless efficiency. Carolann gleaned from students further along in the program that Nathaniel commuted by bicycle from the house on Bishop Street he shared with his wife Eleanor, an alcoholic scold from a Mayflower family. He carried on with female students, but only the French ones on loan from the École Normale.

At thirty-nine, Carolann was older than Nathaniel's typical Parisian pixie, but what she had in her corner was years of civic success. This was a woman who had led record-breaking fundraisers and strong-armed aldermen into new stoplights and squeezed cookbooks out of housewives and band uniforms out of school boards. The failure of her pizza party spoke not to her hostessing skills, she concluded, but rather to a department-wide lack of conviviality.

Our Welcome-Wagon Lady had been there before. Her solution was offering coffee and doughnuts every morning in the wood-paneled department lounge on the third floor of Harkness Hall. She would transform the space into a Parisian café, minus, and this she would insist on, the cigarette smoke.

She drafted a memo and took it to Nathaniel Gates' office. "That is such a lovely blouse you're wearing," she said to Diane Bluder. "Did you find it here in town?"

Diane Bluder scratched the back of her head with a pencil.

"Might you give this to Chairman Gates?"

The envelope was lightly perfumed. "This is in reference to what?" Diane Bluder had been there before too.

Accustomed to the ways of bureaucracy, Carolann expected a series of increasingly intimate one-on-ones with Nathaniel Gates before her proposal went to the ombudsman; three days later, quite to her surprise, she found a check in her box for one hundred dollars, a key to the storage room off the lounge, and a typed sentence of encouragement on office stationery.

Her next step was finding shift workers among her classmates. Peter Facciafinta's arm-flapping rush from the Hadley desk recharged her batteries. They toured the common area. Taken in sum, the oilskin lampshades, the limp, flame-retardant curtains, the orange vinyl sofa cushions pocked with cigarette burns, the old magazines swollen from dozens of thumbs, and a half-finished puzzle of a Swiss village on a banged-up coffee table reminded Carolann of a television documentary she'd seen about life behind the Iron Curtain. They didn't square, she said, with the elegance of my portrait and the cabinet of china. Her searching look at me, and her query about my identity cemented my growing fondness for her. Peter declared that I had invented the Sippy Cup.

Peter loved her plan for Franco-American nourishment and immediately placed a call to an uncle on the supply side of things. Soon the two were playing slapjack behind the desk. Peter's *sotto voce* commentary on the dreariest inmates marching into the elevators sent Carolann into gales of laughter. He was a very naughty boy, this boy of her Gates.

While retrieving a wayward ten of spades from the floor, she smelled pizza. This was no ordinary pizza, but a wood-fired white clam pie from Sally's, one of the two famous pizzerias in Wooster Square. Looking up, her eyes traveled the side seam of a superbly packed pair of dungarees. This was no ordinary delivery boy, but a glossy-haired stag whose hot hand of introduction held hers three seconds longer than was polite. When he turned to set down the box, the push of his ripe, mounded behind might have been the slap of a porcupine's tail, so sharp and instantaneous were the needle trails he left across Carolann's chest.

It was sexual shapeshifter Luca Lucchese, back at Hadley, but not for his jean jacket. As they discussed doughnut varieties and dickered over coffee brands, Luca worked Carolann over with the same rough magic he'd used on Silas at Partners Café. He touched her arms; he chewed her crusts; he brushed a crumb from her cheek; and most intriguingly, he declared, with fingers that gently shaped the air around her neck and shoulders, that the power of Astarte was in her aura.

"Astarte? Really?"

"She's the Phoenician goddess of love and fertility."

"Well yes, but how—" began Carolann.

"You think I'm so uneducated?" said Luca.

Peter giggled. "My great-aunt Benita reads palms at all the Italian festivals."

"You two are really related then?"

Luca's intoxicating shrug confirmed Carolann's notion that he had swiped all the male genes in the family for himself.

"My mother does palms and charts. And when I was a little bambino, she taught me all about the goddesses. Isis, Shiva, Ceres, Hera, Minerva, Venus, Diana, Astarte. She was so nuts about girl power, it got her excommunicated almost. I did not wish to offend you, Carolann."

She began to blush. "No offense taken."

"Let me say instead that you have the *abbondanza*."

"That means abundance," said Carolann.

"*Si, carina,*" said Luca. The sudden slit of his eyes was a second slap from the porcupine's tail. This time the quills made a hash of her thighs.

The trio got down to business. Peter would donate a dorm fridge for the milk. Luca would borrow an industrial-size coffee pot from St. Bernadette's. They'd begin with a standard cinnamon, powdered, jelly, and cake mix. The exotics would come later. There was a baker in Branford who owed Luca a favor, if he could just get at those Yellow Pages right above their heads.

"I'll get them," said Carolann. She stood and reached for the shelf.

"Allow me," said Luca.

As he passed behind her, Luca made a tight space even tighter by pressing his penis between her buttocks.

Blood beat in Carolann's ears. Her fingers itched. Her throat dried. It had been years since she had been approached from behind; Lou Chudek had a tricky back. And how much heat was this man packing? As Luca reached and pressed some more, she opened her eyes wide, wider, but, preoccupied with her surging senses, she missed the scornful look Peter was sending his uncle's way. Bisexuals made him tired.

After Luca released her, Carolann's mind cleared enough to make a decision. Locking eyes with a Sèvres shepherdess in the glass cabinet, who was as flushed of cheek as she was, but in control of her woolly charges, Carolann decided that her motion for the body of Nathaniel Gates could be tabled for the time being.

Blake scholar Lakshmi Dawat re-adjusted the cymbals on Becky Engelking's fingers. "No, Becky, I said the thumb and the forefinger. Like this."

Lakshmi held her arms in fifth position and curled her hands inward. Becky hesitantly followed suit. Her neighbor was so graceful, she made Carolann feel like Tobacco Girl Number Five in *Carmen*. The soapstone elephant next to Lakshmi's toothbrush glass didn't help her confidence.

"Lovely, Becky. You are very nimble."

"You are too," Becky answered quickly. "Now what do I do?"

Lakshmi began to rotate her hands in opposition to the larger sweeps of her arms. "Tinkle."

Becky dropped her arms. "I could never do that."

"Then you'll never get a Brahmin man."

"Well, I'm not sure that I want one," said Becky. "You said they were chauvinist pigs."

Besides which, she reminded herself, from a Full Gospel standpoint, Brahmin men were headed straight to the pits of hell.

"Close your eyes and let the cymbals speak."

Becky closed her eyes and tried to tinkle. After some unpromising clicks, she discovered that the cymbals made a stirring ring if she rotated her hands in a certain sinuous way. Moving her arms up and down created a contrapuntal effect as the pairs of cymbals crossed paths in the air, then spun away from each other. Her hips began to sway, the hem of her skirt twitching in hypnotic counterpoise.

She opened her eyes. Lakshmi was nodding encouragement. What next?

Becky's Punjabi makeover had come about after a shared lunch of ham salad and curried eggs. Clearing the table, Lakshmi mentioned, with an enigmatic smile, that her Victorian poetry professor was bent on proving that Elizabeth Barrett Browning had written most of Robert Browning's verse. Becky, sensing a challenge to her own feminist credentials, explained that the *soprano* exerted dominion over all musical creatures, male *and* female, then, weighing in on the Browning marriage, repeated some wisdom from her voice teacher, Estrella Cincha: "Who can ever really know what happens between two people?"

Lakshmi moved to the sink with her saucepan. "Ah yes, true love. The Western invention. The all-purpose cleanser, stronger than dirt."

"You don't believe in love," gasped Becky. "Lakshmi! You shouldn't be cynical!"

"Love has inspired some fine verse and some fine singing, but little of use. Love and its utopian obsessions remind us that we have so very little to do with our hands. I clean my fork—"

"Oh, dear. Egg is hard to get off. Try using cold water."

"—and then what, I am to think of love?" continued Lakshmi. "Love distracts one from thinking that someone else should clean one's fork. What endures is *power*. Love, which is held up as the pinnacle of human selflessness, which is in itself a form of human subjugation, buttresses the institution of human subjugation, which is the source of power."

The appearance of a big idea in multiple clauses made Becky's head spin, but she remembered La Cincha's advice to "absorb like the sponge." "Yet there must be love in India," she countered. "What about your parents?"

"They submitted to the conjugal station as a means to ensure the transfer of property. My mother brought her cattle to my father's barn."

The farm reference led Becky straight into Brent Fladmo's arms, and an easy objection. "You just haven't met the right guy, Lakshmi."

"My parents have already selected a groom for me."

"No! Who is it? Tell me!"

"The gentleman in question is waiting for me to complete my studies. After Oxford and Yale, I intend to apply to business school at Rice University. Sharat will not wait forever. I have three younger sisters. He may choose among them."

"But he wants *you*."

"I am the contracted choice of his parents."

An actual bartered bride! La Cincha would flip. "What's he like?"

"I have never met Sharat."

"Suppose he's really cute?"

This was hypothesis. Becky didn't really think an Indian Indian could be as cute as Brent. However, to be fair, she began to imagine Brent with jet-black hair and ebony eyes and skin the color of maple syrup...eyelashes as curly as a calf's...in front of him, a peacock trailing his fan...

"What if he's *gorgeous*, Lakshmi?"

"Then I would seduce him with some giddha."

"What is giddha?"

"Come, I will show you."

And that was how Becky found herself whirling and bangling with the girl next door. After mastering the cymbals, Becky looked longingly at the rainbow of saris in the closet. Before she could object, Lakshmi was lashing a pair of them around her waist. The midnight blue and hot magenta silks caressed her shoulders. The addition of an ankle bracelet and silver earrings with multiform pendants gave Becky the power to destroy temples. From a makeup bag Lakshmi drew a vial of ground lapis powder and dressed Becky's eyelids. They looked in the mirror. There was one course of action. Although they spent oodles of time together eating breakfast and listening to records in his room, Becky was still waiting for a first forward pass from Brent. She must giddha for him.

Becky lost her nerve at his door, so Lakshmi, keeping firm hold of her wrist, knocked and knocked again. They pressed their ears against Brent's Snoopy message board, but all was still. Yet then—the gratifying sound of applause from down the corridor. Becky turned with a sudden, serene dignity.

Lakshmi's engineer friends Venkatesh and Arup had spotted her from the dining pen. One was tall, the other short, and they were always together. They invited Becky for kheer in Arup's room. Becky dimpled at their entreaty and, rather like Jane addressing Tarzan and little Bomba, said, "Kheer? Tell me, what is *kheer*?"

"Rice pudding with rose water and pistachios," Lakshmi tartly interjected.

"Sounds scrumptious," said Becky.

As Becky jingled westward with the Indians, the object of her pagan transformation was idling in an open doorway on the eastern end of the floor, pimping a rice pudding with tamer flavors to be found at Naples Pizza on Wall Street.

"It's really delish, Silas."

"I said I'm waiting for a phone call," said Silas, with unmistakable ill humor.

"Some other time then," said Brent.

Put me down for the twelfth of never, thought Silas. Closet cases gave him the willies, and moreover, Randall had told him about Becky's dibs. Silas knew better than to cross a dramatic soprano with a weight problem. "Shut the door, will you?"

We now leave Temple Street to watch Walt Stehlik manage the stage at the Yale School of Drama. We venture ahead of Nixie, whose need for him was more acute than ever. While continuing to pluck the motif of Nixie's stale eggs, which would lead to birth defects, feeding tubes, and a mountain of debt, Pauline Bolger had added a new string to her lute: *That paper*, which was an aggrieved mother's substitution for "the doctoral dissertation." When was Nixie going to finish *that paper*? How long did *that paper* need to be? She could always get a law degree after *that paper*. Nixie was tempted to change her phone number.

At 217 Park Street, Debi Fleer, the first-year actress playing the part of Helga Two in the avant-garde play, had just locked herself in the bathroom. It was up to Walt to flush her out and into her breast prosthesis, two feet of green foam rubber with a kiwi-sized nipple. He called for a break and picked up his tackle box.

One problem of Yale's drama school is its tendering of expectations. The promotional literature says Shakespeare and Schiller, but, given its number of Oscar-nominated alumni, it is impossible for the students not to hear Miramax and HBO. It's an Ivy League star factory, with as many as eleven-hundred hopefuls auditioning for a sixteen-member acting class. That translates into forty-eight infantile, narcissistic monsters running amok during any afternoon of rehearsals, with only six Walt Stehliks on hand to tighten their restraints.

"Debi, do you want to tell me what's wrong?" Walt asked at the door. He heard the spin of a toilet paper roll.

"If you need something softer for your nose, Debi, I have tissues." Walt also had at hand aspirin, Band-Aids, throat lozenges, Q-Tips, No-Doz, Tampax, lollipops, comic books, and a bee venom kit.

"I think you're doing a great job as Helga Two."

Debi spoke. "Everybody hates me. I look fat."

Walt avoided the time-suck of discussing an actress's weight. One had only to glance at Helgas One and Three, long-necked blondes with ballerina bodies, to know what the matter was. Debi, five-feet-three with frizzy brown hair, was the token Hermia in a class of Helenas. "Oh Debi," he said, "you've discovered such a clear spine for Helga Two that I think that the others are intimidated."

Discovered or uncovered, the *spine* is the most helpful tool handed to Yale drama students. Directors invoke the elusive *character spine* to affirm or to castigate actors and the sacrosanct *dramatic spine* to railroad playwrights into revisions. Walt was using the spine as all-purpose blandishment, but it backfired. Debi began slamming things around in the utility cabinet. "Great," she said. "I've got the backbone of a burn victim with a big green tit. I want to be in another play."

"You were cast in this one, Debi, because you're up to the challenge. Now why don't you splash water on your face and come out, so we can all go back to work."

"You can kiss my tuchas, Stehlik."

Debi Fleer had read too many Hollywood biographies and was not, it seemed, going to come out of her trailer, so Walt played his ace of trumps.

"You give me no choice then but to report to Merle that your behavior is unprofessional." Merle Edmister, Dean of the Acting Program, rewarded his favorites with title roles and punished miscreants with confidants, crones, and walk-ons. Invoking his name led to actor freak-outs.

Debi freaked out. "Nooooo!" she cried. "I'm not unprofessional!"

There were sounds of heavy things falling. The rest of the cast gathered behind Walt for a listen as Debi cleared the utility shelves. The only sentence anyone could make out in the melée was, "I am not a meatball face! I am not a meatball face!"

Nixie Bolger, suddenly beside him, cocked her head at the door. "What's her name?"

"Debi Fleer," said Walt.

Nixie set her briefcase against the wall and knocked sharply. "Debi, this is Nixie. Nixie Bolger. I need to use the facilities."

The door opened a few inches. Nixie slid in sideways and before the door shut again, she could be heard to say, "That's some costume you got there, Debi. I love the theater."

Three minutes later, both women re-emerged. Before assuming her position for the dance number, Debi apologized to the room for delaying rehearsal in an unprofessional manner.

"Sorry to interrupt all y'all," said Nixie, smoking glamorously in the corner, her coyote coat draped over her shoulders. "I was looking for Walt."

"Could you come back around eight?" he found himself saying.

It was another lonely night in Room 303. Fanned across Silas Huth's bedspread were *The Interpretation of Dreams, Oedipus Rex*, a yellow highlighter, a nail file, and a ravaged package of pink sugar wafers. A bottle of Bacardi stood on his desk, and Billie Holiday sang the blues on his turntable.

Silas was culling ideas for his final Oedipus assignment, a fifteen-minute presentation Gidwitz called an "angle of entry." This provocative term, upon which Gidwitz had declined to elaborate, had induced widespread panic and an involuntary raspberry from Nixie Bolger. Silas had begun with Tiresias, the bad penny of Greek tragedy. On a simple story level, it was a mystery to Silas why Oedipus would listen to word one from the blind, hermaphroditic know-it-all. Nana Eagle Eye had taught him early on to slam the screen door on Jehovah's Witnesses.

He closed his eyes. What a grind grad school was turning out to be. He would finish the Gidwitz, then write a seminar paper, then two more, then endure another three semesters of hermeneutical potpourri, do a year of research in Paris, write his dissertation, screw his way through the MLA conference for a decent first posting, teach intro courses, churn out articles, scramble for tenure—the material of his life stretched before him, an endless bolt of dun-colored burlap. He'd wind up teaching at a cow college in East Jesusville, Oklahoma, a tale from the crypt like Pierre Humay. Silas knew there were so many easier ways to be. With his looks and charm, why couldn't he just seize the day and swag the loot in Manhattan? But the plague was raging two hours south, and why dwindle into an urban clone when he had a free, four-year ride at *Yale?* Deep down, Silas knew he lacked the Holly Golightly gene. Heedless he was capable of, but not spontaneous. Spontaneity had not gotten him out of Fruitland Acres.

World-weary, half-lit, sick of his own company, Silas capped his highlighter and thought about sharing his funk. Nixie had left on a cloud for the drama school. His reliable comedy partner Randall Flinn was at the library. Hanging around the kitchen was open season for Brent Fladmo and Pierre Humay. Partners was a hike, and his sweater would wind up smelling like smoke. Moreover, Luca Lucchese might be passing two-for-one rum and Cokes to a fresh victim. After all these weeks, Luca's rejection still stung.

Self-abuse required the least effort. Silas unbuttoned his jeans. Flopping back onto his bed, he felt the nail file poke his shoulder. He rolled over and screamed. His breath spun a gratifying shower of pink flakes from the cookie package to the floor. He screamed again, just to watch more wafer dust take the plunge.

Taking revenge where he could find it, Silas brandished the file, stumbled to the closet, pants at his ankles, seized Luca's jean jacket from a hanger, and let it rip. The instrument was insufficient to the task, but he kept hacking. So focused was his passion that he didn't hear the knocks at his door.

Carolann Chudek peered in and saw Silas on the rug, red-faced and barelegged and sprinkled with black threads. She spread her arms as she kneeled to receive him. "What's wrong?" she asked.

"Trouble is a man," he snarled. "You wouldn't understand!"

Try me, she thought, and began fishing in her purse for a Kleenex.

Carolann's man trouble—occasioned by the selfsame Luca—wasn't of the "Why won't he call?" variety. The afternoon they had gone for the coffeepot, he and Carolann parked at East Rock and mated in a pile of movers' pads like zoo animals. His smell, taste, size, sounds, and stamina were so utterly *other* than Lou that the experience felt less like adultery and more like a master class in structural biology. Or that's what she told herself when searching her soul for guilt or remorse. Finding none, she risked mentioning in a phone call home how tired her legs had been feeling. Lou's suggestion to "get more regular exercise" she took as a directive for more twist and shout in the back of Luca's truck.

Smoothing the bristles of Silas's crew cut, Carolann felt the wet of his tears soak her skirt. It had been years since Ricky and Ronnie had let her comfort them this way. She missed their young, sweet selves so much. "It's okay," she murmured. "Shhhh, it's okay. Mommy's here."

Oh dear. What a thing to say to Silas. Were I wearing pearls, I would have clutched them.

Silas went rigid. He snuffed in an unbecoming amount of nasal fluid before asking, "Why are you in my room, Carolann?"

"I was wondering whether you might like to sign up to sell doughnuts and coffee."

Silas had heard of her plan. He rolled out of her lap into a drift of crumbs. "I hate doughnuts. They make me puke."

"They do not, goosie. It would only be a couple of hours a week."

"Don't call me 'goosie,' Carolann. Do not *ever* call me 'goosie.'"

"Nobody hates doughnuts, Silas, not really."

"They absolutely make me puke," he replied truthfully, while covertly pulling up his trousers. This Tiresias wasn't going to bring *him* down. "Don't tell me what I like and don't like. You're not my mother."

"Why don't you want to help out?"

"Grad students are supposed to be miserable, Carolann. And if you ask me, better you should spend your time learning the language."

Carolann began to blush. "What do you mean?"

Silas began to impersonate her French. Subjects and verb endings didn't agree. Masculine articles mixed with feminine endings. There were pauses, stutters, clicks, repeats, hems and haws and halts, ludicrous false cognates and mangled tenses, a word salad rendered in the flattest of Midwestern accents.

When he finished, Carolann gave as good as she got and struck the spot that Silas alone had been blind to."Who was your mother?" she asked. "And who was your father?"

He slammed the door after her and howled to the heavens above. God Almighty, who had often played the role of fantasy father during his childhood, was said to live up there.

When Nixie returned to Park Street that night, Walt led her into the basement home of the Yale Cabaret. Unplugged lengths of electric cable hung from the grid like ailing pythons, and the room smelled of mildew and sawdust. A giant chicken-wire hoopskirt was bolted into a platform under the proscenium arch. Walt was racing against the clock to complete a dirt mound for a production of Samuel Beckett's *Happy Days*. It was a lot of work for one six-performance weekend, but insiders maintained that the best theatre in America happened in the student-run space. Meryl Streep had made her final Cabaret appearance only seven years before. (Sorry I am that La Streep did not in her time at Yale take a room at Helen Hadley. True-to-life tales of her doings would doubtless find me a publisher.)

Nixie removed her rings and set them in an ashtray. She picked up a hammer.

"Put me to work, Walt."

"I thought maybe dinner first, Nixie."

"Later," she said, hitching up her slacks. "I had a big lunch."

"Um, I don't need you to hammer, but you could help me mix this."

Backlit, with a sack of plaster of Paris over one shoulder, he looked to Nixie like a *sans-culottes* in the French Revolution, building a barricade so that the poor might have bread. "We have to cover that frame," he said, pointing to the wire skirt. Before long they were kneeling face-to-face, kneading plaster in a washtub. "Those are my fingers you're squeezing," said Walt.

Nixie apologized, but she wasn't sorry.

They poured the plaster over the hoop, and while it dried, Walt explained drama school ins and outs over burgers at Kavanaugh's Pub. Rival directors were holding production meetings at rival tables attended by rival designers and playwrights and dramaturgs. Only the actors table-hopped. Unshaven men, their fisherman sweaters and non-functional scarves reeking of smoke, slid into their booth for a second to trade gossip and snitch fries. Actresses falling out of their clothes would air-kiss Walt and bum cigarettes from Nixie, whom Walt introduced as the miracle worker who had sprung Debi Fleer from the bathroom that afternoon.

In this land of gaudy opinion, her Burly was a different man. He spoke a breakneck blend of technical terms, insider jokes, and play titles. The rumble of his laugh was a new strain of music. As his fiercely flung superlatives lifted into the cobalt cushion of smoke above their heads, Nixie had a new determination: if, as the chamber of commerce posters were proclaiming that autumn, New Haven were the Paris of the eighties, then she and Walt would be its Sartre and de Beauvoir.

On their walk back to the Cabaret, Walt fell silent. The temperature had dropped. Winter was in the air. Nixie dreamed of a first snow with Walt, flakes catching in his beard, a second pair of socks, backgammon and flaming brandies by the fireplace in the common lounge. They came upon the Thirty-Cent Lady, who had picked a doorway at the corner of Chapel and Park as her bed for the night.

"Thirty cents, please," she asked. Nixie and Walt dug into their pockets.

Whether the Thirty-Cent Lady represented a failure of supply-side economics, or psychotherapy, or urban policy, is lost to history, but she was as known in her time at Yale as Noah Webster or George Herbert Walker Bush were in theirs. Her request of thirty cents was reassuring. Not a dollar, not a couple of bucks, or the passive-aggressive "Whatever you can spare," but thirty cents. No private crisis or global ill was too big to solve if this one woman's survival bore so modest a price tag. The Thirty-Cent Lady's well-being assured one's own, the thinking went, so it is not surprising that her donor base viewed her as a good-luck charm or a portable wishing well.

Walt dropped a quarter and nickel into her fingerless glove without breaking his stride. A streetlight cast his retreating shadow in front of the women, and Nixie, who had stopped to open her change purse, found herself saying, "He'll be good with children."

The Thirty-Cent Lady closed her hands around the coins, but made no reply. Where had *that* come from? Nixie wondered. Where had that *come* from?

She heard her name. Walt was standing in the golden light of the open door. The stamping of his boots on the brick felt like a summons.

They sang along to an oldies station and sloshed buckets of paint onto the plaster. Nixie matched each of Walt's gestures with an economy of her own. They connected electric cable while the paint dried. When all was ready, he entered the mound from behind. To test the plaster, he asked Nixie to shimmy up the slope. She reached the top and he popped his head through the opening. She found herself staring into the fondant chocolate of his eyes. The vapor of their mingled breath hung in the subterranean air.

"*Ah les beaux jours,*" she whispered.

"Huh?" he said.

"The French title of *Happy Days* is *Ah, Les Beaux Jours*. Beckett did his own translation."

"Wow. I haven't read the play."

To hold fast to the moment, and to keep herself from sliding down the hill, Nixie joined her hands around the back of Walt's neck. "That's my neck," was all he had time to say before her lips found his.

With the plaster barrier immobilizing his hands, Nixie seized advantage and enslaved Walt with her kisses. She tracked his face with lipstick until he was moaning her name. She moaned his name back, and they rubbed noses, a simple Inuit gesture that aroused her more than anything she recalled having done with Stavi along the Riviera.

Walt dropped into the mound at last. Spread like a starfish on a brown plaster beach, Nixie listened to him flap the dust off a canvas drop cloth and spread it on the floor. At last he tugged on her boot, and she slid downward into his crouching form.

Later, on her solo walk home—Walt had to spray the paint with a fixative—Nixie fantasized that she was already with child. She stopped again at Park and Chapel to tuck a five-dollar bill into the frayed pocket of the pea coat worn by the softly snoring mendicant.

Rounding the third-floor corridor, Nixie noticed light seeping from under Silas's door. She paused and listened to a snatch of Nat King Cole before she decided that Becky should be the first to hear the news. She yawned, stretched her arms high. Sleep would feel so good.

On the other side of the door, Silas was a wild-eyed wreck. Carolann's question had planted him deeper in the Oedipal paradigm than Gidwitz or Freud or Lacan had, deeper than she herself would ever know. The aftermath of her visit had required the rest of the rum and a roll call of American song stylists. In the wastebasket was a snowdrift of discarded letters to Nana. All bore variations—jaunty, lost, accusatory, fretful—of the topic sentence, *Who were my parents?*

Chapter Four

By Veteran's Day that year, the Commander in Chief had announced the formation of a national holiday celebrating the birth of Martin Luther King and invaded Grenada to prevent its becoming a "Soviet-Cuban colony." The IRA was taking a rare breather in Northern Ireland, but a suicide truck bombing of Israeli headquarters in Tyre, Lebanon, had left sixty dead and thirty wounded, leading to air reprisals on Palestinian positions. Around the world, ceremonies were being held to commemorate the 500th anniversary of Martin Luther's birthday just as a corporation in Bellevue, Washington, unveiled a brand-new product called Windows. This operating system extension that permitted the simultaneous viewing of unrelated application programs lit a long and winding fuse for a revolution to rival, if not exceed, Luther's.

Closer to home, Randall Flinn's talent for listening was in constant use. He supported Nixie's and Becky's romantic campaigns, celebrated their incremental victories, and should he hear a swish of slippers in the night, readied tissues for their tears. He and Silas kept up with film-society offerings, attending everything from *The Searchers* to *The Awful Truth*, *Gallipoli* to *La Strada* to *Pink Flamingos*. Silas favored motion, while Randall could be satisfied with picture, so their post-mortems were sometimes fierce. Their first spat was over *Barry Lyndon*. "But the cinematography!" said Randall all the way home. "But the plot!" screeched Silas, stomping to his room, furious that he couldn't convince Randall that action mattered more than art direction.

About his own life Randall was recondite, but his chastity strengthened his position as moral monsignor to the third floor. In addition to

weekly mass and his nightly rosary, he was known to pop into The Church
of St. Mary's any time of the day for solace.

Two days after Nixie and Walt's plaster play date at the Cabaret, Randall was taking out a package of chicken thighs to defrost when he noticed
Silas in the dining pen clutching his Texas Pete with white-knuckled
intensity. (Silas put hot sauce on everything.)

"Are you okay, Silas?"

Silas pushed out a chair with his foot. "Coffee?"

"Maybe later. I'm just on my way to church."

Silas stood with a clatter. "Take me with you," he cried, thumping
the bottle against his chest. He looked a perfect Magdalene: frowsy bedclothes, downcast mien, and two days of stubble. His interior was no less
turbulent. His answer to Carolann's terrible question—"*I am a foundling.
That means I was left to be found and my parents can never be found.*"—failed to
extinguish the network of ruby filaments blinking in his stomach.

"Do you have time to get dressed?" asked Randall, who hated to miss
the beginnings of things.

"St. Mary's is throwing distance from here."

"I was never good at games."

"It's right out *back*," Silas said.

While he waited, Randall rinsed out Silas's coffee cup and gingerly
scrubbed several leprous-looking plates in the sink. The church bells had
begun to ring when Silas returned in a jacket and tie. "Sorry," he said. "I
broke a shoelace."

The Church of St. Mary's, the second oldest parish in Connecticut and
the birthplace of the Knights of Columbus, is an impressive Romanesque
Revival edifice. Silas halted so abruptly on its precipitous front steps that
an old woman stumbled into his back. He was staring wide-eyed at St.
Joseph in a niche. "I haven't been to Mass in like five years," he confessed.
He had generally skipped services in favor of chapel, choir, confessional,
and crying-room couplings.

Randlall took his elbow. "A return to the sacred mysteries might do
you good."

During the processional, as Father Grasso and his retinue passed with
the crucifix, the creaking swing of the censers made Randall, kneeling in
meditation, wish he were an altar boy still, going to bed with simple prayers

and waking up to achievable tasks like European capitals and moving the decimal point. Matins, lauds, prime, tierce, sext, nones, vespers, compline. In a mere eight months the Monastery of San Pietro would make an altar boy of him again, and the canonical hours would wash his mind clean of Hadley debris: Nixie getting laid on a basement floor. Pierre Humay's periodontal malfeasance. Silas feasting with panthers and polluting him with blasphemous images.

Mass had scarcely begun when Silas yanked at Randall's elbow, causing his missal to smack the kneeler.

"What is it?" asked Randall.

"Look," Silas breathed. "Look at the altar."

"I *am* looking at the altar. I am following the service."

It didn't matter now who his parents were, dead or alive, or that Carolann had gotten his goat, or that Luca Lucchese was a dirt bag. Silas would even cease to think of sending Peter Facciafinta into the Big Diabetic Sleep, because God had chosen this Sunday to reveal His new plan for His second son. "Look at that acolyte, Randall."

Randall looked first to Silas. Lips parted, hand cupped upon his breast, his friend was caught in a moment of beatitude. It was as if an unshaven medieval angel, in wood with polychrome traces, had touched down and then flown off before Randall could measure its wingspan.

"Which one?" asked Randall, unsettled by this peep into Silas Huth's soul.

"Left of the flowers."

Randall recognized a catalogue-ready all-American from his department. "Oh," he replied. "That's Bill Goris."

"Who?"

Randall went down to pick up his missal. "William Goris. He's in my Ruskin seminar."

Silas looked from William to Randall with unflattering skepticism. "You mean you *know* him? He's heaven."

"He's saintly, I'll give him that. He does the flowers here."

Silas bent down next to Randall. To see them in conference below the pew, they might have been centurions casting lots for Jesus' robe. "But he's not gay," said Randall, trying to nip things in the bud. It was one thing for Silas to hold forth in Randall's room, quite another to sully his place of worship.

"Looking like that?" scoffed Silas.

"He is in a cassock."

"And he does the flowers? Get *real*, Randall."

A hundred voices tolling "Christ have mercy," called them up for air.

Silas changed Communion lines so William Goris would hold the paten beneath his chin and was equally bold during the post-service social hour in the basement. "Randall tells me you're in his department," he said, shaking hands.

"That's correct," said William, who bore his advantages with ease. "I'm here to study the history of the compote."

Silas choked and dribbled Kool-Aid on his tie. Had he heard right? Absurd (and actual) dissertation topics were already a running gag between Silas and Randall. (e.g., The Semicolon in the novels of Madame de Staël. The paper cutouts of Swiss *silhouettiste* Jean Huber.) "The compote?"

"Yes."

Add it to the list, thought Silas. "Would that be the dish or the…dish? I mean the food—the fruit compote in the dish?"

"The ceramic or metal dish for holding the food," answered William. The *compotier*, as it were.

"Compotes change over time then," said Silas, with dimples.

William laughed, and Randall felt a curious stab inside. He realized he didn't want Silas to launch a romantic campaign and leave him behind. He liked scrapping over the movies and people and books, even if he lost. Or let Silas win. Of William Goris he had given little thought except to be impressed by his insights in seminar and his commitment to St. Mary's. William couldn't light a room with mayhem, or incite mirth in others the way Silas Huth could.

Silas had worked many a man out of his cassock. The semi-sacred setting only upped his game. He pointed to a Red Cross poster. "Do you give blood, William?"

"I do. I help out on the blood draws too."

"Do you hold the hands of anxious parishioners?"

"It can happen," said William.

"If they faint, do you wake them with a kiss?"

Now it was Randall's turn to choke and dribble.

"That has yet to happen," said William.

Silas pushed one last time. "Next blood draw is Thursday. Is it a date?"

William excused himself and went to talk to some women in puffy hats. Silas had overplayed his hand, and Randall, who had been searching for words to express that Bill Goris wasn't right for him, was relieved.

Becky Engelking's voice teacher, Estrella Cincha, bore the shoeblack bun and flowing drapes of her profession, but, like so many in her field, had never adjusted to retirement. Her makeup—bird wings of rouge, a mulberry-sized beauty mark, eyebrows like the brushstrokes on a Japanese declaration of war—could be read at thirty yards, helpful preparation should a pupil be stricken and need a last-minute replacement. Yet even those teachers backed off the stage have their favorites. When Becky Engelking began her studies at Yale, Estrella Cincha had reached the point in her own timeline when she could no longer remember who she herself had been before the implacable call of *la voce*; Becky reminded her of a certain full-skirted farm girl from the pampas who had boarded a bus to Buenos Aires once upon a time. Falling prey to Becky's sincerity, done in, as it were, by doctored souvenirs of her own youth, La Cincha decided early on to share her secrets of dramatic breathing with her pupil. Her "Argentine Way" would give Becky's voice shimmer and light. It would make her a diva: choice roles, recitals, recording contracts thick and soft as sealskin.

Becky made steady progress; her throat was more relaxed, her tone was creamy like the flan, her breath control stronger, her roulades more dazzling, but then, in November, a plateau. Something was pressing on her instrument, and La Cincha knew what it was. Love: the wellspring of temperament that scored and charred the artist like a churrasco steak. Her Beckitá might master the Argentine Way from a technical standpoint, but La Cincha worried that her foursquare musicality might get her no further than guest appearances with the Pittsburgh Pops.

"You love him," she announced one afternoon. "You love this boy who eats with you the rice puddings at Naples."

Becky sat on the piano bench to cover her adrenalin spike. The severity in her teacher's tone dashed any pleasure Becky felt at having the lock of her heart picked. "How did you know?"

"I know everything!" La Cincha retrieved a bottle of Pernod from her bottom desk drawer. "Beckitá will tell La Cincha all!"

So Becky told all, from her first walk with Brent on the green to his boyhood tractor accident, from his near-translucent eyelids to his favorite Mario Lanza recordings. When she finished, La Cincha went to the window to pass sentence. The waning autumn sunlight made fire of the golden gourds bobbing from her earlobes. "You have a passionate nature, Beckitá," she said. "We are both passionate women from the plains. So it is important that you must make your first lover your slave. You must humiliate him, not be humiliated by him."

"Brent doesn't humiliate me," said Becky. "He respects me."

"Oh, *la povera*," said La Cincha. "Oh *mia poverina*. You say he removes the crusts from the bread."

"Yes, he does. I don't understand," Becky said, suddenly frightened. "He cuts them off with a knife."

"He has a toast rack."

"He can drive farm equipment."

"His pajamas have fishies on them."

"They're fire engines!"

"He makes the chew-chew."

"It's mustard chow-chow. Spicy hot. It won a prize at the state fair!"

"He has *never* kissed you."

Becky felt herself rushing headlong into an accident she'd unconsciously spent months steering around. As she stood, her surge of anger made the piano bench topple and release a tempest of sheet music. "Brent Fladmo is not gay!" she cried.

"Look at me, Beckità." To temper the blow of her final piece of evidence, La Cincha held out her hands in comfort, but to Becky the chopsticks in her bun were crossbones on a bottle of poison. "He plays the organ."

Becky cried "No!" swept up her things, and ran into the cold.

"He's straight," she wanted to shout to the windswept clouds, but she hadn't the breath to support it. She knew, *everyone* in the music world over the age of twelve knew, that male organ players are always always always gay. Becky had done her best to protect Brent from dorm mantraps like Risa Brandex and Faye Kringle, but now, fleeing to the safety of her room, La Cincha's *coup de grâce* beating time in her head to mocking toots from a disco whistle, Becky was forced to consider the bevy of male mantraps—Peter and Scott and Pierre and Silas and—Oh God—what might have been going on behind her back all these months was too ruinous to contemplate.

She changed clothes in a rage. When Brent returned from work-study at the music library, if he even looked at her the wrong way, *a gay way*, she would fling the colander at his head and take back all of her records. En route to the kitchen to start her spaghetti, she saw Lakshmi waiting for the elevator with Venkatesh and Arup. They were bundled up like three brown kittens. One had a scarf, one had a hat; Lakshmi had the mittens.

"Becky! Happy snow!" said Lakshmi.

Becky looked over to the dining pen. Fat flakes were melting on the windows.

"Come celebrate," said Lakshmi. "We're going to the Whitney Winery."

"I wouldn't dream of drinking on a school night," she sniffed.

Lakshmi pointed to the colander. "But you eat, yes?"

The men smiled eagerly. Becky wished she could remember which was which. First snows *were* an occasion and better, she thought in a flash, to have gone missing when Brent did come home. If he cared, he'd come looking. "I'll just be a minute."

What are now referred to as fern bars were in vogue as the seventies became the eighties, a brief season before the unsparing hunger of Reagan's army of tort specialists and bond traders seeded the re-birth of the steakhouse. A fern bar like the Whitney Winery served sincere Chardonnays, spinach salads with bacon, and quiches of the day. While Becky knew not to expect El Morocco, she didn't realize that, far from living it up Brahmin-style, Lakshmi and Arup and Venkatesh were loading up at the chafing dishes for the price of a ginger ale. Becky could have suggested that they not take advantage of America's bounty, but sitting tall and soignée in a bank of deer and sword ferns, she decided it was more tactful to repair the trade imbalance by drinking whiskey sours for all. In very little time she was holding court with tales of Iowa blizzards and frostbitten digits, treacherous Brent forgotten and her cocktail napkin a still life of orange rinds and cherry stems.

Happy hour gave way to dinner seating, and the Indians said farewell. While a jazz combo set up in a corner, the remaining Jarlsberg and pepper jack cubes were carted away, but Becky, tighter than a tick, stayed put and signaled for another round. Listening to the musicians jam on "Proud Mary," she became aware of a gentleman, in a tie of stockbroker red, making eye contact from the bar. There was gray at his temples, and his homburg and briefcase were placed on the stool beside him. He ran his finger around the rim of his beer glass; she shook her hair. He ruffled the feather in the hatband; she traced a cheekbone with a drink stirrer. He sucked beer foam from his salt-and-pepper mustache with his lip; she pensively touched her clavicle. Finally, he tilted the face of his watch in her direction.

After four whiskey sours, Becky was ready to give him the time. "Doo doo doo doot, doo doo doo doot" wailed the saxophone. This was the way it should be, she thought, man and woman coming together, Brent Fladmo and his spicy chew-chew could go to Sodom while her red-tie daddy-o hitched a ride on this riverboat queen…doo doo doo doot! Becky was just about rolling down the river and out the door with a total stranger when a cold something goosed her neck. She nearly toppled into a pillar.

"I've been looking for you everywhere, Beck! Nobody knew where you'd gone to."

He had come for her. Becky turned. "You asked people where I was?"

"Well, duh," he giggled. His nose was moist.

"Oh Brent, I've been right here."

"That's what Lakshmi said."

He was holding her hands; he wasn't letting go. She must catch her breath, sober up. "Lakshmi is such a dear," she said.

"You won't believe this—" Brent was breathless too.

"What is it, Brent?"

"Faye Kringle passed a worm!"

"What? Who? *What?*"

"Faye passed a worm!"

"What do you mean, 'passed a worm'?"

"Faye has had a worm inside her for two years. It was a parasite she got on that dig in Syria. She said it was fifteen inches long."

"That's the most disgusting thing I've ever heard," replied Becky, and she burst into tears. From the corner of her eye, she saw a homburg settle onto a salt-and-pepper dome. It had been close.

"Have you been drinking?" Brent asked with a frown.

"No. I'm just glad to see you. Hold me."

"Sure," he said. She felt his grip through the down of his jacket. "Let's go home and see Faye. She is one tough camper. I know if I had a worm—"

"Don't say that! You'll never have parasites, Brent. I promise."

"Don't cry, Beck. Faye's fine. Do you want my hankie?"

Brent Fladmo wasn't gay. He was *Midwestern*. He held her, and held her up, on the walk home through the happy happy snow.

Three fresh inches fell through the night, ideal conditions for the début of a French Kaffeeklatsch. Early the next morning, through a bow window high in Harkness Hall, Carolann Chudek watched the flakes cluster on the oak boughs. The sight of the undergraduates tacking against the wind on the flagstones below pricked her heart. Ricky and Ronnie would rather die than admit it, but the novelty of roughing it without Mom had worn off. Lou, on the other hand, saw no reason to disguise his need; he begged for her return, bribed with promises of sectional furniture and island getaways. Their attempt at phone sex was a different kind of embarrassment, especially when measured against her blowouts with Luca Lucchese. She could only tell them all to hang on until Thanksgiving.

Through another leaded window she peered at the plastic sheet and duct tape "township" on Beinecke Plaza, built across from the president's office to protest the Yale Corporation's investments in South Africa. This was common practice at the most liberal campuses of the day; evidence, however faint and unremembered, that America's young had looked up from its navel at least once between the Vietnam War and Occupy Wall Street. Shivering under a blue tarpaulin, two students were proffering anti-apartheid leaflets. The wind kept knocking over their "Free Mandela" placards set on rickety easels. Carolann made a note to fill them a thermos next time and give them any leftover doughnuts.

She began rearranging her wares with the corn-on-the-cob tongs she'd brought from home, purposely avoiding the gaze of Jean-Jacques Rousseau, who was one in a series of canonical engravings that ran the perimeter of the department lounge. A pioneering advocate for the rights of children, Rousseau wouldn't have approved of a mother leaving her boys to pursue a doctorate.

A soft ticker in the corridor made her heart race. A wheel paused in the doorway. She turned. It was he. Even holding a dripping, one-speed Schwinn, Chairman Nathaniel Newbold Gates was a presence of such unique majesty that Carolann repressed an impulse to kneel and blot his trouser legs with the masses of her hair.

Unique to Carolann, but familiar to me. Replace the bike helmet with a beaver, and the fogged half-glasses with *pince-nez*, and the department chair could have been my father or any one of my seven uncles, or my forsaken fiancé. They're tall, rector-ish New Englanders, whose weedy builds, sloping slightly at the shoulders, are kept in trim by morning Grape-Nuts and squash twice a week. Nathaniel Gates's russet hair was streaked with gray, and it curled a bit, as it did now, when damp. Habituated to privilege and command, yet guided by thrift and industry, a man like Nathaniel Gates is the platonic ideal of the Yankee facing ever east, a man who ventures beyond the Hudson River solely by federal appointment.

Carolann waved her tongs and burbled, "Beignets, monsieur. Café et beignets."

A woman alongside a thirty-cup percolator was a surprise finding in the department lounge. Professor Gates set his kickstand. "What's all this then?"

"C'est café, monsieur," she said. "Et ça, c'est…les doughnuts."

His pale blue eyes lifted over his half-glasses. "Is this a pledge drive? United Way?"

"Non, monsieur. Je suis une élève ici."

"Vous êtes étudiante, vous voulez dire," he said.

"Yes. In my first year I am student. Je m'appelle Carolann Chudek. You gave your permission to set up coffee and doughnuts for the department."

"Ah yes." Chairman Gates relaxed and shook the water from his helmet. Then he seemed to forget where he was. "Well, carry on," he said, aiming his foot at the kickstand.

Carolann knew how to keep a man close. She pulled a book from her satchel and pressed it against herself. "*Plots and Pleasures* changed my life."

He smiled. Like his hair, his teeth were good for his age and all his own. "Did it really?"

"Oh yes, Professor Gates, your insights are deep inside me."

He looped the chinstrap of his helmet over the handlebar and dug out a cracked leather change purse that looked to have come over on the Mayflower. He bought a cake doughnut, and as Carolann fixed his coffee, he autographed her copy of his influential study. When asked about her courses, Carolann's enthusiasm for Runteleh Gidwitz cast a pall she sensed but didn't understand. How could she know that her professors were locked in popularity contests of their own, and that Gates thought Gidwitz a condescending fraud?

"À la prochaine, monsieur," she said, brushing his fingers as she relieved him of his empty cup. One doughnut would lead to another, she thought, as he steered his Schwinn away. By Christmas they'd be feeding on strawberries dipped in chocolate. Rare steaks to improve the color in his cheeks. She'd help him with his posture too.

"What's the big idea handing out free coffee, Cranny?" asked a voice that made her neck prickle.

He'd come in as silent as a cat. "Luca," she said in lowered tones, "Don't call me that here. My name is Carolann."

Luca Lucchese tipped the contents of a pair of sugar packets into his mouth. Then, as a chaser, he drained the cow creamer. "I like Cranny better. Now tell me who that was."

"That was our benefactor, Nathaniel Gates. He paid for his doughnut."

Luca flopped into a leather chair. It let out a protesting whoosh. The coffee table barked as it met the heels of his ostrich cowboy boots. "You have the hots for that prune."

Luca's intuition maddened Carolann. "That is a falsehood! He is my intellectual guide, and I cannot wait to meet his wife Eleanor. Why were you spying on me?"

"C'mere." He had the dickens in his smile. She shook her head. "Put down the tongs and c'mere," he repeated.

Again Carolann surveyed the room: the radiator steam blurring the glass over the portrait of Descartes, the snowflakes melting against the leaded panes, a signed copy of *Plots and Pleasures,* and a hot Italian lover with skin as smooth and fragrant as a bowl of peeled almonds. "Just for a second," she whispered.

This pursuit Rousseau approved of, but a fresh customer halted her progress.

"Ma chère Carolannda, I heard about your cafeteria and had to see for myself." Jasmina Wha-Sab was cooing at the doughnuts as if they were baby chicks. "They are so cute. How do you ever find such things? *Ma, Luca! Come sta lei?*"

"*E sempre cosi, ragazza. Cosè fa?*"

Luca caught Carolann's eye. "You know each other?" she asked.

Jasmina shook snow from her Hermès babushka. "I see exactly what you mean, *caro*. Carolann has made a brilliant idea with her doo-nuts. To help people is so beautiful. I cannot wait for my shift to begin. I will buy an apron," she drawled.

"You told Jasmina about the doughnuts, Luca?"

"Luca knows that I am an officer of the Graduate Student Senate, and always I look for ways to improve lives. He called to me with your hospitality, which I know *naturellement* from your *grande soirée du pizza*. This," she said, denting a jelly doughnut with a fuchsia nail, "is an improvement. I vision a franchise in every department."

"Really? I've been open only a half-hour," said Carolann.

Jasmina dropped a bill in a Styrofoam cup and air-kissed her exit. "I will convene my committee *tout de suite*."

Everything was happening so fast. The tip of an ostrich leather boot snaking its way under the back of her skirt stifled Carolann's feeling that Jasmina was stealing from her. She giggled her way into the storage room to refill the cow creamer.

Carolann would have fared better in the end had she worried less about Jasmina and more about Silas, who was heading down the hall that very moment with a prepared apology. He knew that in order to be free for the resplendent purity of William Goris, drawing blood two blocks away at St. Mary's, he had to clear his conscience and apologize to Carolann for his bad behavior.

Even at twelve paces, her merchandise made him sick to his stomach—his aversion to doughnuts was neither feigned nor explicable—so he held back in the doorway. Carolann was nowhere in sight, but there, in a leather chair, with a back issue of *Eighteenth-Century Studies* spread over a leg, was Luca Lucchese. He and Silas locked eyes for a neck-prickling moment, then Luca winked.

What was he doing in Harkness Tower, of all places? Unless he was there to snake the drains, Luca had no business mocking the academy with his footlong phallus and lack of education. Silas's shock was so great that instead of defending his territory and screaming, "Shit heel!" he fled down the stairs and almost crashed into an undergrad holding out a petition clipboard for him to sign.

Silas raced across Beinecke Plaza, then paused, breathless, in the Memorial Hall rotunda. To prepare for the Anglo Angel, he needed to clear his mind of the Dago Devil. There wasn't time to swing back through the dorm for a shower, so he blotted his armpits in a basement stall and fluffed the nap of his coal-black hair. Silas and William would definitely look hot together.

Before leaving the rotunda, Silas touched a finger for luck to the sword pommel poised between the legs of a naked hoplite carved in the marble. This marble soldier guards the roll of the Yale men who have died defending their country. Harvey Harris Bloom B.A., *Class of 1863*, Charles Webster B.A., *Class of 1863*, George Stanley Dewey, *Class of 1863*, Henry Clayton Ewin, *Class of 1863*, Francis Kern Heller, *Class of 1863*, Zalmon John McMaster, *Class of 1863*, Frederic William Matteson, *Class of 1863*. There are thousands of names engraved in the rotunda. Because he keeps watch over the dead, the hoplite can never leave his sacred office. He and I nod to each other, but don't speak.

Registering donors in the church basement, William Goris smiled at Silas's nervy quip about parting with a *compote* of hemoglobin. He seemed to be promising even more when he asked whether Silas had had sexual contact with men, but Silas's winsome affirmative caused William to frown and fold the registration form in half.

"Is there something wrong?" asked Silas.

"I'm sorry, but the Red Cross isn't accepting donations from men who've had homosexual contacts."

"I gave blood in Arizona just this spring."

"It's a policy response to the AIDS epidemic."

It was Silas's second shock of the day. Who among us would appreciate the insinuation that one is tainted, or worse, marked for destruction? Silas got loud, fast. He was not dirty or ill or a drug addict or Haitian; this was flagrant discrimination, and if you stopped to consider how the Catholic patriarchy had invented faggotry, here was hypocrisy of the greatest magnitude, and he, Silas Huth, would write the diocesan head and expose all.

William did his best to separate the Church of Rome from the ministry of Clara Barton, but Silas would not be shushed. Donors began sitting up on their resting cots. A squadron of nuns was bearing down on them when William asked Silas if he'd like to talk things over at Clark's Dairy, where he dealt an even rougher blow. William was gay, but celibate. For purely health reasons he was going to wait until more was known about how AIDS was transmitted before he would express himself sexually again.

Silas's hissy fit at this news exceeded Carolann's post-*mudderfug* milk bath at Atticus Books & Café. When asked to leave the restaurant, Silas stuck William with the check and, heedless of the slush, ruined his best pair of loafers in a bitter trudge back to Hadley.

Every now and then, the rule of three, which applies to comedy and celebrity deaths, is violated, and bad things happen in fours. Finishing his supper that same night in the dining pen, Randall Flinn heard a crash, then the plummy voice of Pierre Humay.

"Don't be that way, dear boy. Come, give us a kiss."

"Get your hands off of me, you creep!"

That was Silas. At the sound of glass breaking, Randall ran to investigate.

Pierre's ox-like hips had pinned Silas against the stove. Wriggling against the bulk, Silas was trying to swat Pierre with a slotted spoon. Pierre, his tongue extended in lascivious concentration, had slipped a hand under Silas's sweater in order to rub his stomach; the other plumped a breast. To Randall's trained eye, they looked like an ithyphallic satyr confronting a boy on a Greek amphora, or a bath mosaic at Pompeii, or a woodcut from a Medieval beast fable, or a Beardsley drawing. A trope for every age, in any case.

Catching sight of Randall, Pierre let go of Silas and fell back against the wall with such force a cabinet above their heads popped open and released some roaches into the fray. Silas screamed and started battering the counter with the spoon, catching Pierre's hand instead.

"Violence is unnecessary. You have rebuffed my advances. I shall retreat."

"Don't you come near me again, you big fat fruit!"

"This is a terrible misunderstanding," Pierre said to Randall. His comb-over, askew on his heated pate, looked like the lattice crust on a cherry pie.

"Trying to bugger me in the kitchen?" shouted Silas. "What's to misunderstand?"

"You had led me to believe that my interest was reciprocal," replied Pierre.

There was an ugly pause, then Silas lunged. Randall caught him and retrieved the spoon before someone lost another molar. Pierre scampered away. Silas burst into tears and slid against the refrigerator to the ground.

What was it about my residence that led its citizens so swiftly to what Thackeray calls "the waterworks?" Randall offered Silas soda, an ice cream sandwich, a hand to stand him upright, anything to quell the racking sounds of his misery. Finally he dropped two paper towels in the direction of Silas's fists and crouched to remove the broken glass in a pool of tomato sauce on the floor. For a moment there was just the click of glass pieces.

"I didn't lead him on, Randall, I swear. You believe me, don't you?"

"I believe you, Silas."

"Really?"

"Really. Pierre is too old for you anyway."

"He's not *that* old, actually, it's the teeth," Silas said with sudden science. "I've done older." He blew his nose. "I fucking hate snow."

"Tell me."

Silas motioned for the roll of towels and led Randall through his Day of Exodus—Luca at Harkness Hall, William and the blood draw, William at Clark's Dairy. Silas's complete *joke* that he was thinking of answering the personals in the *Gay Times* had prompted Pierre's ambush at the stove.

Randall was too alarmed to censor himself. "The personals? You promised Nana Eagle Eye that you would settle down. You said you believed in love!"

"I do. Love was going to be William."

"The personals are just about sex! Why are you so promiscuous?"

"Why are you yelling at me, Randall?"

"Because you've slept with four dozen different men, that's why, and I worry."

"Well don't. I can take care of myself."

"Fine!"

"Fine!"

Unused to being called on his contradictions, Silas the Prize flounced to a window and began burning holes in the frost with his thumbs. As his anger ebbed, his talent for negative thinking took over, and his ego began to shrink. He was a promiscuous, heedless, foundling slut and look where it got him—felt up by Lady Henna Comb-Over, and Randall, who cared, mopping up the mess. He was trashier than Luca Lucchese and Peter Facciafinta put together. He deserved everything bad that happened to him. The plague would find him.

Silas decided to share. "Sex is my power," he mumbled. "Sex and close reading. They're all I'm good at. They're what got me out of the muck."

Having said it, Silas couldn't take it back. It felt surprisingly okay. Randall nodded but didn't believe. Sex and close reading were Silas's instruments to power. His animating force, the essential goodness in him that Randall knew was there, were gifts from God. He found a spatula in the dishwasher and began an awkward transfer of tomato sauce from the floor to the garbage can.

"That's why I'm a slut," said Silas. "Now you tell me why you're a virgin."

A new voice spared Randall from this discomfiting topic.

"Hey—do either of you jokers know where I can find Nixie Bolger?"

"Who wants to know?" said Randall.

A petite brunette in a floor-length down coat the color of a persimmon extended a gloved hand. Obeisance was clearly her due. "Ms. Cassandra Fleer wants to know."

"I thought your name was Debi Fleer," said Randall, taking her hand.

If Debi was surprised that a stranger with a bloody spatula knew her name, she wasn't letting on. "I changed it. I thought Cassandra up on my way over." She undid the snap on her free glove with tiny, perfect teeth. "My shrink thinks I dream up these names to hurt my father." She checked her watch. "Miss Nixie Bolger has twenty minutes to get herself to the GPSCY Bar and nab Walt Stehlik."

Nixie hadn't spent productive time with Walt since their coitus on the set of Beckett's *Happy Days*, so her blouse was off before her door was even closed. Experienced in dressing to please, Debi and Silas moved Nixie so adroitly through clothes and accessories that Randall hadn't the room to feel embarrassed about seeing her in her brassiere. Helping Debi back into her puffball while Nixie drifted through a second cloud of Jontue, Randall agreed to come along. Silas had said he needed a drink after his hellish day, or maybe twelve, and Randall felt it his duty to keep bad things from happening in fives.

Sanctioned amusements for the graduate population were scarce. The Graduate and Professional Student Center at Yale—acronym GPSCY— was the one public space on campus where fun might be attempted. Outside, the GPSCY building, a Gothic Revival error wedged between the *Yale Daily News* office and the School of Graphic Arts, gave the impression of having passed like an unhappy governess through many families. Inside, the well drinks were inexpensive; there were darts by the bar, pool tables beyond, a patio in summer, a dance floor above, and everywhere a supply of cheap, cerebral drunks.

The foursome gathered out front, by a bike rack topped with a crust of snow. "Now, I'm not promising anything," said Debi.

"Leave that to me. Fix my hat, sugar," Nixie said to Silas.

"Oh God, straight people." Silas tilted Nixie's fur kolpik just so, smoothed her hair, and followed her through the door.

Randall, his courage flagging, cupped his hand around the match Debi was trying to light. "Sounds like a big crowd in there."

"It's always full," said Debi.

"Drinking on a school night…I don't know."

"Get in there."

Debi checked his coat and plied him with screwdrivers. Randall knew better than to tire her with the Italian Baroque, so he shifted the spotlight to her artistry, upon which she was eager to dilate. Debi Fleer had been the biggest little star the Cleveland Playhouse had ever seen. Her Anne Frank, her Cinderella, and her Gretl von Trapp had drawn attention from talent agencies, but her father had insisted she finish high school. Yale was, as they say, inevitable. Randall wondered how the new, avant-garde play was going, so Debi, committed to working from a place of truth, blithely mowed down Helgas One and Three, who were holding forth to their own admirers by the dartboard.

At the other end of the room, beyond the pool tables, Becky Engelking, who had arrived earlier at the GPSCY with Brent, was using her powers of persuasion to get the deejay to play "The Bunny Hop." Time spent with the Indians had reinforced her interest in exposing them to stateside pleasures. Venki and Arup were already mad for tuna melts. When the current club hit segued into a timeless intro, darts, pool cues, and beer cups paused a moment in disbelieving hands, then were hastily set aside in an exultant rush to the floor.

The Americans drew in the foreigners. In minutes, the line had doubled and tripled back on itself, an entire universe bunny-hopping in drunken, grade-school communion, the mirrored ball above bouncing happy reflections off the corrective lenses of five continents. The only holdouts worth mentioning were Nixie and Walt, necking with great feeling in front of a Palladian window draped in thick green velvet.

Afterward, a grateful throng pressed against Becky—good practice, she thought, for backstage at The Met. Someone proposed that she run for the Student Senate. Someone clamored for "The Hokey Pokey." An art student presented her with a rabbit sketched on a bar napkin. Venkatesh had gone to fetch her a goblet of golden Chablis, but all Becky really knew was that Brent, hopping directly behind her, had stolen second base during the dance. It was all starting to happen for her. She had a man, her music, and the common touch.

In her ecstasy Becky felt more than ready to grab a microphone and teach the world to sing, but it was Nixie's turn now to leave her mark upon the party. She released her Burly and strong-armed the deejay into playing "Rock Lobster," a two-year-old club hit. As the song began its atomizing throb through the speakers, the savvy began to jerk, whip, flail, and rattle their limbs. The invitation to impersonate crustaceans was less controlled than the invitation to make like a rabbit. Brent Fladmo, palms up and out like Atlas bearing the Earth, rotated like a dung beetle. Arup performed quick squat thrusts like a Cossack dancer. Venkatesh hopped on an imaginary pogo stick. Debi and the other Helgas were doing Martha Graham; undulating from neck to knees, hair flipping over and back, they were a grove of willows lashed by a tempest. Silas was all elbows and knees and fists, as if he were trying to punch his way out of an old, useless skin.

On the lyrics, "Down Down Down," Queen Nixie's subjects obeyed her order to hit the floor. The magnitude of the pent-up force in all the bodies twisting, communing, and evolving underwater was making Randall, standing stock-still at the edge of the bacchanal, nervous. He was just contemplating a move to a fire exit when the guitar shifted to an ear-splitting riff, and the dam broke. Nixie screamed "Up!" and her kingdom leaped to its feet and began to frug double-time.

Randall threaded his way over to Debi. He took the plunge and began to dance, carefully and, he hoped, on the beat. On the second round of "Down Down Downs," the Helgas Three flopped onto their backs and began to arch and collapse their spines like inchworms on acid. Burly Stehlik's leonine head of hair beat against Nixie's thigh like a dust mop. Randall twisted lower, all the way to the floor. Finally, he lay flat and started to spread himself into a starfish position, Nixie's starfish position. The bass pulsed through the wood and into his palms. His little round glasses played catch with the mirror ball, which felt as far off as the North Star. His hair was damp with sweat. The world smelled like beer, smoke, and wet wool, and then Debi rolled on top of him.

Chapter Five

Plots and Pleasures, so crucial to Carolann Chudek's journey of liberation, was a title that might also serve to describe the interactions of Randall Flinn and the strong-willed Debi Fleer. Her forward roll at the GPSCY Bar set in motion a plot for Randall to call his own, one rich with spiritual conflict, physical obstacles, and, alone among those of his peers, moral anguish. The pleasures were rife, but, to use another neologism of the age, *problematical*. Simply put, Randall knew that Debi imperiled the salvation of his immortal soul.

Randall had the superego of an eldest child. He had believed the drug movies in junior high: a puff of reefer on Friday led to an arm stick of heroin by Sunday. His parents maintained that they both had been virgins on their wedding night, which provided Randall with evidence that sexual intercourse led inexorably to marriage, children, and chaos. Moreover he was bound to a catechism peculiar to Irish Catholics. Its first article of faith is *No One is Looking at You*. Second, third, and fourth are *Who Do You Think You Are?*, *You are Last in Line*, and *It's Just Waiting to Die We Are*.

It might strike you as odd that Randall proved unable to resist Debi Fleer in Connecticut when only the year before he had outwitted Judy Ellis in Michigan, but I think the change was environmental. Randall wouldn't turn Debi out, not only because his body was overdue for physical connection, but also because his room, his space, his *life* had become crowded with the love slaves of Helen Hadley Hall. The very air he breathed was streaked with the pastel trails of their whizzing candy hearts. The part of him that wanted to be a Ken doll down there had begun a scrimmage with the part of him that wanted to belong. This meant ego, heresy, and a world of troubles, but Randall had a time-tested way to deal with external pressures, and St. Mary's, as we know, was right out back.

"What sins have you to confess, my son?" The priest had a sibilant *s*, like a little whistle.

Randall crossed himself and took the plunge. "I kissed a girl, a young woman, for fifteen minutes. We were lying on top of each other…" Randall paused to let that sink in. "…in front of a lot of people."

"Have you kissed young women before?"

"Yes, but we never Frenched." Judy Ellis had chain-smoked unfiltered Camels.

"I see."

Randall paused to listen to a heavy, rolling scrape outside the confessional. He pictured a barrow of paving stones and a knot of parishioners ready to cast them his way.

"This woman called me on the phone last night. She wants to do more of this, I can tell."

"No one else can make you defile the temple of your body, my son. Resist all temptation to wickedness." The Old Testament diction raised Randall's hopes for a stern ruling. "As penance, say two Hail Marys and a Glory Be."

"Is that all?"

"Bless you, my child," the priest whistled.

"But how do I get her to stop?"

"Go and sin no more."

Randall tripled the penance and stopped returning Debi's calls. This was an effective strategy until his volunteer work left him open to pillage.

At the urging of Jasmina Wha-Sab, the Graduate Student Senate had approved an expansion of Carolann Chudek's hospitality. From the moment she had slipped her strong, maternal hands around his, Randall could refuse Carolann nothing. His franchise was inside the High Street Bridge, a Gothic overpass that led into the History of Art Department. Although Randall had never sold a thing in his life, he discovered that he wasn't someone who could pretend he had no relationship to the product. If forced behind a card table with a two-gallon coffee pot, a stack of napkins, and a tray of doughnuts, then he was going to have to verbalize the dilemma. Carolann's treats became his glazed, powdered, and cinnamon-twisted sons and daughters in search of good homes. Randall bullied them, and they, in turn, revealed to passersby their dreams of love, fame, and fortune. The children knew they were a drain on their father's precious time; as eleven o'clock approached, the drama intensified. Randall would threaten to devour the last of his litter à la Saturn or Thyestes, and they would beg to be bought. Compassion led to steady purchase; Carolann was soon having a second dozen delivered to the High Street Bridge.

More troubling than these visits from the stork were those of Debi Fleer. She'd listen to Randall's improvisations, which she likened to the spirit of the true *commedia dell'arte,* then pull him into a broom closet for ten-minute breaks that left him rumpled, stupid, and ventilating draughts of yeast-and-Shalimar-scented air.

On the day that Debi dragged him to second base, Randall sought guidance on campus at the St. Thomas More Center. Instead of the grille and kneeler, there was Sister Anne across the table, looking in her short wimple and knee-length skirt like one of Pharoah's waitresses. Instead of the traditional blessing, she asked Randall to tell her what was upsetting him.

"This woman—I won't tell you her name. This woman has been coming to my doughnut stand, and we make out in the closet, and this morning we engaged in some petting. NOT heavy petting."

"You are a doughnut vendor," said Sister Anne.

"Of course not. I'm a graduate student."

"Then you sell doughnuts part-time, Randall."

"Who told you my name?"

"You did."

"Right. So Debi came to my table before class and…she took me into the broom closet and…she nipped my earlobe with her teeth and…that was bad…and then…"

Randall hung fire. Debi had squeezed jelly from the pore of a doughnut and spread it on his lips. After licking it off, she had taken his hands and placed them on her breasts. They began to move of their own free will…

"How did it make you feel?"

"Wonderful. Sinful. Bad."

Sister Anne hung fire.

"It *is* a sin," said Randall, closing his eyes. "The nuns taught me that. Other nuns." (He almost said *real nuns.*)

"Are you pure, Randall?"

"Of course I'm pure. She says it's not a sin for her. She's of the Jewish faith."

"Ah," nodded Sister Anne. "I think you should re-examine, and then determine for yourself, with the help of prayer, your own conception of carnal sin. If and when Debi makes you uncomfortable, just say no."

Randall opened nettled eyes to the stained-glass window behind his confessor. *Just Say No?* With centuries of scripture and commentary, not to mention the lives of the saints and martyrs behind her, could Sister Anne and her clear nail polish not improve upon the anti-drug nostrum of Nancy Davis Reagan? He crossed himself to end this brush with collegiate Catholicism, made comfortable and relative for modern man.

Doughnut blow-bys eventually ceased to satisfy either party. Debi's phone messages now said she would be "dropping by the dorm later," yet not specify a time. Waiting for her arrival was a fretful rotation of nail-trimming, pillow-plumping, and decades of the rosary. She would sweep in and back Randall onto the bed. Inhaling Shalimar as if it were a phial of ether, Randall would feel her breasts land like pontoons, and then—hours of horizontal pleasure.

One icy Sunday Randall tramped up North Street all the way to St. Aloysius, the anchor of a once-thriving Polish community in New Haven, and got right to the point. "A woman touched my penis last night."

"By accident?"

Comic timing was not a bad thing in a confessor, Randall decided, and the priest's Old World accent lifted his spirits. "Okay, she rubbed it."

"Was it through clothing?"

"At first." Then Debi had yanked off his pants by the cuffs. "I should have kept my shoes on."

"Shoes are good obstacles."

"I didn't let her take off my underwear. But then..." Randall gave the priest time to imagine what had happened next.

"An emission?"

"No, I stopped her," Randall answered harshly, not in reproval, but because he was getting aroused in church, a sin he was *un*prepared to confess. "And I didn't touch her below the waist this time."

"*This* time?"

Sweet Jesus, at last a priest who *understood*. Randall could have wept with relief.

"Basically Father, she wants to go all the way and isn't going to let me have any peace until we do."

"Do you want to get married and start a family?"

"Not at all. In fact I intend to join a monastery next August."

"Are you Polish?"

"Excuse me?"

"Monk is okay, but the church needs children. Why not marry this girl? No more sex worries."

"*Marry* her? I don't think we can even have a conversation."

"This way you can have cake and eat it too."

"Are you saying my penance is marriage?"

"Yes."

"How about if I just don't see her again?"

The snort Randall heard was dismissive and definitive. "You will see her and you will go all the way. This far, you cannot go back to the holding of hands."

This advice wasn't Old World. This was pre-Hittite. Randall crossed himself and fled.

I trained as a chemist. Chemistry is a stable field, subject to scientific law. Over the last century, in trying to understand my left-brained charges, I have been exposed to a host of literary fashions. Every twenty years another "New Criticism" is there to process. One generation exults in the plenitude of literature, the next thrills to its essential nothingness, and etcetera. The phenomenon is not unique to *belles lettres*.

Infrequently, the ideas of some titans shape many fields simultaneously. Darwin and Freud, Einstein and Ferdinand de Saussure were four such titans. It is not for me to decide whether Jacques Lacan is among their rank, but his interdisciplinary influence has persisted several decades after his death in 1981. One of Lacan's primary assertions, if I may, is that the human organism only exists during its speech-acts, or *la parole*. Silence is nothingness.

By Thanksgiving, Silas Huth had abridged this Lacanian dictum into "If said, then true."

Gidwitz and the persistent lack of a boyfriend had made of him a sleepless, peevish wreck. He had begun to worry that when he wasn't speaking in order to exist in the world, who was he? Where was he? And was he subject or object? Equally troubling was a recurrent nightmare about a mysterious stranger, whose face was made of bumblebees and who bludgeoned Silas with a bouquet of tulips. Every evening Silas prayed that his pre-conscious would return to traditional libidinal themes, and by four every morning the Bee-Man would have buzzed him awake. Any additional fragments he might have been able to record as dreamwork evaporated on contact with the waking world.

Finally, one morning in early December, he woke again from this nightmare and decided to take action. In order to discover his identity, he decided he must visit the oracle during her office hours. It was either that, or go mad, or forgo speech altogether and die a martyr to the Lacanian *parole*.

"Come in," said Professor Gidwitz in her unplaceable accent.

He expected her lair to be strewn with the bones and blood-matted scalps of dissenters, so the chintz curtains, the bowl of paper-whites blooming on the windowsill, and the chain of paper clips on her desk blotter were disorienting. As was the package of Gauloises caught in the mouth of a black clutch.

Why would Gidwitz need a purse? What else was in there? A pistol? Strychnine? Tampons? Silas refused her offer of a smoke, sat in a chair, and began babbling in French about his angle of entry. She waited until he had run out of breath and answered him in English.

"Begin at the beginning, Mr. Huth."

Her smile was inviting. What color was her lipstick? Was that lipstick? Could he ask?

It was the Gidwitz Effect at two paces, so Silas did as he was told. He began with his unknowable heritage, his upbringing in the trailer park, his cultural identification with Nana, his social insecurities, his boyhood habit of reading volumes of the encyclopedia, the manhandling of the Jesuits, his facility with text, his sexual intrigues, and his search for love. Although he was his own favorite subject, Silas was unaccustomed to monologue, but Gidwitz kept saying, "Go on." So he went on, drawing closer to the present. As he revealed the most recent slights from Luca Lucchese and William Goris, and the loss of Scott Jencks and the Bee-Man nightmare, and most of all, his need for an authentic, anchoring self, he found himself drawn to a ruby-tasseled pillow on the black leather *chaise longue*.

As if reading his mind, Gidwitz said, "Feel free to lie down, Mr. Huth," but the change in position made him self-conscious. He stared at a water stain on the ceiling for what seemed like forever and listened, in an indigo silence, indigo being the color of the twilight deepening in her office. Radiator steam. Footsteps in the hallway. Clock ticking. Wind whistling. The oracle smoking. Inhale. Exhale. Tap of the ashes against the ashtray. Disapproval, disdain, contempt.

But then, finally—"Why are you afraid of me, Mr. Huth?"

"Because everybody is," gasped Silas.

"That's not why you're afraid of me."

"Because you have a widow's peak."

"That's not why you're afraid of me."

"Because my balls are in your mouth!"

"That's not why you're afraid of me," taunted Gidwitz, her voice steady against the stream of Silas's temper.

She ground out her Gauloise. Silas, riven by the loss, let someone else speak for him. "Katrinka isn't afraid of you, you stinky cow!"

Runteleh Gidwitz sat forward in her chair. "Who is Katrinka?"

"I'm Katrinka, dumbbell."

"How old are you?"

"I'm seven."

"Where do you live, Katrinka?"

"I live in a windmill, with tulips all around."

"So you are a Dutch girl."

Katrinka bit her lips to keep from giggling.

"What do you look like, Katrinka?"

"Can't you see me?"

"Not very clearly. It's gotten so dark out."

"My hair is in braids, and I wear an apron over my skirt and a starched white cap with lacy flaps."

"Is your hair blonde, Katrinka?"

"Yes."

"Do you wear wooden shoes?"

"What do you think?"

"I think you do."

Gidwitz snapped on her desk lamp, and Silas startled. The first thing he saw were her hands glowing under the light. "Excellent, Mr. Huth. I'm afraid the hour is up."

"Nooooooo," said Silas, kicking his feet against the couch. But pique swiftly turned to need. "Can I come see you again?" he asked.

"When you get angry with me again, you may come back."

"But I'd never get angry with you. You're so pretty."

"Maybe next time Katrinka would like to sit on my lap."

Silas kicked again, and then a third time. He liked the sound. It cleared his head at any rate, for he asked her who Katrinka was. Then, rising from the couch, he was amazed to see her reaching to him with open arms, as if she needed a hug.

He backed out of the room using his balled-up coat as a shield. Had he just called her pretty? Did she just give him a boner? Could he get expelled for it?

Advent was Randall's favorite time of year, but the candles on the wreath, the odor of fresh-cut pine boughs, and the crèche on the lower altar at St. Mary's provided no comfort that December.

Familiarity with Randall's case had bred a measure of contention in the priest with the sibilant *s*. "There are other parishioners waiting, young man."

"'Young man'? What happened to 'my son'?"

The priest sighed. "What is the matter today, my son?"

Two inches below both of Randall's knees, on the crest of his shins, like soft spots on a stone fruit, were a pair of oval abrasions.

"Rugburns, Father."

"What are rugburns?"

"Hickeys on your knees. Not your knees, my knees. They're friction marks. A scourge. I woke up with them this morning."

"How do you get them?"

"They come from rolling around on the floor, or rugs, or bedspread when you're...going at it pretty strong."

The night before, stripped to his underpants, and kissing her breasts, Randall had moaned that he was in danger of losing the last of his self-respect. At that Debi had drawn back and said, "Please, I can only take so much. I'm leaving." He ought to have let her dress and go, but Randall, so late out of the gate, was not ready to forgo the shudders, the limits leaped, the smeared swell of their faces. He beat her to the door and lifted her to his chest. Carrying her to the bed, he felt pride in playing the dominant role in a *tableau vivant* known to artists of every age (and medium) and achieved sexual climax on his third step.

Debi had understood. "Honey, what a breakthrough," she purred.

"Scourge or stigmata?" the priest asked.

"Is sarcasm necessary, Father?"

They held their tongues in common defeat.

"Say something, Father. Please. I don't know what to do."

"You want to sleep with this woman, don't you?"

From the ceiling of the confessional Love's manacles dangled like tongues of fire. Randall had a Lacanian moment of his own and spoke his wish aloud. "Yes," he replied. "Yes I do."

"God's mercy is infinite."

"Meaning?"

"You can atone after."

"As long as my repentance is sincere," Randall responded automatically.

A priest had suggested he commit fornication and destroy the grace of God in his heart. It was a very low moment. Had he the money, Randall would have taken the next flight to Umbria and begged for early admittance to the Monastery of San Pietro. So now, having exhausted all the Holy Roman outlets in New Haven, Randall sought wisdom from a secular authority, wife and mother Carolann Chudek. Handing over the till one morning after a doughnut shift, he mentioned his vexing abrasions to her. Alas, there was no balm in Gilead with which to heal his sin-sick soul, for, with a great clap of her hands, Carolann had exclaimed, "Rugburns!" then raised her skirt to show him hers.

Silas alleged otherwise, but Peter Facciafinta could read, and he read newspapers. By the end of 1983, the Center for Disease Control in Atlanta had estimated that there were 3500 cases of AIDS in the United States. Of those 3500, 1500 had died, and nearly every case was a male homosexual. The identification of the HTLV-1 virus was fifteen weeks away, so there were no truths besides the death count and a list of symptoms.

Through his reading, Peter became aware of a forty-page pamphlet printed that May called *How to Have Sex in an Epidemic: One Approach*, published by an outfit called "News From the Front." He procured a copy. Its final line, "What's over isn't sex—just sex without responsibility," made an impression.

One day a sign appeared above the honeycomb of Hadley mailboxes and in the elevators:

ATTENTION ALL GAY AND BISEXUAL MEN.
URGENT MEETING IN TV ROOM.
THURSDAY AT 6 PM.

For all anyone knew, a theme party might be in its planning stages, so the atmosphere in the TV room that night was raucous, with the gallery holding its breath each time the door opened. Several prayers were answered when Tómas Suovonemi, a dreamy Finnish political scientist, slid in at five after six, red as a lingonberry. Four men stood to offer him their seats.

Peter began. "Hi guys. Thank you all for coming, and welcome. I've brought us all together to have—"

"To have an orgy!" shouted someone, rather predictably.

"Maybe later, Sergio. No, I've brought us all together to have a discussion about AIDS. Acquired Immune Deficiency Syndrome. AIDS."

There were gasps and groans. Some made to leave, but Scott Jencks said, "You should stay and listen. This is life-and-death stuff."

Peter continued in the pall the word "death" had produced. "I don't have that much to say, guys. Except I know I'm scared." He held up his copy of *How to Have Sex in an Epidemic*. "There are some useful ideas in here. I'll make Xeroxes and leave them at the desk. I called the health clinic, and they recommended that I canvass your responses to what you know about AIDS. The point of tonight is to hear what you all have to say. Think of it as one of your research projects. Scott will write down everybody's thoughts."

"Anonymously," said Scott, clicking his pen in a down-to-business way.

A dour Yeats scholar named Victor Dobbs got the ball rolling by saying, "What's to know? You get it, you die."

"It takes years to get it," said someone else. "It takes, what do they call it, *repeated exposure*."

"You only get it if you do poppers."

"You only get it if you, you know, *take* it."

"No, you only get it if you swallow semen."

"You only get it if you live in gay ghettos."

"You only get it if you have sex in public toilets."

"You get it only if you sleep with Haitians."

"You get it only if you sleep with old men."

"No, only with old men who *give* it."

The stronger the assertion and the more circumscribed the *only*, the better everyone felt. No matter how contradictory the statement, voicing it chased the bogey out of the room. No one could acquire the cancer if he was sharing advice about how to avoid it. But then, as Peter began to hand out a stack of half-sheets from Health Services, the room lurched violently again. If Yale recognized the existence of the plague, then Yale would not be able to protect them. The bogey began rapping on the door with the tip of his scythe while Peter read out the symptoms. The quaintness of that initial half-sheet—night sweats, swollen glands, excessive fatigue, rapid unexplained weight loss, diarrhea, undulant fevers, purplish lesions, thrush—seems medieval today, a warning scratched out on sheepskin for a deserted village.

"Guys, I know this is a lot to deal with," said Peter, "and really there's no way any of us has it, but I don't think we can keep pretending AIDS isn't happening."

"I don't think it helps to think about it," said Pierre Humay.

"There's nothing we can do," said Victor Dobbs.

"Not true, Vic," said Peter. "*How to Have Sex in an Epidemic* says wearing rubbers when you have sex is a good idea."

"Are you kidding?" said Silas Huth. "Can you imagine blowing a man with a rubber on? Condoms are for straight people."

This sentiment occasioned several minutes of derision toward heterosexual folkways and the airing of hazy thoughts about gay liberation. Peter steered them back to the question of protective measures. Sean O'Connell said that he made sure to get plenty of rest. If he had sex on a Friday night, he waited until Sunday to have it again. Al Zini said he didn't have sex with more than one person at a time. Chuck Diller said he made his boyfriends take showers with him before sex. Peter, pleased that the group was opening up, said that if he wasn't forever in love with Scott, he would make sure to boil his dildos. Someone else said he had stopped swallowing. When someone said he would henceforth stop taking it you-know-where until a cure was found, there was a burst of applause, and the gathering began to take on the quality of a tent revival, with gaudy abjurations the new order of business.

Tómas Suovonemi finally raised his hand.

"Yes Tómas," said Peter. Heads turned to look at the dimpled, blond demigod.

"My solution has been not to have sex with anybody in this country. I will be celibate until I go back to Helsinki. There is no AIDS in Finland."

"You won't even kiss?" asked Peter.

"No kisses until Finland," he said.

"No sex at all. Wow. Write that one down, Scott," said Peter.

"They call it 'celibacy,'" said Silas, disgusted by this second instance of William Goris's self-defense.

"But Tómas," said Al Zini, "doesn't that get hard?"

"It gets very hard," replied Tómas, not intending to bring down the house.

In the midst of the laughter, the doors to the TV room swung open and a voice was heard shouting, "Seek death and ye shall find it, sinners! Cast out the Sodomites from the temple of the Lord!"

Becky Engelking strode to the front of the room, a white leather Bible clutched in both hands like the tablets of Moses. She rarely made a show of her religion, but these were desperate times. A certain organist from Clear Lake had skipped breakfast with her not once, but twice that week. Then

La Cincha had forced her to accept that "the brushing of the boobies during the bunny hop" obeyed the laws of gravity and not desire.

"This is so not cool—" said Scott.

"Silence, catamite!" Becky pushed at Scott with her Bible, then flung one arm high to heaven and began to preach, her eyes darting about the room. "It is written in holy scripture that man was not made to lie down with man. It is SIN! It is against GOD! Do you see where your sin has led you? God has sent this disease to destroy you. AIDS is the scourge of men-loving, it's worse than all the plagues of Egypt. You will all sink into an everlasting hell of boils and blood. Hell is like this very room, but it's HOT, and you can NEVER LEAVE! You must BEG for His forgiveness."

"This is a closed meeting, Becky," said Peter.

"SILENCE for the word of the Lord, you picklebiter! Where is he? Where have you taken him?"

"Where is who?" asked Peter.

"You know darn well who, Peter! I saw the two of you eating rice pudding at Naples Pizza this afternoon!"

The mob started to buzz: *"Catamite?" "Picklebiter?" "Does rice pudding mean what I think it means?"*

Silas Huth got to his feet in the middle of the room. "Shut your hole, Becky, and get out of here right now. You have no business frightening my friends."

"Fire and brimstone ARE frightening, Silas, and it's time you all LEARNED it!" She turned back to Peter. "I saw. I saw what you did. You went to Naples with him. And you are going to hell for it fast as devil's lightning."

"I was at Naples with him," said Peter. "But do you want to know what we talked about?"

"I most certainly do not," she lied.

"Your 'friend' wanted to know what I thought he should get you for Christmas."

Peter's whopper caught Becky so completely off-guard she stumbled into the television. A high heel gave way, pushing her ankle to the floor. The mob took another moment: *"Him?" "Who is 'him'?" "Hags are always the last to know."*

Silas, meanwhile, had gone purple. "Take your Bible and your lardass out of here, Becky, before I shove you through the doors myself."

The pain in her ankle spurred the temper in Becky's voice. "I'll bet you have it, Silas," she shrieked. "I can smell death upon you. The wages of sin is death! Judgment be upon all your heads!"

These last slurs riled the stupefied witnesses and set Silas in motion. Amid an escalating roar of oaths and jeers, Peter began pushing Becky backwards toward the double doors. It was going to be close. Peter yelled to Scott, who grabbed Silas and held on tight until Becky was ejected, followed swiftly by her sprung heel, which Silas had scooped up by the television and winged through the doors just before they swung shut. The last thing anyone heard in the melée was her plaintive, "Why do you all have to be this way?"

Randall Flinn had no cause to be at Peter's meeting, but heard all about it when Silas walked into his room later and gestured to the bed. "Do you mind, Chester?"

The young men had reached the nickname stage. Chester was Silas's nickname for Randall, in homage to true-blue, but danger-averse Chet Morton, best friend to Frank and Joe Hardy in the Hardy Boy *Mysteries*.

"That's what it's for," said Randall, who had been writing letters. He smiled to think of Debi Fleer asking permission to sit on his bed. He had one more day of peace while she was in technical rehearsals for the avant-garde play. He capped his fountain pen and moved over to his easy chair.

Silas shucked his loafers and told the tale. He had calmed down enough to be impressed by Becky's use of *catamite*—"a boy kept for homosexual practices." She had risked ridicule for acting on her beliefs, however demented they might be. In response, Silas had felt the need to stem the tide of her hateful predictions as best he could; everyone was already in so much shock from having to discuss the syndrome.

"That was a great thing you did, Silas."

Embarrassed to be caught in a good deed, Silas bent his head, keeping one hand tucked into an armpit while the other picked at the bedspread. Randall could see him as a little boy with a dictionary open on his lap, memorizing his way out of Nana's trailer. Black hair in the same buzz cut, a glint in his eye, verbal and mean to anyone who crossed him on the playground, including, or most especially, four-eyed targets like the undersized Randall Flinn.

Silas was not an ostrich about the plague, but like many men of this era he held his superstitions close. In his case, after absorbing Lacan—"If said, then done"—he had stopped using the four-letter acronym. Naming it would invite it in, would make it happen inside him. Not naming it was his pro-phylaxis. But since Becky had just now put *it* and him in the same breath, he began pressing at where he thought his lymph nodes were. Neck. Tho-rax. Armpits. They might have bloomed with disease during her tirade. He tensed his thighs in case that might flush out any enlarged nodes in his groin, then broke the silence with, "You're a believer, Randall. A true believer."

"I am. You know that."

"Why do you think God is doing this? Why has He sent this to us?"

"If history is any precedent, I don't think we're meant to know these things."

"Is Becky right? Are these the wages of sin? Am I a sinner?"

"It's not for me to judge you."

"Maybe Becky knows something I don't."

"Take that back," said Randall. "You *don't* have it, Silas. I pray that you don't. Every night since I met you I've prayed for that."

Believing in the beliefs of others was a helpful habit in Silas; it trumped superstition and pushed bad thoughts away. He pulled off his sweater. He threw it at Randall and stretched to the desk lamp. He was surprised to see on the blotter a sepia-toned postcard of a male nude. "I spy Randall, I spy!" he whooped, holding up his discovery.

"That's from Judy Ellis," said Randall. "She sends them with her letters."

"Really? Why?"

"She claims she'll do whatever is necessary to stimulate me."

"Does she know something you don't?" Silas had his suspicions about Randall, but because he wasn't physically attracted to him, he had let them be.

Randall laughed. "She likes to think she does. She sends me female nudes too. In her most lunatic moments, she imagines scenarios we might undertake with a third person."

"Are you that difficult to stimulate?"

Less amused, Randall rolled his trouser legs to his knees. "You tell me, Buckaroo." Buckaroo was Randall's nickname for Silas, an homage to the *vaqueros* of the Old West. Privately he called him Tumbleweed, which was a tribute to Silas's lanky frame and sexual availability.

Even in dim light, Silas saw the rugburns. "Debi? Debi Fleer?" Randall nodded. "Why didn't you tell me?"

"I didn't think you'd be interested."

"Are you kidding me? You're my best friend. This is big news, Randall. This is huge."

Randall's secret delight to be designated Silas's best friend required he make a joke of the situation. "No, Judy is huge. Debi is cumbersome."

"Have you—"

"Not yet."

"Are you going to?"

Randall's sigh was exaggerated. "Like Bartleby, I would prefer not to."

"Tell me. Tell me everything."

Randall recast the tragedy of Debi and the Doughnuts as a poker-faced farce for Buster Keaton. Silas was laughing himself sick until Randall pulled an art book from his shelf, *Il Coro di San Pietro in Perugia* by Don Giovanni Garattoni and told Silas about his ultimate monastic escape.

Silas was—what? Outraged? Stricken? Something had dropped in his stomach, and he had gone as pale as his coloring allowed. He snatched up the book, as if its confiscation would make it impossible for Randall to enter the cloister. "You can't go to Italy."

"Why not?"

How could Silas explain that he had never had a best friend before, a Chester he didn't want to sleep with, or wasn't planning to sleep with, or wasn't already sleeping with, or hadn't already slept with—a man to whom he wasn't physically attracted, but nevertheless loved to be around, and didn't compete with, and looked for at the end of every day? Silas couldn't explain that Randall's plan was tantamount to desertion, because, flipping through the plates in *Il Coro di San Pietro in Perugia*, resisting the urge to tear them to bits, he was only just figuring these things out for himself.

Silas pitched the book to the floor. They loved books, so both flinched at the potential harm in the gesture. "You can't go, Chester, because the stones will be cold. And you know how you hate being cold."

"I'll keep that in mind, Bucko."

Bucko was short for Buckaroo.

Chapter Six

Ten days before Christmas, Nixie and Randall were walking to the world premiere of Walt and Debi's avant-garde assignment. All of Yale seemed to be beetling in the crisp, starry cold to concerts, recitals, receptions, and glees. Randall had drawn his arm through Nixie's to help guide her through the ice patches on the sidewalks. A coil of her hair, drawn up about her head for the occasion, tickled his face as she leaned on his shoulder to answer his question about which was her favorite carol.

"'We Three Kings.' I love the sounds of their gifts. Gold, frankincense, and *myrhhhhh*. And their names too. I used to dream I'd marry a man named Melchior."

They paused for the light at the corner of College and Grove. Nixie opened her purse to get change ready for the Thirty-Cent Lady, who was stationed in front of Sprague Hall. Soprano Kathleen Battle, guesting with the Yale Symphony that night, would net her a jackpot of dimes.

"Let me get this," said Randall. With the spirit of the season, he retrieved a dollar and placed it in the palm of the Thirty-Cent Lady's ragged, fingerless glove.

"Thank you, kind sir," she replied in a tone so cultured that it crossed Randall's mind that she might be Helen Hadley, or what remained of me after a fatal case of rugburns cast me into the flotsam of Connecticut society. It was sweet of him to worry, but in my day we were so swaddled in yardages of skirt and underclothing that rugburns were an impossibility.

Taking her seat in the Park Street drama annex, Nixie let her coyote coat fall below shoulders draped in agates and tourmaline and surveyed the crowd while Randall opened the program. His stomach turned over to see the name Debi Fleer committed to the folded sheet of orange mimeo. Theater may be an ephemeral art, but the memories of its practitioners are long and unforgiving. In its literature, The Yale School of Drama promoted "the collaborative process," but Walt and Debi had already learned that only results counted. Their careers, at school and forever after, depended upon the reception of these three performances.

Walt passed them on the far aisle, dressed all in black, with a clipboard and one-eared headset, his hair as wild as a Slavic conductor's. Nixie dug her hand into Randall's thigh. "Walt! Walt!" she sang out, shattering the Parnassian sculpture of her bust and upswept hair. "Whoo-hoo, Walt, break a leg!" Sensing that Nixie was preparing to send Walt something stronger—a kiss, a scream, a good-luck tourmaline—he lay a restraining hand on her arm.

"I want him so bad, Randall."

"Don't let him know it *every* minute."

The play began. Whether it lived up to the hype generated within the drama school is for more qualified chroniclers to decide, but Nixie and Randall had a marvelous time. They had never met characters like Captiva Blench and Carnella Dolorosa, star-crossed misfits who traded monologues in separate pools of light. Captiva had nuclear dropsy; his fingers were splitting open from too much feeling. Carnella, a broken gourd rattling with radioactive seed, had been the most glamorous showgirl in Las Vegas until her partial mastectomy. The audience understood, even if they did not, that their union was the last hope of the world. Helgas One, Two, and Three, housekeeping staff in Captiva's abandoned bunker, were ordered to give cheer to Carnella: the audience held its breath when the trio of actresses burst through a Mylar curtain in their one-breasted prostheses and began to cootch downstage.

Debi's face was painted with a wickedness Randall recognized from their room wrangles, but there was also a layer of sang-froid to Helga Two that kept her at one remove. His extracurricular knowledge stopped at the footlights. That he and his neighbors were all the same to her in the dark was a disturbing discovery. The trumpet licks on the soundtrack shifted tempo, and Debi stole focus. She began to spin her breast in complete rotations, like a plane propeller. The astonished faces of her sisters, who merely swung their teats laterally, made it clear that Debi was improvising. The audience, wild for her commitment to working in the moment, broke into spontaneous applause. Randall was proud, jealous, appalled, and aroused.

The whistling, the cries of "Bravi" that greeted the group curtain call were spontaneous, and the standing ovation so swift that Randall's view of Debi was blocked by her jubilant classmates. Uncertain of protocol, Nixie and Randall let the pack surge ahead of them on the path to the dressing rooms. Randall had assumed that Debi's comparisons of the drama school to the back lot at MGM were an exaggeration, but now, waiting to congratulate her, and anxious about the distance her performance might have put between them, he felt that she, and indeed all actors, were heroic creatures, so much so that when he heard her sudden cry in the claque, he attempted his own feat of bravery and pushed his way through to a humid clearing in front of the dressing rooms.

A curvaceous redhead was chewing out a young man in purple sneakers. Debi, still in her makeup, a robe wrapped tightly around her tiny frame, stood to their right.

"This beast destroyed my work," the woman hissed in the way of all playwrights.

"What are you talking about?" replied the director. "We're a huge hit."

The playwright turned to Debi. "Who asked you to twirl your tit like that? It's not in the script."

"The audience loved it," said the director. "They loved the whole she-bang."

"What do they know? This trull wrecked my play."

"I have a name," said Debi, keeping her head down. "My name is Debi."

The playwright considered this courtesy. "No," she said. "Your name is Debit."

The crowd, which had been feasting on the altercation, groaned foul. Walt lifted his clipboard in a commanding way, but before he could intervene, Randall yelled out, "Debi Fleer's dance was the best thing in the play."

The playwright turned around. "Who said that?"

"I did."

She looked at him. "Who are you?"

"I'm Randall Flinn, and I don't go to this school."

"So you don't know what you're talking about," sneered the playwright.

"Maybe not," he replied, "but I know pretentious slop when I see it."

A partial falsehood: Randall found the play pretentious, but not sloppy. "Debi Fleer was brilliant. You are rude, miss, rude and...and..."

The strain of standing out was getting to be too much. Randall was saved by Merle Edmister, Dean of Acting, who sailed through the hell-mouth, banished the playwright with an eyebrow lift, then bent down to Debi in the hush.

"You were true to your art, Miss Fleer," he said. "You were *spontaneous*."

The rest of the cast stamped and pawed for praise, but the Dean vanished as quickly as he'd come. Randall found a chair amidst a cloudburst of fresh hosannas. Drained by the pile-up of so many unmet needs, he turned from the scene and watched another, happier drama. His thumb at the cleft in her chin, Walt was holding Nixie's throat like the stem of a chalice. She had curled one fist against his chest as they spooned. Her fur over an arm, her shoulders drawing light to her in a roomful of people used to grabbing after it, Nixie was a star on loan from a classier studio.

When Debi re-emerged in street clothes, Helgas One and Three begged for a breast-spinning lesson. Debi, who might have been expected not to share her technique, scheduled an appointment with them in the dance studio. Randall kept back while she attempted to explain, with charming, counterfeit humility, how it felt to receive a benediction from Mighty Merle. The attention upon her was so electric that Randall felt again how he could lose her to a crowd. It was time to tug the rope she had looped around his ankle. He pulled her to him, kissed her full on the lips, and told her how great her performance had been.

"Yes, you made that clear to everybody," she murmured in his ear.

He pulled back. "Was that all right?"

"Oh sweetie, yes. You must always be partial."

He held out her opening-night gift, a Las Vegas snow globe he'd found in an antique store on upper State Street. She shook it and watched the flakes fall.

"It's perfect, Mr. Flinn," she said softly, both to Randall and, he suspected for an instant, to a motion picture camera whirring above his right shoulder.

Nixie and Walt came over, hands locked; Debi gave Walt's behind a big smack. "Thanks, coach. If it wasn't for you and Nixie knocking me into shape that day, I'd be on probation."

Shortly after midnight the two couples parted at the corner of Chapel and York. Walt and Nixie went back to Hadley. Sometime between the Yves Montand record and the soothing finish of "Clair de Lune," Nixie told Walt that she loved him, had loved him since that first trip to the Price Chopper. While her fingers worried curls on his solar plexus, she interpreted, for his benefit, three months of his glances and gestures and utterances and silences. In the retelling, their affection took permanent root, and so they would grow together to fit the dimensions she had drawn for them.

Randall went to Debi's apartment and carefully set all of his clothing, and his watch, on a chair. As he stood erect, and shivering, next to her bed, Debi drew the comforter away from her body and quoted from the play: "O Rexus Reptilius, it's time to dance aslant the mongo branch."

"Is *that* what that line meant?" asked Randall, sliding a leg in.

Debi twined her arms against the headboard like a silent screen vamp and broke the tension. "You, me, here, Sexus Rexus."

Narcissistic, yes, driven, yes—her profession demanded it—but Debi was also very dear. It should surprise no one that an overwhelming majority of actors who leave show business choose as second careers therapies of every possible persuasion.

"I will submit to Helga Two," said Randall.

"Socks too."

"Huh?"

"Take off your socks."

And so it happened. Once the apple was picked, Randall confessed across her pillow that it had been well worth the wait. She was softer than anything he had ever touched or known. Randall had felt the edges of himself released to the slipstream of human endeavor, and no matter how pretentious that might strike anyone, he thought it, on balance, a most wonderful event.

After apples two and three, he was able to doze, but when the light began to gather strength beneath the blinds, he slipped from her bed and drew on his clothes. Everywhere he turned, Debi looked back at him: in

toe shoes and princess costumes, on a horse, at the beach, in plays and mu-
sicals and pageants. He kissed the curls peeping above a down comforter
and crept out of the apartment.

The New Testament provides examples of Jesus appearing in disguise
to test the faithful. Randall was prepared to confess to the first person he
encountered, but the doorman of the Taft Apartments was snoring in an
armchair and the Thirty-Cent Lady had left her College Street posting.
When he got back to Hadley, he took a long shower, then waited until he
knew they were up to call his parents in Michigan. And later, of course,
there would be a trip up the steep stone steps of St. Mary's.

And then, without warning, first semester was over and the Hadley Holiday Bash was in full swing in the lounge. Peter Facciafinta had draped the
corners of my portrait in plastic holly and hung mistletoe from the ceiling
a few inches from my face. As was the case every year, the forbidding
composure of my features discouraged intimacies from all but the most
inebriated revelers.

Becky Engelking, picking crumbs from the yarn whiskers on her
sweater at the dessert table, was, on the other hand, a portrait of *discompo-
sure*. Christmas had always been her favorite holiday, a time for hunkering
down with loved ones, salt-streaked boots in the mudroom, and plenty of
church solos. Back in happier days—only a month ago—when Silas Huth
had insisted she buy the sweater at a Macy's clearance sale, its gingham
dog and calico cat appliqués were joining paws. Now, after her AIDS fra-
cas in the TV room, Silas wouldn't speak to her, and four weeks of snack-
ing away her sorrows had made the dog and cat drift apart like continents.
The pleats in her skirt were similarly stressed.

Brent Fladmo had continued to keep an imprecise, but tangible distance, so Becky's "Is he or isn't he?" roller coaster climbed and plunged
dozens of times each and every day. Every suspicious signifier, like his
Mabel Mercer records—that old bag couldn't sing a lick!—was offset
by something manly, like his barbell set. He threshed, he baled hay. He
could tip a cow for fun. He'd be right at home in the Engelking kitchen, if
he would only commit to a weekend in Ottumwa over break. Becky was

promising a sleigh ride, then a trip to Canteen in the Alley for loose-meat sandwiches. Sunday, after church, she could cheer him on at Twin Galaxies, the brand-new video game arcade everyone back home was raving about.

Nixie came up and put her arm through Becky's. "Did Brent like his gift?"

"He's wearing it, isn't he?" said Becky. She had tied it for him, but tilted her neck away from his lips. After all this torture, first base was his to steal.

"Bow ties are snazzy."

"Maroon looks good on a man," said Becky, repeating one of her mother's sayings.

"Did he get you a present?"

"He did. I received a lovely antique mah-jongg set."

"Huh," said Nixie. "That's different."

This bit of strangeness Becky blamed on Peter Facciafinta, who must have steered Brent away from a piece of jewelry that day at Naples Pizza. She wished again that she hadn't gone on her AIDS crusade. A gay following was as essential to a diva as the right vocal coach, but the dorm fags had frozen her out. If Jesus could forgive and forget, why couldn't they?

Across the room she saw Brent with Faye Kringle, whose thick hair was trimmed short like a boxwood hedge. Brent's interest in Faye's voided parasite was reassuringly hetero, but then Peter Facciafinta jingled by in his elf costume and when the three of them clinked glasses, Becky's roller coaster plunged again. Faye Kringle wasn't a gal who hadn't met the right guy, she was an archaeology lezbo! And mah-jongg was for Jews, Asians, and homos! Oh, for a handful of tiles to raise welts on them all!

"I didn't think I would ever love again," Nixie was saying.

Becky was about to pipe in her customary "Me too," but bridled instead.

"Oh, that's horseshit," she replied. "If you didn't love Walt, you'd be in love with someone else. You know what, I'm sick of you and your gassy boyfriend!"

Becky could be moody, but she was never coarse. "I hope I haven't done anything wrong," said Nixie. "You're like a sister to me." She held out a sugar cookie, but Becky smacked it upward, where it met its death against an asbestos tile. "And Walt is not"—here Nixie lowered her voice—"gassy."

Becky, her body flooded with temperament, gave a snort. "Oh please. I guess love is blind *and* deaf. And it smells like strawberries. I know better. I grew up on a farm."

"Are you nervous about going home? When I left France—"

"For God's sake, shut up about France too. You think you are the only person who ever crossed an ocean? Look around you." Becky flicked a hand. "The lounge is filled with people who worship elephant heads and flying monkeys and don't go on and on about it."

"They might if you listened to them," replied Nixie, on surer ground now. Becky didn't even own a passport.

"I baked cookies all morning with the Indians. But maybe you're right, Nixie," she said. "Let's see if I'm a good listener. Woo-hoo! Venki! Arup! Guys!" Becky motioned to the foosball table. "Woo-hoo! Lakshmi!"

"Now Becky, let's not put anybody on the spot," said Nixie.

Lakshmi shimmered toward them in a gold-and-scarlet sari, every inch a princess. Her eyes were lined in black and her skin was translucent amber.

"You look gorgeous," said Becky, bussing Lakshmi's cheek to show Nixie how accepting she was of foreigners.

"Where is Brent?" asked Lakshmi. "He was telling me how pretty he thought *you* looked."

"Pshaw," said Becky. "I'm the calico cat. Gosh, Lakshmi, I wish Iowa weren't so far away. You'd have such a good time with all us Engelkings."

Venki and Arup appeared. Twenty-dozen tollhouse cookies later, and Becky still wasn't sure who was who. "Tell me something, guys," she said. "Nixie here says I don't care to know anything about your culture."

"That's not what I said, Becky," said Nixie.

"Silence!" Becky tugged at the back of her skirt to make it behave. "I want you to know that I care about every color of the rainbow. I sing in several languages and am very broad-minded. So tell me something, guys."

"Yes, Becky," said Arup.

"What are gay guys like in India?"

"What guys?"

"Gay guys."

"Gay?" said Venkatesh.

Becky made kissing sounds, then wiggled her index finger through the closed circle of her fist. Both Venki and Arup straightened up.

"There are no gay people in India," said Venki.

"No, no gay people," seconded Arup, shaking his head.

Becky stomped a foot. "*Guys*, I wasn't born yesterday. Hadley is crawling with fairies, so India's got to have, like, *billions*."

"No gay people, yes. My father says they are a product of the West," said Arup.

"Back me up here, Lakshmi" said Becky.

"Actually, Becky, I have never met any homosexuals in my country. But I am naive about this matter."

"Heck then, if it's true, maybe I should move there. You all speak English, I should do fine there, right? All I need is a plane ticket and a toe ring."

Becky's laugh failed to lighten the mood. Venkatesh and Arup retreated; Nixie passed the leash to Lakshmi and sped back to the savories table, where she had been gobbling deviled eggs to boost her fertility. She might lock herself in her bedroom in Louisville to write two seminar papers, but that wouldn't keep her mother from sliding law school brochures under the door. Under those conditions, a fetus would be as comforting as an engagement ring.

Leading Becky to a chair by the fire, Lakshmi chided her gently. The men thought Becky was accusing them of being lovers, which was a particular upset to Venkatesh, who had confided to Lakshmi that he had a crush on Becky. And yes, Venki was the tall one.

A few yards south, Debi Fleer lit three candles on a neglected menorah, said a prayer, and gestured to Randall that it was time to head upstairs. She was leaving in the morning on a Caribbean cruise with her father, and the clock was ticking.

"I'd like to wait for Secret Santa," Randall answered.

"Santa Claus can kiss my tuchas," said Debi. "How about I get undressed and warm your sheets? I'll give you twenty minutes."

"We are not having sex in my room, Debi."

"Why not?"

"I told you, I *live* there."

Though she thought Hadley was an unhygienic dump, Debi expected to christen Randall's room nonetheless. His stonewalling was one of several bones of contention. In the eight days since the closing of the play, Randall had spent mornings in the confessional, afternoons in the library, and nights at the Taft Apartments. There *was* no going back to the holding of hands. Randall knew Debi wanted him to be more cheerfully enslaved, wanted a whistle and a smile as he sailed into port three times every night, but he couldn't comply. Nor did he refrain from verbalizing his feelings of loss when she asked him why he had gone silent, or sighed so profoundly, or was wearing out his knees in the confessional. Room 328 was his sole refuge. It had been his mother's suggestion that he keep his chamber off-limits for his own peace of mind. Everyone, you see, forgave Randall except Randall.

Debi slipped her hand into his right pants pocket. He was ticklish and if she got him giggling, it would be all over. "Now let me have that key."

"Nothing doing."

Silas Huth interrupted the tug of war. "Is this 'Find the Salami'?"

"Key first, then the salami," said Debi.

Randall broke free and put Silas between them.

Knowing that strategic flattery of Silas, her only rival for Randall's attention, would strengthen her case, Debi said that although she preferred Silas with hair, she admired his commitment to the role of Katrinka. Silas, since we saw him last, had had his head shaved in the name of Oedipus. It's a perfectly acceptable option today, but in 1983, a bald young man meant anomie or chemotherapy. In either instance, the wearer was given a wide berth.

"Hair grows back," said Silas, trying to sound flip when, truth to tell, he felt his sanity was now a sometime thing.

Four nights before the holiday party, he had been on deadline for his angle of entry. Titled "Speech and Disappearance," it was a microscopically close reading of Tiresias's single line, *"How dreadful knowledge of the truth can be/ When there's no help in truth!"* By three a.m., dazed with stimulants, he began to be haunted by the truth that the Plague of Thebes had reached across the centuries to infect his body too. He parsed his lymph nodes for dreadful knowledge. He discovered a bump under the right side of his jaw, halfway to the chin—was that a bump? He found it, lost it, found it again, went elsewhere, checked back, lost it again. He and the bump played hide-and-seek, his fear mounting until, finding it one last time, he captured it with a pinch of his thumb and forefinger and ran to the medicine cabinet.

In the mirror he saw a little girl with blonde braids and a white lace cap. "Who are you?" he asked.

She giggled. "I'm Katrinka."

"Do I know you?"

The little girl ignored the question and began issuing commands. Her tone was sweet, but her eyes meant business. Silas felt powerless to resist her as she tore up his "Speech and Disappearance" notes, reset his alarm, and pushed him into bed.

He slept like a baby for the first time in weeks. In the morning, she sent him to the Co-Op where she had the barber shear him like a sheep. They bought a wool cap in the accessories aisle and then went to the Salvation Army on Church Street, where they found a striped dress, a white apron, a wicker basket, and a pot of yellow tempera paint. The dusty bunch of plastic tulips in the window was providential, then it was home to Hadley where Nixie, distracted and sleep-deprived from her own Oedipal labors, lent Silas rouge, mascara, and a strand of red glass beads from her mannequin hand.

Katrinka had made Silas wait outside the seminar room until she was ready to speak. When they heard Pierre Humay finish up in the sepulchral tones of a talking Easter Island statue, Katrinka doffed Silas's coat and cap, threw open the door to Linsley-Chit 312, skipped to the blackboard, and spoke extemporaneously. Twenty minutes later, Katrinka sat down and swung her legs on the chair. Silas's own reappearance—was that yellow *paint* on his fingers?—went unnoticed in the even greater spectacle of Runteleh Gidwitz's tears dripping freely onto the seminar table.

To celebrate the end of the seminar, the cohort went to Naples Pizza, where Silas had to pretend that Katrinka was on purpose. She had pelted the class with plastic tulips, but only God (or Tiresias) knew what she had *said*. That was the crux. What had been her angle of entry? Pierre was convinced she'd spoken Dutch. Scott Jencks insisted that Katrinka had ordered the class to "Rape Mommy's hair holes." Nixie claimed she'd learned how to pierce a baby's ankles, and Bobbie Sproull, the *ne plus ultra* in rational apprehension, stunned the group by saying she had heard nothing but the sound of buzzing bees.

Although they are cliché concepts thirty years on, "the inner child," "regression therapy," "past lives," and "channeling" had yet to saturate the media, so Silas had less to work with when trying to work through Katrinka's terrifying guest appearances. Her blonde hair and blue eyes ruled out Native-American tradition, so in the ensuing days Silas drew upon what he did know—cocaine and No-Doz, Hans Brinker, The Boy and the Dike, Anne Frank, Erasmus, and etcetera. When it came to speech and disappearance, who was speaking, and who, or what, might be disappearing? Was Katrinka leading him to the four-letter "it" or was she protecting him from dreadful knowledge of "it"? He had no answers.

On the positive side, the bump under his jaw had vanished and he had no more Bee-Man nightmares. On the negative side, the day before the holiday party he had gotten a letter from Monsignor Bain at Brophy Prep telling Silas to pray for Brother Ted. The doctors couldn't figure out why a twenty-eight-year-old track coach who had never smoked could have difficulty breathing. Silas didn't pray, but he knew Randall would for him, and this was why Bucko needed serious time in Chet's room before he boarded his plane to Tucson in the morning.

"Would you do some Katrinka for me?" asked Debi.

"She's not a party trick."

"She's made you star of the French Department."

"Not like Helga Two," said Silas. "I'd have come to your show, you know. Chet Chester here wanted to keep you all to himself."

"That is so not true," said Randall.

Debi and Silas might have kept up with their "aw shucks" admiration society, but Becky, who had promised to sing Randall's favorite carol, had begun "O Holy Night" at the piano.

If personal issues had led to stasis with the Argentine Way, there was no trace of it in Becky's voice that night. It looped out like a roll of silver satin ribbon, folding Hadley in its shimmer and leading everyone to take stock of his or her first semester. For Randall Flinn, the tightness in his hamstrings, the weariness in his sacrum, and the rugburns were novel physical sensations, no question, but his wanting to linger at a party was the happier surprise. He looked around the room, linking himself to the faces he knew, and filling himself up on the details he had gathered from and had been offered by people so much freer with themselves than he could yet dare to be. The soprano had taken his request. He was becoming a joiner. As exciting as it was for his body to anticipate sex with Debi, it also pained his soul to admit that she was a parallel, but less essential, course in his delayed education. All semester he had been watching the hearts of his friends swell and lift in their chests on the oxygen that the slightest glance or touch from their love objects pumped into them. Tonight all feet but his were bobbing on the floor. Deep down he knew that Debi would not obtain his heart, because he had not offered it. That was his sin. His inkling that she didn't really want it was hers.

The stillness after Becky's pianissimo finish was a finer tribute than the applause. She motioned Brent up from the bench. They bowed together, then Becky silenced the crowd with a regal drop of her hands.

"That was lovely, Brent," she said. "So very special. Wasn't that special?" Becky was hissing her esses like Randall's confessor at St. Mary's. The crowd began another round of applause. "Some of us are wondering, Brent," she continued. "Some of us are wondering whether you're gay."

Brent crumpled as if he'd been sucker-punched. "What did you say?"

"Are you gay?"

"No!" said Brent.

Becky raised her voice. "Well, some of us think you're a faggot."

"Not again," groaned Silas.

"He plays the organ, right?" said Debi. "Case closed."

"Well, I'm not!" said Brent.

"Oh Brent, you can tell us the truth. Are you positive you're not a bungholing dicksmoker?"

Becky had done it again, but this time the end justified the means. Brent backed her to the keyboard and after a sustained, discordant crash of keys, he began kissing her neck with brisk, noisy smacks. Becky's eyes fluttered as she stroked his hair with her hands, and her rhinestone shoe buckles, catching the light, glinted like a ripple of moon on a river.

Silas turned away from the queasy spectacle. Becky deserved a boyfriend, but he didn't think extortion an acceptable means of acquisition. On the other hand, he reasoned, if Brent's pawing went a convincing distance, he could marry her, sire children, have a church music career, become a closeted pillar of society and fend off the plague with private fantasies and a porn stash in the organ bench. Living a lie suddenly seemed to Silas like a fair trade-off for having a life to live.

Debi turned away too and gripped Randall's hand. "Last chance?"

"I said no."

"You'll write to me—or call—from home."

"I'm not going home."

"*What?*"

"I'll be here writing my Francesco de Mura paper."

"I'm keeping you from your family," she said.

They looked at each other carefully. The boy Randall wanted to be for his parents, rearranging the crèche, shoveling the walks, wrapping presents with his sisters, arranging cookies on a plate for Santa, was gone for good. So was the boy Debi had yanked into the broom closet once upon a time.

"Kiddo, I'm calling a cab," she said. "Ciao."

Off she went towards a group of engineers bluffing its way through "Carol of the Bells." Something fell inside Randall, but there was relief too. He'd have to wait and see whether this pain pushed deeper than his sacrum. She waved goodbye. Resisting a last-minute dash to hold the door for her, Randall blew her a kiss and watched his quince-colored puffball push into the cold.

Silas touched Randall's sleeve. "More punch, Chet?"

Randall nodded. "She's relentless. It'll be quiet here. Right now I need silence more than anything I can think of."

"Do you mean silence like at the monastery in Perugia? Do you mean like a monastic silence?"

"I do," said Randall, surprised by the edge in Silas's voice.

Silas considered Randall now. Debi Fleer wouldn't have the plague. Not only would Randall get to live, he had the choice of marriage or the cloister. Unless Italian monks were as randy as Arizona Jesuits. And of course they were. Randall (and America) might be innocent of the ways of ordained predators and their case-shuffling superiors, but Silas knew all about it.

For Silas, being gay was a cult of the elect, a superior calling, because he, Silas, was cultish, elected, superior. Nana and his mentors had elevated him and reinforced this perspective. Silas had never wanted to be straight or prayed for "correction" or pulled a Brent on a clueless Becky. Anyone, he thought, could be straight. Nearly everybody was. Homosexuality required cunning and risk. But this news about Brother Ted made Silas aware for the first time in his life of the concept of negative risk. Jealous of Randall's innocence, enraged by the safety of the breeding kind, he gave in to his fears and did his worst. He sat his best friend down on a pockmarked Hadley couch and sullied Randall's dream of escape by confessing, in the filthiest terms possible, his past at Brophy Prep. He pushed harder by asserting that there would be no quiet awaiting Randall in the cloister; San Pietro would be a bigger fuck palace than Hadley Hall. The sucking and the slurping and the whipping and the slapping and the moaning would make a din to exceed all the circles of *Inferno*.

Randall, as ever, listened attentively, but was unable to look at Silas. He cleared his throat, and responded to Silas's diatribe by saying that he would certainly add Brother Ted to his prayers. He stood, peeled a length of wayward garland from his trouser leg, and headed for the elevator.

Hurting Randall made Silas feel worse, not better. He slumped right and let his bald head grow chill on the armrest. The sound of girlish coos and Fladmo simpers by the piano made him close his eyes. Take me now, he thought. Take me now. I am ready to go.

Under the mistletoe, so close to me I could have tapped their shoulders with the closed fan in my hand, Nixie was resting her head under Walt's chin. She watched Brent reach incontrovertible second base against a faraway wall and smiled. She thought back to the sing-off, held in this same enclosure. Twas many a mountain that she and Becky had climbed since that muggy night in September.

"How much will you miss me over break?" she whispered.

"Twenty-five days' worth," said Walt, rubbing her stomach as he cradled her from behind.

For days he had not left her side, and every morning they had dined on banana pancakes. His strong hands were helping the baby to grow, Nixie thought. Or warming up the place where a baby could grow. "I won't see you again until 1984, Burly," she said.

"Hmmm. Can't wait."

"What will you do without me?"

He kissed her ear. "Laundry."

With the present conquered, Nixie was shaping a determination for the future: she would have tenure at Columbia and chair the Voltaire Studies Society. Walt would stage-manage Pulitzer Prize dramas. After a bedtime story in their apartment on Riverside Drive, bilingual Hannah Bolger-Stehlik would ask Mommy how she and Daddy had met. To be ready for little Hannah, Nixie opened her eyes in order to remember every face and name in the common room, remember the scuffed baseboard, the plaid drapes, the orange upholstery on the blocky furniture, the speckled linoleum, the radish rosettes drying out on the aluminum trays, all their brilliant, connected lives brimming with possibility. Caspar, Melchior, and Balthazar, she thought dreamily. Melchior and his myrhhhh were hers, and here to stay.

Intersession

Perhaps now a biographical sketch while we wait for our love slaves to return from their vacations.

I did not invent the Sippy Cup. I was born in 1895 in Portsmouth, New Hampshire, the second of four children (two boys, two girls), to a newspaper editor and his wife. The Hadleys had been shipbuilders and maritime traders along that stretch of the New England coast since the early eighteenth century. They began acquiring land as soon as it proved prudent to do so. My mother's family, which had held iron mine interests in Lower Saxony, emigrated to Boston from Hanover after the European revolutions of 1848. My parents met at a lecture on "Theosophical Thought" that Henry S. Wolcott gave at the Boston Athenaeum. My father, Gabriel, who was covering the lecture for his newspaper, thought theosophy—table turning, séances, mediums, and the like—was bunkum of the first order. My mother, Eliza, never weighed in on whether Life, and all its diverse forms, human and non-human, is indivisibly One, but I cannot help but feel, more than twelve decades after their meeting, that my ability to communicate to you as a protoplasmic emanation from a portrait in oils lends some credibility to the "Secret Doctrine" set forth by Mr. Wolcott, Madame Blavatsky, and generations of their global disciples.

My mother did allow that the family subscription to the Athenaeum was a way by which she and my aunts could meet eligible suitors. My father was introduced to my mother in the lending library. Staunch and Starch (the pet names my brother Winthrop gave them) were married fourteen months later.

The comforts of my childhood were lavish in the Yankee way: money manifest, but unmentioned. My fascinations as a girl were tribal accounts of the Great Plains Indians and Jane Addams and her work at Hull House. My matriculation at Oberlin College was made from a desire to quit forever New England and social introductions at the Athenaeum. Oberlin's motto, "Learning and Labor," suited me, as did its original charter, which was to train teachers to advance strong Christian principles among the Western settlers. I visualized a future in a pioneer schoolhouse somewhere north of the North Platte River, instructing as diverse a population—Pawnee, Choctaw, Swede, Scots-Irish—as the region afforded.

In accordance with the time, my sexual education was non-existent. An intense crush on my chemistry professor, Marietta Tieman, determined my choice of major at Oberlin. The Periodic Table of Elements, less crowded an academy in 1913, became my bible. In the winter of my senior year, a blizzard forever altered my existence. I was hiking alone in the Carlisle Reservation, far from campus, when it began to snow. Within twenty minutes, I could scarcely put one foot in front of the other. By the time I reached my rooming house on West Vine Street, five inches had fallen. My garments were soaked, my teeth were chattering, and I couldn't feel my hands or feet. Supper was on the table when I pushed through the front door with the last of my strength. Ada Bonner, the serving girl, pulled me from my waterlogged duster and wrapped a sheepskin throw around my shoulders. Other students began unbuttoning my boots, running a bath, fetching heated stimulants, but all I sensed was the pressure of Ada's hands on my upper arms and the quick brush of her bodice against my back.

The bath restored my senses, and Ada brought supper to my room. Her hand supported my neck as she rearranged the pillows. What I felt in that moment, and in those that followed as she fed me broth and brushed my hair, has never left me.

The next morning, I awoke a nethersexer in love with a townswoman. I became as reactive as a halogen. In any moment during those last five months in college, I might exist, like a halogen, as three states of matter. I knew why poetry was written and for what and whom it was meant. And music—oh, I went to every single concert given that spring at the conservatory, my love beside me as her schedule permitted.

Ada was too frightened to settle with me somewhere, anywhere west of the Mississippi. She was expected to marry, support her parents. And so she would.

After a summer of pleading and post-graduate research for Professor Tieman, I returned to Boston in a profound depression. Life continued outside the door to my room. For months I assented to anything that kept it from intruding past the frame of that door. I considered the cloister. I wrote verses. I took pills and potions, but no exercise. I was an invalid in the Alice James manner.

Staunch and Starch eventually resorted to a form of shock therapy. They arranged a marriage with a second cousin, bookish, bespectacled Baldwin, a "gentler" Wigglesworth. They seemed to expect vociferous objection, but as with everything else that year, I let the engagement happen to me. My sister Theda dragged me from my room and coerced me into providing a simulacrum of interest in the duties attendant upon a Brahmin alliance. Three days before the wedding, I wired Ada in Ohio to come and keep house for Baldwin and me. The vigil I kept while waiting for an answer to this crazed gesture cut through the fog in my brain like nitric acid on a plate of steel.

No one knew why I called off the wedding, but I was free. I threw myself into the life of a Boston bluestocking. I might have ventured north of the North Platte, but at the time not a molecule of me could countenance the idea of boarding a train that traveled west of Oberlin, Ohio. Instead I went to work in Salem for Caroline Emmerton. For many years I taught English, arithmetic, and "Americanization" skills for the House of the Seven Gables Settlement Association.

My brothers, Winthrop Dana and Flann Harrison Hadley, were killed at the Second Battle of Ypres. Ada Bonner perished in the 1918 influenza pandemic. I like to imagine she died nursing her loved ones. Theda and I eventually inherited from Staunch and Starch. Upon my death, I gave a portion of my wealth to Yale, which had been Flann's choice for bucking family tradition. My portrait, copied from a photograph, and the vitrine containing the last of my unused wedding china were unveiled at Helen Hadley Hall during its opening day ceremony in 1958.

And there you have Helen Hadley, as well as I know her.

PART TWO

The Show and Gaze of the Time

"Alas for the seed of man."

—Oedipus Rex

Chapter Seven

Anton Chekhov, a professional when it came to observing human behavior, wrote, "Men dine, simply dine, and in that moment their happiness is decided or their lives destroyed." When traveling the distance of years to the start of 1984, I cannot help but wonder what might have happened had Becky Engelking not partaken so fully of that all-you-can-eat Indian buffet in Sioux City. So much depends upon it.

Christmas in Ottumwa had unfurled along traditional lines: earthy Engelking roister, music-making in the parlor, and every part of the pig. At night Becky drew her comforter tightly about her neck and worried about Brent Fladmo's health. How she burned for a follow-up to their duet at the Hadley piano, but he had a wicked cold that kept him from making the drive from Cedar Rapids. His sputum, he said, was bright green. As for hosting *her*, he was far too contagious. For a day Becky complained of a warning tickle in her own throat, but her mother and her sister Tammy were maddeningly indifferent to her hints about an organist whose germs she might have caught.

One evening she was watching the news with her parents when a feature about the AIDS epidemic came on. Her father pushed aside his pie and said, "Those people can't die fast enough."

Becky was aghast. "What people do you mean?"

"All them fags. They make me sick."

"But—but—" They really are people, she nearly added, thinking of Peter Facciafinta's teasing compliments and Pierre Humay's encyclopedic knowledge of opera and even Silas Huth's sense of humor—although that cut both ways.

"But nothing, Becky. The wages of sin is death."

"Amen," said her mother.

With a terrible, shaming flush, Becky recalled issuing those same words of Paul to the Romans in front of a different television set. The speck of disgust in her father's eye magnified the whopping plank in her own, but now, since Brent was really straight, she resolved that in 1984, she must humble herself before another gathering of Hadley homosexuals and sing her way to forgiveness.

The next day she and her mother and sister shopped the white sales in Sioux City. Treating them to their first taste of Indian food at the Bombay Grill was a likely gustatory outcome after four months at Yale and two weeks in Iowa. Yet what would have happened had the women gone shopping in Ames instead? What if Tammy Engelking, fuming at the eight yards of peach satin her mother had bought for her big sister, hadn't goaded Becky into trying every item in the buffet? What if the management hadn't trimmed costs by holding over the lamb korma? What if, on the phone the night before, Brent Fladmo had said he missed Becky too, thereby keeping her subconscious from dwelling on Venkatesh and his reported crush?

But the die was cast. Tammy and Mrs. Engelking consumed a few forkfuls of curried Veg-All, while Becky's large, cosmopolitan bites demonstrated her delight to the nearly empty restaurant. After forcing down a trio of dough balls soaked in rose water syrup, Becky lost her lunch in the parking lot. For two days she lived in a state of distress the Engelkings called "Both Exits, No Waiting." The doctors, fearing dehydration, kept her home in Iowa for an additional week.

Back at 420 Temple Street the Hadley population was on a belated round of intellectual industry before the resumption of classes. Even Peter Facciafinta, under the spell of the media, was having a go with Orwell's *1984* at the front desk. But all—with the exception of Brent Fladmo—took the time to get on the horn to Ottumwa and boost Becky's spirits. Brent couldn't even be persuaded to chip in for a get-well bouquet. His new, spiky hairdo and the Go-Go's album he kept on constant rotation suggested a turn toward the New Wave over break.

At 102 Mansfield Street, in the undulant shadow cast through her window by the spine of "The Yale Whale," Eero Saarinen's famous ice rink, Carolann Chudek licked an envelope, oblivious to the teakettle whistling behind her. Wisconsin had been a lovely interregnum; she and Lou had treated each other with respectful tenderness; she let him take her whenever he liked, which was often enough to prove that he still loved her, and she him. The boys wore their Yale Christmas gear with a pride that touched her heart, and she had cooked them all their favorites. But now the time had come to act upon her New Year's resolution, hatched in seminar the month before when Runteleh Gidwitz had said, in runic response to Carolann's angle of entry, "The gates are open, Mrs. Chudek. Pound at them."

Exactly! No more meeting cute by the doughnut tray, or attempting to soften Mrs. Bluder with free coffee and fashion tips. She must pound away at Nathaniel Gates with all her wiles. Thus it was that, on the fifth of January, Chairman Gates opened a letter marked _Personal_ in his office. Its two pages, supplemented by drawings, outlined her plans for him. The bad French excited him, as did the smears of orange frosting and the references to his bibliography. Before he could alert the university office trained to handle these kinds of situations, his hand was inside his trousers.

Letters arrived every day, each more explicit than the last. Spicy scents clung to their pages; bay leaves and dried pods and cookie crumbs fell from the envelopes. Carolann also enclosed filmy fragments scissored from her lingerie. He was not to reply; he was to touch himself, drench the fragments with what she called essences, and wait.

After following her instructions, he would lower his face in the sink of the office bathroom and turn on the tap. Although he had served in Korea and spent a bachelor year on the Left Bank, Nathaniel Gates had never quite gone to seed. The graduate students he'd had through his climb to tenure and beyond were the routine spoils of academic dominion. Precious little had prepared him for Carolann's lewdness. He had never given much thought to his essences, and now he had a collection of them bagged in plastic behind the Proust on his shelves.

She made him wait a week. The morning Mrs. Chudek was to arrive to "review" her courses, he sent Mrs. Bluder on an extended journal hunt at Sterling and nervously twirled in her chair in the outer office. At 9:45, Carolann pooched her lips at the frosted glass. He let her in and locked the inside office door. She let her coat slide from her arms, then, facing away from him, slowly bent over and withdrew from her striped canvas satchel a doll-sized, rabbit's-fur muff. Two days later Mrs. Bluder was sent to a used bookstore in Stamford and the satchel contained a cherry-topped cheesecake in a springform pan. On their third meeting, she took out a teething ring, and Nathaniel knew he was lost.

Carolann was wise enough to space out their rendezvous. Nathaniel would call her every night begging to know what would be in the satchel "next time," and she would tease him by saying that her studies were more important than any "next time." Wandering the campus crosswalks, his fingers redolent with their conjoined essences, he found himself distracted by a parade of totes and briefcases, purses and backpacks. One morning he pursued a duplicate of Carolann's satchel for three breathless blocks and had to relieve himself in the wine cellar of the Elizabethan Club. One night Eleanor Gates opened her walk-in closet and found her husband trembling by her handbag hooks. For the first time since the Kennedy Administration, they made love on the floor.

Our latter-day Astarte made certain to maintain her freedoms and accepted a lunch invitation in West Haven from Luca Lucchese near the end of January. They hadn't been alone together in the New Year; immediacy was making her blush in the passenger seat. Stripped of his tweeds, Nathaniel Gates had a freckled paunch dusted with reddish fur. When held over her knees, the backs of his thighs jiggled like an aspic. The power of her scenarios had unleashed in him a torrent of talk, but she wished sometimes for quiet. Luca, on the other hand, lifted weights and acted like the favor was his. Watching his leg tighten in his jeans as he downshifted on Route 1, she made a mental note to put a pacifier in the satchel for "next time."

The maitre d' and the waiters at Umberto's greeted Luca in Italian. A Barbaresco was breathing on their table and the chef sent out an impressive antipasti.

"I was the best waiter this place ever had," Luca said by way of explanation. "I started at sixteen as a busboy. Umberto comes after me all the time to buy a piece of the place. The guys here are putting on the dog, because they know how important this lunch is."

"It is?"

Luca tapped the tablecloth with a cherry tomato. "I got a proposal to make, Cranny."

Her sip of wine failed to douse a sudden shower of sparks.

Between bites of veal saltimbocca, Luca outlined his vision for All-Ivy Doughnuts. Celebrity salad dressings, signature ice creams, and the like were taking off in the early 1980s. If an unknown housewife's cookies could wind up in hundreds of malls across America, why, he reasoned, shouldn't the entire Ivy League benefit from the goodness Carolann was pushing in New Haven? Why not, as a next step, let Luca test it out at Brown, two hours east?

Carolann recognized this male impulse—Lou's business had expanded to six stores in the early years of their marriage—but she had concerns. Leaning back against the banquette, she said, "This is volunteerism, Luca, not something to make a living from."

"I know you think I'm just some townie bum—"

"That's not true."

"—with no education, but I want to bust out of West Haven and make my dream happen. You've inspired me."

"Luca, my doctorate is my top priority. I don't know a soul in Providence."

"I've thought of that. I got relatives in Rhode Island. They can do the deliveries, and Jasmina is set to rustle up staff through the Brown Student Senate. You don't have to lift a finger, except..."

"Except what?"

"Except your name has to be on this."

"My name? It's your dream, Luca."

"I'm nothing without you, baby. The way you ditched your family and came out here to change your life is an inspiration."

Unable to reach his hand through the hedge of glasses, she found a foot instead, a foot that answered back.

"You might have to travel to Providence for a meeting or two, but I'll treat you like a queen. We could stay overnight, whaddayasay? Just you, me, and room service."

"It sounds heavenly," she sighed.

"The other thing we need is a rubber stamp from Yale. Something official saying the university is behind it."

"Approvals like that can take months, Luca."

"Nah, all we have to do is get it out of Gates."

Carolann tensed. "I don't see what Nathaniel can do. He has authority over his department, but——"

"He plays handball every Tuesday with the ombudsman. Charles Simms. They were at Harvard together. They go way back."

"How did you find that out?"

He gave a jaunty Lucchese smile. "You don't think I'd present my Cranny with a business proposal without doing the research? Charles Simms gives it the okay, signs a little something, and we're in business. All the tots at Brown will get their milk and cookies."

Carolann thought of Nathaniel's gurgles and the push of his fingers. Milk and cookies indeed. The gates *had* opened. She owed Luca this much.

After they had raised a glass to All-Ivy Doughnuts, Carolann reached for her purse.

"No, baby, my treat. This is our new beginning." He brushed some cannoli crumbs from the pillow of her lips. "You gotta be anywhere now?"

Lightheaded with wine and footsie, Carolann shook her head no.

Silas Huth came back with a cold of his own. It had slipped his mind that Arizona was freezing in the winter, or perhaps it was an unconscious wish for a return to his pre-Lacanian, pre-Katrinka, winsome summertime self. In any case, Nana Eagle Eye's trailer was subject to bone-cracking desert winds, and his heavy coat and warmest sweaters were in New Haven. They watched a lot of bad television from under a pile of afghans, and she made him fry bread and *posole*, but there wasn't much to talk about besides his past triumphs. He might entertain her with sketches of Hadley person-alities, accents included, and spin to his advantage the treachery of Luca Lucchese and the loss of Scott Jencks by one single solitary day, but as for broaching the essential topics wriggling like cutworms in the loam of his consciousness—the plague, Katrinka, Brother Ted, his birth parents— the thought of disentangling one from the other exhausted him before he could begin. He knew Nana was watching him, listening for an opening, but he kept his counsel. When he opened the books he had brought home as fodder for his seminar papers, the French swam before his eyes as if it were a foreign language all over again. The jargon in the accompanying folder of Xeroxed critical articles made his brain hurt. Was the air that much thinner in the desert?

One morning, while Nana showered, Silas called Brophy Prep. His plan to solve one mystery was nipped in the bud when Monsignor Bain told him that Brother Ted had been moved to a Jesuit facility closer to a better hospital. There was no change in his condition, but all were praying for his recovery.

A petrified Silas began to pray too, as best as he knew how—random sets of Hail Marys and Our Fathers and Glory Bes at all hours of the day, plus reminders that "This is the Day that the Lord Has Made." When it was sunny enough to wander the dusty lanes of Fruitland Acres, he led free-form bargaining sessions with God to keep him alive and plague-free and Brother Ted too. And everyone else, while He was at it.

One day it was warm enough to wander as far as Mr. Quigley's place in the northeast corner of the park. Along the way Silas counted all of the plastic flowers Nana's neighbors had pressed into the earth along the pebbled paths to their trailer doors. As a boy, he had loved this colorful, all-weather solution to making pretty things grow in the desert, but now they struck him as an emblem of despair in a perilous world. He prayed that hope and safety and peace come into the trailer community, which at one time had been his entire, and entirely secure, universe.

A rearing bronco weathervane still topped the roof of Frank Quigley's double-wide, a housing perk for being the maintenance chief and sales manager of Fruitland Acres. This bigger trailer was marked by tragedy. Mr. Quigley's first wife and his daughter, driving home from Flagstaff, were struck and killed by a semi that had lost control of its brakes. Silas was five, and had only just been taken in by Nana Eagle Eye. At the funeral, he remembered the smell of incense and the women sobbing and praying and the sight of glassy-eyed Frank, Jr., standing between the coffins. Gripping a silver rail on each coffin, he was stretched like an eight-year-old Christ on the cross. He remained at this post through the entire service, his teeth pressed so hard against his lower lip Silas watched for blood to trickle, Dracula-style, from the points of his incisors.

As he approached the Quigley trailer, Silas's heart began to pound. Frank, Sr. ran Fruitland Acres with a second family he'd started after the accident, but had never put a fresh coat of paint to the blistered, tongue-colored aluminum siding. Spotting a stand of cottonwoods in their backyard, Silas realized that his walk wasn't random. He had come this far for a re-enactment. He clambered up the slats of the corner point of the north and east sides of the fence and stood gazing north-northeast into the desert horizon. New England had been his Promised Land since his earliest boyhood.

Silas made a wide arc behind the trees. Blocking the most direct path to the fence corner were three wooden boxes, more tall than wide, standing on short legs. From the inside of his chest a menacing buzz suddenly overtook him, made Silas double over with its force. He froze, and then he felt a little girl tremble behind his eyes, heard her whisper nonsense syllables in his ears. He never made it to the fence.

"What were the boxes, Mr. Huth?"

A gust of wind rattled the leaded panes on one side of the tower office. The Sphinx's paws were set on her desk just as they had been in seminar, but his fear of her was a thing of the past. "They were beehives," he nearly shouted. "I forgot that Old Man Quigley kept bees."

"Go on."

He uncrossed his legs in order to stamp his right foot. "You think I don't know what 'go on' means? I didn't just fall off the doughnut wagon." (Silas had meant to say "turnip truck" here.)

"That is apparent, Mister Huth. I gave you Honors Plus in seminar."

"Yeah, well, thanks but no thanks." She'd also gifted him with a little Dutch stalker.

"Tell me about Mr. Quigley."

Before coming back to Yale, Silas had scraped through every boyhood memory of Frank, Sr. and Frank, Jr. and come up with nothing, no molestations, or pet killings, or devil worship with hex signs, only the bees and the colossal dread he had felt to be in the Quigleys' backyard again.

"He's no Oedipus, if that's what you're after."

"And is that who you are after, Mr. Huth?"

"Oh *please*," he snorted. "If Katrinka is in there, I must identify with Antigone. I just want you to help me get rid of her."

"Why would you want to be rid of her?" she said.

"Why would I *not* want to be rid of her?" he answered matter-of-factly, to counteract the undertow in her voice.

"To further the work of the unconscious. Does she appear often to you?"

Silas avoided mentioning her four-letter trigger. "She's not an hallucination."

"I would like to meet Katrinka again, spend time with her."

"She'll never munch your rug."

Gidwitz let that provocation pass. "I want to get to know her, write about her, extend the literature."

"You already have tenure."

"I sense a lot of hostility from you, Silas."

"It's that obvious, huh?"

She ground out her Gauloise, fingered the chain of paperclips on her desk. "I think you are afraid of catching AIDS."

The room spun. "No!" cried Katrinka. "NO!"

Katrinka ran around the desk for help. The nice lady held out her arms, took Katrinka into her lap, and rocked her. Then the nice lady tugged one of her braids and kissed her. Katrinka giggled.

"What's so funny, Katrinka?"

"Your mustache tickled my cheek."

"Do you hear the bees now?" asked the nice lady.

"Oh no," said Katrinka. "They've gone to sleep."

"Are you tired too?"

Katrinka snuggled in closer. "I am. I am."

Mother and daughter, or aunt and niece, rocked and snuggled until the Bingham Tower clock, chiming the half-hour three floors above their heads, cleared the mist in Silas's brain. When he saw where he was, he rolled out of Runteleh's lap, barking his shin against her desk on his fall to the floor.

"Suck my dick, you vampire!" he said, crawling to the door.

"Very good, Mr. Huth."

He hobbled out of her office. On his way back to Hadley, he was so discombobulated he stiffed the Thirty-Cent Lady, which everyone knew was bad luck. Everyone wanted a piece of him, and there wasn't enough to go around.

It took a dorm emptied of Americans for Randall Flinn to get a taste of what he had originally envisioned Yale would be like. Over break he spent his afternoons reading and writing in Sterling Library. It felt positively monastic to be tucked inside a carrel in the sixth-floor stacks, the insights of scholars past carved and inked into the sides of his desk and on the little shelf above his head. The mullioned windows cast streaks of wan winter light on his notes; the air smelled of iron and of leather dust; and Randall would pause with pleasure to listen to the creaking cage of the old book elevator, then to the soft hobble of a shelver, bent with age, rolling a full cart of treasures to the end of every row.

He gloried in the Mass of Christmas Vigil at St. Mary's, sang carols with a full throat and open heart, and ignored as best he could the growing pile of message slips from Debi left for him at the front desk. On New Year's Eve, after a carillon concert at Woolsey Hall, he and Lakshmi Dawat rang in 1984 on the Hadley roof. They'd brought a bottle of port for fortification, recited Blake, Tennyson, and the Brownings from memory and had made it halfway through "The Eve of St. Agnes" before their teeth began to chatter. Descending the rickety metal ladder behind Lakshmi, Randall, whose rugburns had faded, made his resolution. Second semester he would mount—and stay astride—a higher horse. That would mean breaking with Debi and avoiding any conciliatory gestures from Silas Huth. He would take meals in his room, use the stairs instead of the elevator, and redouble his academic efforts.

Twelfth Night had come and gone, and Randall was hardly the King of Kings, but the day before classes began, he received three visitors bearing gifts.

Debi was first, caroming into his room with a Bendel's bag. She kissed him and plunged her hands up his shirt for warmth. He yelped from the cold.

"Honey, we have to dye my hair!" she said.

"We do? Why?"

"I got it! I got Irina! I checked the call-board! We start tomorrow!"

The drama school call-board was the barometer of thespian worth. Mighty Merle posted new cast lists every week, and his assignments were scrutinized with the science the court physicians once brought to royal waste at Versailles. Going from Helga Two to Irina, the prettiest Prozorov in *The Three Sisters,* was solid indication of Merle's confidence in Debi.

Randall, holding her tight, forgot his resolution in a trice. "Why do we have to dye your hair?" His body had a better idea.

"Irina's an aristocrat. The dye's in the bag. It's a honey blonde."

Randall couldn't picture it. Debi had frizzy brown curls, and two weeks in St. Kitts had deepened her complexion. "What about a wig?"

"This is the first-year 'realism project,' Chekhov, Ibsen. A wig isn't realism."

"Neither is hair dye."

"I have to kill with this part. My whole career depends on this part."

"I thought your whole career depended on Helga Two."

"How can I be truthful wearing a wig?"

"I've seen a fair number of aristocratic portraits. Russians aren't always blond."

"Irina is. The peasants are brunettes."

"That's realism?"

"No, Randall, that's theatre."

She pulled her hair on top of her head. She arranged tendrils about her cheeks and attempted many fetching angles in the mirror. "Oh Randall," she said mournfully, getting into character. "I don't know that I've ever been this happy." She hopped over to him and pushed him down onto the bed. "I've missed you, bubi."

"I've missed you something bad too, and you know why?" he said.

"Why?" she asked.

"Because you are bad," he said, and it was the truth.

Debi began to undo his trousers. Then something different started to happen. He twisted away. "What are you doing?"

"What does it feel like I'm doing?"

"I'm not going to say what it feels like you're doing."

"I'm giving you a bj. Trying to."

"Oh no, don't do that. You don't do that."

"I don't?"

"You said you didn't do that. You said you'd never do that."

"Well, I'd like to do it to you, because I'm so happy."

"NO! And I mean it."

Randall had raised himself onto his elbows and was trying to slide his legs out from under her. His sword and shield, the envelope from the Monastery of San Pietro, was out of reach.

"This is what all guys want, Randall."

"I am not *all guys*, and you are not changing my mind about this, *ever.*"

To pretend that nothing was wrong, he helped her dye her hair in the utility sink. After dinner at Clark's Dairy, he walked her home and they made careful love in her apartment. Two hours later, around ten, Randall was trying to frame her assault in a letter to his parents when Nixie swept in to announce her engagement to Walt Stehlik.

"No!" he cried. "You can't be!"

"I am!"

"You can't be," he repeated.

They stood a yardstick apart and began flinging retorts at each other like Punch and Judy.

"Randall, we're in love."

"Are you sure?"

"Sure what?"

"Sure that he asked?"

"Of course I am."

"Where is he now? Why isn't he with you?"

"He just went off to Kavanaugh's."

"You're engaged and he went off to Kavanaugh's?"

"They're starting Chekhov tomorrow."

"*Three Sisters.* Debi's playing Irina."

After his humiliation with Debi, the joy in Nixie's face, shining through her exasperation, was more than Randall could bear. He put his arms up to protect his head, as if he were afraid she might strike him, then did something none of his friends had ever seen. He began to cry.

Nixie pulled tissues from the box on his dresser and sat down with him, rocking him on the bed while she told him her story. That afternoon, she and Walt had wandered north on Whalley Avenue, a dangerous idea to anyone besides young lovers. Pawnshops, "Takeout-Only" joints, store-front churches, and liquor stores lined this route out of town, but the sun was warm, and before long they had given away their laundry quarters.

Nixie paused in front of a building with bars on every window. The graffiti spray-painted on the sidewalk—"Kid Killers" and "It's a Child, Not a Choice"—led her to suspect that this was an abortion clinic. During her vacation in Kentucky, there had been row after row with her mother about her responsibility to make new life.

"I want to have your children, Walt," she said.

It was the Pampers moment again, but from her side of the aisle. Her admission hung in the air as they kept walking. She was conscious of nothing except the sound of their feet keeping time with the pounding of her heart.

Suddenly Walt said, "Look."

Across the street was the Whalley Avenue Diamond Exchange, an emporium famous along Interstate 95 for its hectoring billboards. The store was closed, but "Engagement Rings a Specialty" blinked one of the neon signs.

"It was just a silly thought," said Walt, and Nixie said, "I'll marry you, Walt," and they kissed, and that was that.

They cabbed back to Hadley and wrecked her room. While Walt showered, Nixie made scrambled egg and bacon sandwiches. After he went off to his meeting, she crawled back into bed. Holding her knees to her chest to promote fertilization, she began to plan. Becky would be her maid of honor and sing. She had come to Randall's room to see if he'd agree to do one of the readings.

Randall lifted his head from the soaked collar of her chenille robe. "Can I make one suggestion?"

"Absolutely."

"Hold your knees up *immediately* after. It's not supposed to work if you've gotten up to fry bacon. But more important," he said, blotting his face, "I would be honored to read at your wedding."

Nixie, hoping for a less complicated reaction from Becky, left to call Iowa to share this moment that she said every girl dreams of. Randall, cheered by the thought, pushed her out the door. Nixie was not a girl. She had crafted this triumph with the skill of Elizabeth Tudor. That she could see herself as a girl in this moment was part of her improbable glory.

He had brushed his teeth and was stowing his toothpaste in his medicine cabinet when a third visitor knocked on the door. Randall nudged it open with his foot.

In a short brown robe and corduroy slippers, Brent Fladmo, his legs the color of beeswax, was holding a wooden tray with a cup and a teapot on it.

"Brent," said Randall, "you'll never believe this. Nixie and Walt just got engaged."

"That's wonderful, Randall. Just super. I was wondering—"

"She wants you to play at the ceremony."

"Super." He paused briefly. "I was wondering if you knew where Silas was."

"Silas?"

"Mmm-hmm," said Brent, pursing his lips.

"Silas *Huth*?"

"He's finishing his Racine paper. He told me to bring him tea at eleven o'clock, but he's not in his room."

Randall took in the selection of teas arranged in a tidy circle on the tray. There was also a paper napkin, folded diagonally, a teaspoon, and some sugar packets from Naples Pizza tucked in the saucer. Everything, he thought, except an origami rose in a bud vase.

"He had almond tea last night. I think he prefers the herbals," said Brent, pursing his lips again as if to say that if we are to improve the world, we must begin with its smallest details.

Randall nodded blankly. In his experience Silas was a coffee drinker. But was that true? Had it ever been true? Since Silas's return from Arizona, when forced to acknowledge one another in the kitchen or the corridor, they nodded but never spoke. The forty yards separating their rooms might as well have been forty miles. Chester missed Buckaroo, simply and terribly.

"Which tragedy did he pick?" Randall asked, vexed that Brent Fladmo of all people would have this piece of information after he had spent months listening to Silas jaw about Racine's blindingly severe vision of human passion.

"*Brittanicus*. He got a great idea yesterday afternoon. Right after our walk. He's so smart," sighed Brent.

They'd taken a *walk*? A walk *together*? A walk to *where*?

"He's brilliant beyond all human understanding, Brent, but I can't imagine where he'd be. Did you try the computer room?"

"Good idea. I don't want this to get cold. Nobody likes lukewarm tea," he said with a final purse of his lips.

"No, they don't."

"Good night, Randall."

"Good night, Brent."

Having conveyed what he wished Randall to know, Brent simpered off, the mousse crust on his spiky New Wave coif catching the light, his baby steps preventing a spill.

Chapter Eight

Chekhov was right. If Becky Engelking had not eaten that Indian buffet in Cedar Rapids, she would have returned to Helen Hadley on schedule, and her presence would have kept Silas Huth from sleeping with Brent Fladmo, and then Randall Flinn might have made it through the year unaware that he had fallen in love with Silas Huth.

Randall spent countless hours pondering this peripety. Silas admitted that sex with Brent would have been out of the question were Becky in the barn. But would Randall have ever seen clear to his own heart without the appearance of Brent and his infernal teabags? As he lay awake the night of Nixie's engagement, throwing a foot outside the bedclothes every twenty minutes to lower his temperature, Randall didn't resist the realization that he was in love with Silas. Once the arrow had struck its mark, it was clear, if not obvious; follow the clues, Randall, read your discourse, Silas himself might have said. Randall looked for Silas at the end of every day; he made him nervous; he made him laugh; he loved to make him laugh in return; he was bossy and shallow and vain and beautiful and impatient and mean and reckless and impossibly bright. The variegated chips on his shoulder were so many pieces of diamond confetti.

What Randall did resist was the warped shaft Cupid had drawn from his quiver. No glimpse of Helen being borne across the Ionian Sea had lit his lamp. No apparition of Mme. Arnoux embroidering on a riverboat. Not even a stranger across Hammerstein's crowded room. No, his love had taken wing upon the proprietary purse of Brent Fladmo's lips. As the chains of his enslavement wound tight about him that second semester, Randall would find other reasons for this turn in his life, but for the present, he had to admit that he had fallen for Silas Huth because Silas would spend himself upon Brent. Vanity pricked, Randall was in love. Damnation might follow hard upon but, testing the edges of himself in bed that night, he felt as if a fever had broken and clarity was filling him up like water rising in a bathtub.

The last thing Randall would ever do was reveal his feelings to Silas, but the first order of business after classes the next day was to get to the bottom of Brent.

There was no answer at Room 303. He knocked louder. At the thought that Silas and Brent might be tumbleweeding in there, he kicked the door.

"Silas, this is me. Randall. Are you in there?" "Me" felt like a new word. Randall was a different me. Would it show?

"Door's open."

Would *he* look any different?

Hunched in a corner of the bed, his back up, Silas was a cat facing a pill. A beauty mark had suddenly been placed on his left cheek for Randall to notice. Randall went to sit in the desk chair and skipped any discussion of their break at the holiday party or their fortnight of freezing silence. "Is there someone you're avoiding?" he asked. "Someone bearing almond tea?" Randall imitated the dip of Brent's lips.

Silas groaned long and loudly.

"*Brent Fladmo?* You've made fun of him for months and now you've slept with him. You slept with a figure of fun, Silas." Castigating his love was a safe outlet for the pleasure he felt to be alone with him after so many weeks. "There's hope for Pierre Humay after all. I'll go tell him to floss."

"You will not." Silas crossed behind Randall and pushed his shoulder aside—the first touch—to retrieve a crumpled package of sugar wafers behind his desk lamp. Just below his chin an oval scar stood out against the stubble of his beard. What was the story behind that? "Have a cookie."

"I don't want a cookie. I don't ever want a cookie that you gave me."

"What's wrong with you, Randall? I'm the one with the problem."

Randall could have made his confession right then and there, told Silas what his problem was, but he didn't want it to be over. Silas would be chasing or fleeing love his whole life long. This might be it for him.

"Tell me, what is so irresistible about Brent Fladmo? His musical fingers? His repartée?"

Cheeks bulging, Silas tried to speak while Randall discovered that his nose crooked slightly left. They glared at each other, Silas's eyes so emerald, Randall had to hook a leg through the chair to steady himself. Silas swallowed, took a deep breath, and Randall bit into the first of a dozen sugar wafers.

Out of consideration for Becky's feelings—Silas insisted upon this point—he had kept his distance all fall, discouraging Brent's evident crush with brisk politeness. Unlike Pierre Humay, Brent crossed no physical boundaries; he relied instead on moist glances and conversation starters cribbed from Nixie's *Oxford History of French Literature*. But then, two days ago, Silas, wallowing in a masochistic funk generated by his trip to Gidwitz's office, agreed to take a walk with Brent.

In addition to its windowless secret society buildings, Yale has, tucked behind slender-staved iron fences in odd corners of its territory, some other mysterious, antiquarian structures. They contain the archives of eclipsed departments, or anthropological bequests, or even the maiden great-nieces of scholars gone to their graves. It was to one such property, an ocher-colored clapboard house on Whitney Avenue, that Brent led Silas in a lightly falling snow, patches of which were already massing like pristine football pads on the twisted boughs of venerable chestnuts.

It was obvious that New Wave Brent had spent his vacation screwing his courage to the sticking point. The foreknowledge appealed to Silas's fatalistic streak. If Fortune could reward Peter Facciafinta with Scott Jencks, then Fortune would sacrifice him to Brent Fladmo. When the moment arrived however, snowflakes clotting the bangs of Becky's chunky cavalier, there was a whiff of egotism in the request. As they stood in the center of a gentle incline ringed by glossy-leaved holly bushes, Brent asked, "Do you want to kiss me as much as I want to kiss you?"

It being Fortune's pleasure that he should submit, Silas rejected the question as unworthy of reply, closed his eyes, and waited.

Brent's tongue broke the seal of his lips like a motorized spade. Silas responded with subtler motions, but Brent kept on digging. The thought that he would have to teach Brent how to kiss made Silas want to sink into the snow and let it drift over him until he died of exposure. When Brent pulled at his rear end, he got annoyed and broke the embrace.

"Why were you annoyed?" Randall asked.

"Because he didn't know what he was doing," said Silas. "This is what it was like." He reached over and jabbed his index and middle fingers into Randall's triceps. "His tongue was like a shark fin."

"Ouch," said Randall, enjoying the touch nevertheless.

"Told you."

They left the yard that time had forgotten and went to Brent's room. Since the attraction was one-sided, Silas had spent no time imagining what the Fladmo body might be like. Naked before him, he found it larger than it had any right to be, with firm maws and dense, hairless hams. The tongue tracking his neck and chest felt like a grocery-store sticker gun. As the object of pursuit, Silas believed he should have been granted more control over the proceedings, but Brent kept rolling on top of him with entitled grunts, and the timing, he realized, was a disaster. There could be no slipping away "for a good night's rest" in the middle of the afternoon. When it was all over, Silas trained his eyes on the ceiling, removed the hand roaming his abdomen, and asked about Becky.

"The poor thing," giggled Brent.

"What about the Christmas party?"

"I rubbed her boobies some. That was it."

"Have you ever slept with a woman?"

Brent rolled on top once more and said, "The thought of a vagina makes me want to vomit."

The crudely expressed fear, the thought of poor, unsuspecting Becky, and the clammy "Don't we all feel this way?" subtext revolted Silas. He heaved himself sideways and found the floor with a foot. "I just got a really good idea for my Racine paper," he said.

"Come back later," said Brent, trying to sound dirty.

Roughly five quarts of water had boiled away in the plug-in teapot by the time Silas returned. Brent opened a fresh tin of butter cookies while Silas racked his brain for the name of the girl who gets pushed into the lake in *An American Tragedy*.

"Roberta Alden" said Randall, interrupting.

"You've read Dreiser?"

"Finish your story."

They had just about settled in for the night, Silas teetering on the furthest possible edge of the bed when Brent whispered a suggestion.

Silas paused, looking, as they say, green about the gills.

"What?" asked Randall. "What did he say?"

"He said…'Do you want to fuck my ass?'"

Randall choked on some sugar wafer.

"He was *presuming* again." Silas cranked open the window to let in a little air. "As God is my witness, this was my last mercy-fuck ever."

"Mercy-fuck? So you did it with him?"

"I most certainly did not. It's an expression, Randall."

"Meaning?"

"Meaning never sleep with someone because you feel sorry for him."

Randall, now on the floor leaning against the dresser, remembered something else. "What about last night? How could you go back to him a *second* time?"

Silas groaned again, but his burden was lifting as he reached the final reel.

"He showed up with tea and I swear to you, Randall, I thought he was going to tell me he loved me. I don't know how he found me in the computer room. I said we needed to talk. I said he was a really nice guy, fun to be with and all, but that I was in a three-year relationship with Frank Quigley, Jr., and it—"

"Hold on. Who is Frank Quigley, Jr.?"

Silas shrugged. "I don't know. Some trailer kid from my childhood. And so because of Frank, it wouldn't be fair to Brent if we got emotionally involved."

Randall slipped his hands under his thighs. The cold pressing into his knuckles made him shiver. "Did you say that you would always be his friend?"

"I did."

"And did you kiss him one last time in the computer room?"

"Why are you being sarcastic, Randall?"

"I'm just trying to visualize." Coffee cup lids and crumpled printout sheets, two men kissing, one in a robe and slippers, a tray of tea things balanced on a volume of Racine's tragedies.

"Do me a favor."

"Anything," Randall replied.

"I need you to tell Brent that Frank Quigley means everything to me."

"Does he?"

"Of course not. I don't even know where he is. It's just a name."

"Should I quote you?"

"If it's too much to ask—"

Randall stood, flipped on the light switch, and bound himself to Silas's arrogance. "You're awful, you know. You really are awful."

"Don't think I don't know that," said Silas, smiling anyway.

"You said he was fun to be with. That, I think, is the lowest."

Silas laughed. "You're probably right." He stood and stretched his arms and neck. Randall wondered again about the scar, the size of a banana label, under his chin. "I've missed you, Chester," he said. "Big-time."

"Yes," said Randall, his voice shaking.

The next day Randall found Brent on the common-room couch. His posture, hands folded in hope, ears pitched for any mention of his swain, illustrated the page of catechism Silas had unknowingly prepared for Randall, a catechism Randall had memorized in the night: Don't buy cookies. Don't let him know how you feel. Don't take the lead. Don't assume anything. *Never* make him feel sorry for you.

Nixie now knew that there was no pleasing her mother, *ever*. Over the phone Pauline had greeted her daughter's big news with "Walt *who?*"—as if Nixie had not been bending her ear with the name for the last four months.

"Stehlik."

"Stay—lick?"

"Yes, Mommy. He's Lithuanian. Both sides."

"A hard-working people. They can run to fat. Does he drink?"

Where *did* Pauline keep that set of ethnic stereotype flash cards? Nixie wondered. "He's not fat, Mommy. He's twenty-two. He's studying stage management at the drama school."

"A younger man," her mother clucked. "It was bound to happen."

"Only four years!"

"Younger men are easily disappointed. Does he know about you?"

The decades of rebuke in her mother's voice infuriated Nixie. "Do you have any idea what you are saying? Have you ever approved of a single thing I've ever done?"

Pauline switched gears. "What does a stage manager do?"

"They call the show. The show doesn't go on without Walt Stehlik."

"He's in the theater? Nixie, there is not one thin dime to be made in that profession. You'll be living in shinbone alley with a—he's not airy-fairy, is he? Daddy and I were appalled at all the strange characters in that dorm we dropped you off at."

"Mommy, NO! He's straight. He's got a beard and a deep voice, and we are getting married in May—"

"I thought you wanted to finish *that paper*—"

Nixie stifled a scream. "I am going to complete my *dissertation* in a couple of years, but for now, I am still taking classes and getting married to the man I love, and I hope you and Daddy will come to the wedding."

"You're not going to have it in Louisville? Everyone here will think you're preggers. Are you?"

Nixie was ready for this sally. "No, I'm not pregnant. And I decided years ago that I would rather stick needles in my eyes than undergo any wedding you were in charge of."

She drew in a lungful of smoke while her mother processed this decision. Nixie knew the expense and the logistics would be too much for her parents. She and Walt had met at Yale and wanted to tie the knot in front of all their new friends.

"You don't have to be rude about it," said Pauline, relief in her voice. "We're thrilled for you, naturally. Here—let me put your father on."

Nixie was relieved too until she read a couple of bridal magazines. Respectful of foreign customs, she jotted down "Jordan almonds" and "ivory satin runner" and "cake knife w/tassel" from their hyperactive articles until the list of ponderables began a second page on a brand new legal pad. But ever the straight-shooter, she went to Mansfield Street for the next best thing to a mother: Carolann Chudek, who poured her a cup of coffee, pulled the pad from her hands, and flipped it facedown on an end table.

"Food first."

"Excuse me?"

"Let's start with the menu."

Carolann was never happier than when planning a party. Her initial theme for Nixie and Walt was high New England (read Nathaniel Gates): lobster salad with a whisper of celery seed, a raw bar, poached salmon with dill sauce, fresh peas, new potatoes, cold beef tenderloin with horseradish, corn pudding for a savory, mounds of watercress, maple ice for the palate, and gooseberry fool—*if* in season. The cake was a separate discussion.

Given Walt's loan burden, Nixie confessed to limited resources, so Carolann was cheerfully downshifting to a state park clambake when the door to her bedroom swung open and in walked a half-dressed man Nixie had never seen before. Bed hair, aquiline nose, a sinuous stride, dark, mocking eyes—this couldn't be Lou Chudek.

"Did we wake you?" asked Carolann, anything but embarrassed.

"Nah. I couldn't help but listen in..." The stranger came over and kissed Nixie on both cheeks. "Congratulations, *ragazza*!"

When he broke free to introduce himself, she began to cool her hands on a large Venetian glass paperweight on the coffee table. Luca Lucchese... Where had she heard that name before?

"Nixie girl, Italian is the way to go. Leave it all to your uncle Lu." Luca buttoned his shirt and looped his belt as he improvised a menu. "A modest antipasto, chicken parm, vats of ziti, fill up on bread, get shitfaced on the vino, cake and cannoli, and you call it a day. The secret is portion control. Umberto over to West Haven owes me big-time. He'll sweet-deal me."

"My mother is allergic to tomatoes," said Nixie.

Luca found the notion of a tomato allergy uproarious. "Then she hasn't got the *abbondanza*. Okay, la mamma gets a plate of scungilli with olive oil, make her feel special."

Watching him buzz through Carolann's kitchen, drumming the counter, eating cold cuts straight out of the fridge, shutting the door with his noteworthy behind, Nixie saw a man who got things done, and it relaxed her. He tugged on a pair of ostrich cowboy boots while the women studied the shift and release of his pistons. "I can do you for eleven dollars a head," he finally declared. "Cheaper than a clambake, and you won't get sand on your veil."

"That's incredible," said Nixie. "Are you sure you can do it for that price?"

"Nixie girl, you're starting out in life with your goombah. I salute that. The margin will be tight, but guess what—you picked May 26th for the big day, am I right?"

"That's right."

"Well, that's a very big day for my Cranny too," said Luca.

"It is?" said Nixie. Who—or what—was Cranny?

"It's her birthday." Carolann mouthed the word "forty" to Nixie, and Luca grinned. "So I take that coincidence as a sign that you get to start life at eleven dollars a head, and me, I get to overcharge the next guy. Is it a deal?"

"It's a deal."

There was a goodbye kiss so sizzling that Nixie averted her eyes.

"Ciao, bella. A stasera."

Carolann zipped up his ski jacket and patted his shoulders. *"A stasera, caro."*

The door slammed. Carolann turned to her wide-eyed guest, a smile playing at the corner of her lips. "Shall I put on another pot of coffee?"

For the first time since his discovery of self-pollution, a shift in Randall's life went unreported to the Flinns. His parents and the eldest sisters, Irene and Bridget, were sympathetic problem-solvers, but the problem at hand was that Randall wasn't convinced that his problem had a name other than love. His faith proscribed homosexual conduct, but Randall bore no illusions of ever crossing that line with Silas Huth. A thorough grounding in history and the history of art made Randall less susceptible than others to the mandates of Leviticus. There was nothing inherently wrong in loving another man in the manner of the Greeks, or of Gilgamesh and Enkidu, or David and Jonathan. As Randall went about his days, thrilled to have acquired a new lens through which to experience the world, and to enlarge the world of himself, he knew he would die for Silas, if asked, but he wasn't sure, in point of fact, whether he need ever kiss him. For the time being, Silas was a Mannerist portrait: elongated, virtuoso, cool, "in quotation marks," and unreal.

Lust was not a factor. As befitting any love slave, Randall was more caught up in the delicious process of generating reveries, tinting them, embellishing them, lending them shade and contour and depth. (I recall here, with a phantasmal blush, my own halogen springtime state with Ada Bonner in 1916.) Did wanting to train with Silas to New York to catch the da Vinci anatomical drawings show at the Met, then dine in a restaurant with tablecloths, constitute an impure thought? How about a weekend touring the mansions of Newport? Or, much closer to home, taking Silas to a Vincent Scully lecture on American architecture? That Randall could dream thusly, and still recite the rosary every night, seemed like the greatest gift of all.

And yet you say, citing a want of continuity in Randall's character— and yet—Debi Fleer was sin. Debi Fleer was hellfire and damnation. Debi Fleer had taxed his knees, but now, living for Silas was a magical rewinding of the clock. As long as Randall never made a physical move, or declared himself to his beloved, he felt he was safe.

Safe until the next time he found himself across the pillow from Debi. Randall hadn't meant it to happen—he never did—but one night after Chekhov rehearsal, alert to a slackening in her rope around his ankle, Debi induced a very high temperature. Randall brought aspirins, takeout soup from Claire's Corner Copia, and a small bouquet of posies. Her miraculous recovery transmitted a different fever to Randall. Fondling her, urging himself against her, he began to replace her with thoughts of Silas, at first against his will, but then with increasing agitation and, finally, with an indecent release.

That was a sin, but what sin was it? How did one apportion the trespasses?

"Did you tell Debi what happened?" asked the sibilant Father Daley at St. Mary's. Prolonged association had put names to voices. At this juncture, Father Daley and Randall might have met for face-to-face pastoral counseling, but Randall still craved the anonymity of the Fourth Holy Sacrament.

"Of course not."

"I suppose you're right. It would be ungallant on top of everything else."

"Exactly," said Randall.

"Did she try oral again?"

"No, she knows better than that."

"Good. That's too close for comfort." Father Daley paused. "Silas-wise, I mean."

His confessor was sounding—and with the grille between them, Randall had only words and tones to interpret—almost giddy to hear him speak about his life-altering feelings. Recalling his Christmas Party rupture with Silas, Randall risked a new avenue of inquiry.

"Silas told me that there are a lot of homosexuals among the Catholic clergy."

"Ah."

"This he knows, believe me, from actual direct experience."

Father Daley sighed. "God gave all of us a libido, Randall."

Freud *invented* the libido, but Randall let that pass, because he knew Father Daley was going out on a casuistical limb.

"Moreover, He gave us the choice of how to use it."

"Or not."

"Exactly," said Father Daley.

"So are there *practicing* homosexuals in the church?"

"No, Randall. That is a sin."

"But it's not a sin to have these feelings, Father."

"Not *per se*. It's not like President Carter lusting after women in his heart."

"Well, he's a Baptist."

"Exactly. Protestants cut the cake into much thinner slices."

Randall pondered this. He imagined Martin Luther would have an iron ruling for his situation, but the point was moot, since Protestants didn't have confession. The Church of Rome had had many more centuries of coalition-building and glorious artmaking and inglorious deal-cutting and excommunication and torture. It had generated reams and shelves and libraries of moral fidgets. It had spun bolts of velvet drapery to conceal the crowbar of doctrine. When Randall made his escape to Perugia in September—but hold! Perugia!

Hold indeed. Since the moment brown-robed Brent had come to his door like a thief in the night, Randall hadn't given one thought to his vocation. The torch of Silas had reduced all other sources of illumination to penlights and kitchen matches. How could Randall be leaving for Italy in only eight months? Never again to see, hear, stand in the presence of his magnificent mortal overlord?

"Randall, are you there?"

"Yes, Father Daley," he replied, distressed to think that, in loving Silas, he had lost his vocation. That was the thing about vocations. You had them until you lost them.

"God's mercy is infinite, and He forgives all sins—"

"That's what you said last semester. The sin then was that I didn't love Debi. But," he pleaded, "I love Silas. Do you believe me when I say that?"

"I do."

"You do? Bless you, Father."

"But Randall, nothing sinful has happened between you. From what I've heard you say today, nothing sinful will ever happen between you. So I want you to stop punishing yourself. God's mercy *is* infinite, but I want you to show some mercy to yourself."

For the Irish Catholic this was heresy. "It's not mine to give."

"It is, my son," said Father Daley, in a tone of grim force that astonished Randall. "I want you to think long and hard about that. I want you to pray to God for the ability to forgive yourself."

"And my penance?"

"*That* is your penance."

Randall traveled the short distance between St. Mary's and Hadley, his mind in a muddle. Getting out of the elevator, he heard a rising, arpeggiated wail from the direction of Nixie's room, but Randall didn't rush to its source. A composed stride would steady him for the part he had agreed to play.

Becky was wedged on the floor between the closet and the bookcase. She was struggling to draw her legs up towards her chest, to make a ball of her grief, but her great, racking swallows of air prevented it.

"How did she find out?" Randall whispered.

"Peter Facciafinta," said Nixie, breaking up a chocolate bar for extra solace.

"Did Peter say who Brent was with?"

"He was with Silas!" screamed Becky. "You all knew, and you didn't tell me. Why didn't anyone tell me? I thought you were my friends. I'm so humiliated, I could die."

"We are your friends," said Nixie. "We love you."

"I couldn't wait to come back to Yale," she choked. "Now there's no reason to be here. I'm just a fat girl with no friends."

Lakshmi Dawat slipped into the room. "I don't want to hear you use those words, Becky," she said. "You are a healthy, beautiful woman. Inner and outer, yes."

Becky sobbed harder. "You can say that, Lakshmi, because you're skinny, and because you're beautiful in India. I'm a sow, a heifer, an oinker, a pig! I hate this, hate this, hate this!"

She began to smack her body. Randall knelt and grabbed her ankles. Her tears were threatening to take him under too. Seven doors down was Brent, alone and miserable and shunned for acting on his need. What would happen to him were he to dare act on a prompting from his heart? What refuge would he find from his need of Silas Huth?

"Becky, I want you to listen to me," said Randall. "You are a child of God. You were made in His image. If you hurt yourself, you hurt Him. Now stop this."

Becky did stop, either from exhaustion, or because she had revealed the deepest of her wounds. She lay winded, rocking slightly, facing the wall, the first among them forced to surrender her chains.

"I am a child of God," she murmured.

"You must never forget that."

"I must never forget that," she repeated.

"Prayer is a power."

"Prayer is a power." Nixie tapped Randall's head with a roll of paper towels. He unspooled several sheets and held them out.

Becky began to dry her eyes. "Brent Fladmo is one of the damned," she said. "I knew it all along, but I wanted to save him. And Silas is a flaming faggot who corrupted him."

Lakshmi and Randall each took an arm and pulled her to a sitting position. Randall, who knew more of the truth, resisted correcting her. An abridged version of what had really happened between Silas and Brent exceeded his present narrative abilities.

"Becky."

"Yes?"

"Try not to judge them. Try to forgive. It won't be easy, but it's for the best."

A piece of Toblerone got her thinking. Forgiveness wouldn't be easy, but it would be for the best *one day*. Deep down, the tiny temperamental part of Becky was telling her that the pain she was experiencing upon her manumission from Brent Fladmo would serve her art. These raw feelings—rage, sorrow, humiliation, revenge, self-pity—were the stuff of opera. She must remember them, draw upon them.

Lakshmi and Randall helped her to her feet. At the doorway, Becky told Lakshmi she was beautiful in America too. Lakshmi gave a mocking bow and replied, "There are other gods guarding the Ganges, yes?"

Becky thought for a moment. "Venkatesh," she breathed, dropping the wet towels into Randall's hand.

Silas bounded into Randall's room one evening without knocking. "Amazing news, Chet!" he cried.

Randall, rattled in a good way by any entrance of his new reason for being, set aside a monograph on Gainsborough. "What is it, Buck?"

"I just got off the phone with Nana. Monsignor Bain called her up this morning."

"And?"

"Brother Ted is out of the hospital and returning to Brophy in two weeks!" Rubbing the stubble on his head, Silas looked like a convict just given a governor's pardon. "That means he doesn't have AIDS."

Randall, who knew all about Silas's lexical superstition, was puzzled. "Did you just say what I think you said? AIDS?"

Silas's smile in this moment made Randall's heart swell. He would do whatever he could, firebomb Perugia, garrote the Abbot, to keep such jubilance alive in his friend.

"And if Brother Ted doesn't have AIDS, then I don't have AIDS."

"But why are you able to say the word now?"

"That's my other news. I went to see Gidwitz again."

"Really?" Randall detested the woman sight unseen, thought her an unwholesome Freudian mongoose. In other words, she was his rival. "Why see her again?"

Silas gestured to the bed. "Do you mind?"

"That's what it's for," said Randall.

Silas kicked off his slippers and started in. Professor Gidwitz had summoned him with a note in his department mail slot. Not wishing to wake up in her lap again, he had stood in the hallway and insisted they meet any place but her office. She picked up her black clutch, and he followed her to the department lounge, which was empty but for Jasmina Wha-Sab tending the coffee pot. Silas stifled his nausea at the sight of her doughnuts and watched Jasmina's eyes bug when her literary (and personal) goddess claimed one end of the red leather couch and actually beckoned to Silas to come share it with her.

Silas took a wooden chair instead and sat, knees together, across from Gidwitz. Encircled by the stern, engraved faces of everyone from François Villon to Victor Hugo, he felt like Susanna before the Elders. The topic, three guesses, was Katrinka. He listened while Gidwitz offered him a stunning academic opportunity: would he like to spend the summer on fellowship with her at the Collège de France, conducting videotaped Katrinka sessions? She would transcribe, and together they would analyze them and co-author a book.

Jasmina, eavesdropping, nearly ululated with homicidal jealousy, but Silas remained rational. Gidwitz creeped him out, and Katrinka freaked him out, but one did not reject a free summer in Paris out of hand. Here was a dissertation, a first book, and an eventual tenure-track position anywhere in the country.

"Would I have my own living space?" he asked.

"Of course."

"And you wouldn't have a key?"

Her "tsk-tsk," as if to say what a naughty little boy he was, failed to reassure.

"And a stipend?"

Gidwitz named a very generous amount.

"What makes you think I'll just do Katrinka on command?

"Because I know the trigger."

She reached over with a slip of paper from her purse. Just as Silas was about to take it, Jasmina had come round the couch with her tray.

"Would anyone care for a doo-nut?"

"No," snarled Silas, his gorge rising at the smell. "Back off."

Jasmina swiftly backed away, but his vehemence intrigued Gidwitz. "Is there something the matter, Mr. Huth?"

"Yeah, there is, Professor Gidwitz. Why am I not allowed to hate doughnuts? Last I heard it wasn't illegal not to love them."

"Interesting. When did you first eat a doughnut?"

He found the question ridiculous. "How the devil should—" But then he flashed on three upright boxes in a back yard and a sticky china plate— "...I used to eat them all the time at the Quigleys. Nana said they were a big nothing and would never buy them, so they were a forbidden fruit. Frankie was addicted to them."

"Frankie?" asked Gidwitz. (And Randall.)

"Frank, Jr. We were friends then."

"You are friends no longer?"

Silas couldn't answer, because his mouth suddenly felt like the bottom of an hourglass filling up with sugar. The sensation, worse than Katrinka, threatened to stop his breathing, The French authors began to spin above his head, merging into one terrible, punitive canonical father boasting a beard of bees. His stomach became a volcano of rising dough, swelling, expanding, pushing, searching, seeking a target. Eventually the dough would force its way through his navel and blast his flaming, sugared guts all over the lounge. He and Jasmina and Runteleh would perish in the fire of his magma. To save them all he reached over and snatched the slip of paper from Gidwitz's lap.

He read the four-letter trigger and the choking, searing matrix of terror inside him evaporated instantly. "Ha," he said. "I could have told you that."

"Will you say the trigger for me, Mr. Huth?"

"Nothing doing, Runteleh," he said. She gasped at the use of her first name. He looked at the length of her, from boot heel to widow's peak, with a contempt she didn't entirely merit. Across the room, he saw Jasmina snorting lines of cocaine off the doughnut tray in an effort to calm herself.

"Runteleh Runt Runtie," he sneered. "You think you're the pick of the litter, but you're the runtie runt runt."

Gidwitz was ready to speak, but he cut her off. "And don't *you* say the trigger—because if you do, you will never see me—or Katrinka—again. Is that clear?"

She began fingering the clutch in her lap. "Very clear, Mr. Huth," she answered. Arousal had intensified her untraceable accent.

He sauntered home, very much the prize, very equal to Yale and its peculiar personages. Nana's update on Brother Ted took the final onus off the virus. AIDS AIDS AIDS—he didn't have, wouldn't get, it; he could compose a song from the happy news, if it weren't so blasphemous.

Silas pulled off his sweater. He threw it at Randall and stretched out on the bed, bringing his hands behind his head. "Christ, what a day, huh?"

Night had fallen. A wind had begun to whistle through the poorly caulked windows, but Randall resisted warmth and light. Fretting in his leatherette chair, he had two questions for his love. One: Was the sugar-mouthed character that called Gidwitz the runt of the litter a third personality, a nasty brother or cousin to Katrinka?

Silas batted that aside—clearly there was some Quigley juju lurking inside him that would have to come out someday, but no, that was bona-fide Silas.

Two: Was Silas going to go to Paris with Runtie?

Silas turned to face Randall. His white T-shirt gleamed in the dark. "I don't know yet," he said. "The good news is I can do anything I want now. Because I'm going to live."

He jounced on the bed with another burst of joy. When his hands brushed the rosary Randall kept beneath his pillow, he remembered something important and sat up.

"Thank you for your prayers, Randall. For me and for Brother Ted."

Randall had no reply for that. His prayers were a given.

"And...I've been meaning to apologize for saying those things about priests and monks at the Christmas party. I was overstating the case. There have to be *some* who don't suck cock."

Randall winced, but silently accepted the apology.

"It's just that I hate the idea of your not coming back next year."

Randall's eyes glistened with words he couldn't say.

"I don't want you to go to that monastery in Perugia. It's selfish, so sue me, but I can't help feeling that way."

Randall managed to nod, and Silas, to manage his own vulnerability, began to rummage through the books on Randall's desk. He brought the titles close to his eyes in order to read them. *Gilgamesh? The Hunchback of Notre Dame?* Silas moved to a bookmark in a leather-bound volume—"Beauty and the Beast" in French? Then, to a bookmarked page in Edward Lear's

Nonsense Songs. "'The Owl and the Pussycat?' Lord, what class are these for?"

You, Randall might have said to the T-shirt glowing in the dark. The seminar of you. Instead he began:

> *The Owl and the Pussycat went to sea*
> *In a beautiful pea green boat,*
> *They took some honey, and plenty of money,*
> *Wrapped up in a five-pound note.*
> *The Owl looked up to the stars above,*
> *And sang to a small guitar,*
> *'O lovely Pussy! O Pussy my love,*

Silas squinted and read along, "*What a beautiful Pussy you are,*" and they finished together:

> *You are,*
> *You are!*
>   *What a beautiful Pussy you are!*

Randall, warming his hands inside Silas's sweater, recited the remaining stanzas of the Lear. Then they went back to the top and began again. It wasn't Keats or Shelley, but it more than met Randall's needs. As a boy, he had never sat up in a pup tent with a friend and a flashlight and a box of Graham Crackers. Silas would never be more beautiful than he was that night, when all Randall could follow him by was the afterimage of his T-shirt and the movements of his mouth.

The next day Randall went to the Taft Apartments. Debi was memorizing lines in her kitchen. A postcard of Chekhov leaned against a juice glass in front of her script.

"Take off your coat, doll," she said.

"No. Will you marry me?"

A good actress goes with her first impulse. "Are you kidding? You're gay," she said.

"I'm what?"

"You're gay, Randall."

He sat down, stunned. They looked at each other.

"Is that a no?" he asked.

She burst out laughing, ran around the table, and held him tight. Randall detected a trace of professional sparkle in her sympathy, as if she knew one day she could draw upon the scene they were playing. She told him it was a mark of distinction in a woman to have had one boyfriend—but only that one—who turned out to be gay. She said he was a wonderful lover, they must always be close, and he must bring his first boyfriend to meet her, preferably backstage after a major performance.

The one thing Randall needed to know was whether she had slept with him out of pity.

"What do you mean by that?" she asked.

"I mean, because you felt sorry for me? Was I a mercy...a mercy you-know-what?"

"A mercy-fuck?"

"Yes," he said, detesting the term. "Was I a mercy-fuck?"

"Oh baby, no. Don't ever think that. Three times a night? Are you kidding?"

Randall had proposed to Debi because he had promised God he would marry the first and only woman he'd slept with, but deep down he knew he had proposed because during the time he'd spent repeating "The Owl and the Pussycat" with Silas in the dark, he had felt full-strength what had consumed the Bards and the Old Masters when they sang or painted yearning. He had glimpsed the empyrean. He had been warned.

Chapter Nine

By the first of February, 1984, the Apple Corporation had introduced its first Macintosh personal computer for a list price of $2,495; President Reagan had announced that he would run for a second term; and Randall Flinn had tripled his doughnut sales. The children sacrificed to his professional ambitions first semester had been transformed into pairs of star-crossed lovers who must never be parted. No customer in the High Street Bridge could leave without a cinnamon twist *and* his powdered sugar sweetheart. Or a coconut coquette *and* her peanut prince. The love triangles that formed on a moment's notice provided the ripest dialogues. When his romantic sublimation had begun to move four dozen per shift, Carolann sent novice vendors to Randall. The day Lakshmi Dawat came to observe, he indulged her second passion (besides Blake) and together they sold several Scarlett and Rhetts, two Melanie and Ashleys, a Dilcey and Pork, and a pair of cream horns posing as the Tarleton Twins.

After Lakshmi had left, one of Randall's professors stopped by and, over a glazed doughnut, told him that his seminar paper on Francesco de Mura's "Bacchus and Ceres" had been so dazzling, in both its scholarship and its expression, that not only would she shepherd it to publication in *Baroque Studies*, but also she had insisted that the History of Art department fund him an additional three years. He needn't even apply—he was in, if he so chose. Randall barely registered the academic compliments, for he was already spinning three more years in the vicinity, region, or principality of Silas Huth.

As for our Arizona picaro, a new adventure began that month. Hacking through Chrétien de Troyes' *Erec et Énide* had replaced lying upon the Oedipal couch as the most intensive labor for the first-year French students. By semester's end, they were supposed to be able to translate old French and demonstrate a cursory knowledge of the tropes and tangles of medieval romance. Gilles Betterave, a visiting professor from Lyons known more for his lustrous bush of electrically charged white hair than for any theoretical capacity, was their guide.

One afternoon in class, a logy Silas shifted his gaze to the pewter-colored sky. Snow was forecast, and he was daydreaming about his long underwear. Union suits made him feel sexy, like an unwashed logger in a camp in the Yukon, but with Valentine's Day approaching, he rued that there was no one to unbutton him. The Fladmo fallout had kept him from sparking elsewhere in the dorm, and he had had to conclude that William Goris wouldn't translate Brother Ted's recovery into a clean bill of health for Silas.

Someone's slump into sleep pushed a book to the floor. In the clatter, Silas noticed that Scott Jencks was staring at him from across the seminar table. Silas hunched his shoulders in a "What gives?" gesture. Scott responded with a tilt of the head. The column of his neck swelled and strained the charcoal cowl of his sweater. Sliding his fingers along an imaginary beard on the left side of his face, Scott rolled his eyes toward Professor Betterave. This was gestural French for "this is so boring." Silas wiped his cheek stubble in agreement, then resumed doodling in his notebook.

As they filed out of the classroom, Scott drew Silas by his sleeve. "Hey, your hair is growing in," he said. "It's nice and shaggy now."

Silas shrugged with the indifference of an unwashed logger. When he complained about falling behind with *Erec et Énide,* Scott offered to come to his room with a pot of coffee so they could work together.

It was a sweet gesture, but after ninety minutes of Scott running semantic circles around him, Silas began to wonder if Peter Facciafinta was ever going to ring the dinner bell downstairs. But then, an unlikely moment of semiotic thickness: lying on his stomach on Silas's bed, Scott reached for his mug. "What is *con mar fui?*"

"Weren't you listening in seminar?" said Silas. "*Con mar fui* is the great mystery of Old French. Even after centuries of speculation, they can't solve it. They don't know whether it's an oath, a locative, a verbal construction…"

"Right, right. Sorry. *Con mar fui*. Like Fermat's Theorem," said Scott.

"Yes, exactly," bluffed Silas, who knew nothing about math or science or whatever it was whoever Fermat was was trying to figure out.

"You look fried, Silas."

"Long day."

"Do you have Mahler's Fourth?"

"What? I mean, no. Why do you ask?"

"Mahler's Fourth Symphony is my favorite tranquilizer."

"I prefer Satie for that," said Silas, unable to sheathe the blade in his voice. Scott Jencks apparently knew everything except *con mar fui*. They'd have made a terrible couple. Too bad he couldn't have figured that out months ago.

"I'll loan you mine. It's the Elly Ameling recording." He made a face. "Peter prefers show tunes."

Silas closed his dictionary. Wisecracks at Peter's expense were an ancient reflex, so he simply said, "Peter."

"Peter," Scott sighed. He was sitting up now, twiddling his pencil. He gave Silas a full-bore gaze with his cornflower eyes, which Silas broke in a charged silence, turning away as if that might cool the tongues of fire he had felt start atop his ears. He noticed the worn spots on the knees of Scott's corduroys and in the creases of his crotch. There were crescents of perspiration at the armholes of his shirt.

"Peter and I haven't had sex in six weeks," said Scott. "Not once this entire year."

Silas was struck speechless while Scott, who had said too much, tidied the bedspread and wound the cord around his percolator. "It's tough. We live together in a room this size."

All Silas managed to say before Scott left was, "That's not fair."

It didn't seem fair to Randall either, when Silas played his brand-new copy of Mahler's Fourth Symphony, the Ameling version, and reenacted the scene for him. Several times.

The legal pad list began to worry Nixie again. A bride-to-be is urged to rely upon her maid of honor, but with strategic memory a new cultivar in the truck garden of her temperament, Becky kept pretending not to remember that Silas was a groomsman and that Brent was playing the organ. Whenever Nixie asked Becky what she wanted to sing at the ceremony, she offered "Blue-Tail Fly" or "It's Raining Men." Let Brent Fladmo accompany that!

Walt had been no help either. Nixie would wait up late, but when he returned from *Three Sisters* rehearsals, he would shed his clothes and stop the gentle nag of her questions with sleepy, instinctive couplings, like a bear drinking at a stream. In the afterglow, she would ask him if he loved her, and he would squeeze her tight, pinning her to the wall until they both fell asleep. The attention was welcome, but she still needed a list of Stehliks to invite.

What Nixie needed most was someone to tell her a wedding cake didn't require a special knife, with or without a tassel. That someone was Randall, who ruled that the dress came next. One overcast Saturday he hustled Nixie and Becky to the Chapel Square Mall, a site seldom traversed unless one was in search of cotton candy, a chicken box, or a prostitute.

Chapel Square had a Macy's as its anchor, but it was a Macy's with the ambiance and inventory of a strip-mall Korvette's. Nixie had been hoping for a gown along traditional lines, but her broad shoulders, small bosom, long waist, and large hands ruled out the rack of sleeved and cinched fantasies tucked in a sad little corner marked "Bridal."

To regroup after this disappointment, the trio sat down for coffee in the food court. The shoppers were mostly young mothers with children, and teenagers circling the arcade of dollar stores and bargain jewelers. The wet-coat smell, the shrill echoes on marble, and the floor streaked with slush trails compounded their gloom.

"These women are our age, some of them," said Nixie, after a deep pull on her cigarette.

"I was thinking that very thing," answered Becky.

"My best friend Ruth from high school has three kids, can you believe it?" said Nixie. "Her husband travels all the time. She never gets out of the house."

"My cousins all marry by the time they're twenty-five," said Becky.

A young couple at the next table, named Tony and Donna, were arguing about whether they could afford movie tickets. It was Valentine's Day, practically, said Donna, and they never went anywhere. Tony was working construction part-time, until his back got better, but rejected Donna's suggestion that they move in with her mother in Hamden. Even though there was plenty of room, she wouldn't make room for Sparky, the dog who was Tony's best friend. If Donna was so fired up to see a movie, it was up to her to find a hair salon that would pay her what she was worth.

What a mistake for the Hadleyites to seat themselves in this other New Haven, a city that had received more urban renewal funding per capita than any other during the fifties and sixties, yet remained (and remains to this day) a divided disaster of haves and have-nots. What was Nixie's "paper" compared to Donna's saving up for a degree in cosmetology? They listened to more squabble—Tony's lecherous father, a busted vacuum cleaner, a temporary crown—drooping lower and lower into their chairs until Becky noticed that someone dressed like an Eskimo was waving at them.

The approach of Pierre Humay usually cast a pall, but not today. "How fortuitous to find you abroad," he said, making a slight bow. "I have been buying some necessaries. May I?"

He pulled back his fur-lined hood and sat down, rolling the top of his pharmacy bag to conceal the box of Miss Clairol.

"We're looking for a wedding dress for Nixie," said Becky.

"We struck out at Macy's," said Randall.

"I looked like a fullback," said Nixie.

"I understand your frustration with the current modes," said Pierre. "Have you ever been to 'Illyria Lady,' a *boutique d'occasion* I frequent on Upper State Street? My cousin Frieda in Ottawa deals in vintage lingerie. I make purchases for her." Pierre paused, daring them to disbelieve him. "The proprietess carries exquisitely crafted wedding garments. There's one in particular I have had my eye on, ivory satin, from the forties—"

Nixie stood up. "Let's go."

Randall fumed all that way back to Hadley that Pierre Humay had hijacked their day. Stopping out front, he told Nixie to go on without him.

"But I want you there, Randall," she said. "A girl only gets one wedding dress."

Randall smiled despite himself. There was that "girl" again. Through the plate glass he watched Peter Facciafinta put up the mail. Some Indians were playing foosball. A Chinese woman with a daring home permanent was dragging an immense sack of laundry out of the elevator. Silas was upstairs listening to Mahler and/or staring into his mirror. It was another Hadley Saturday. How many more would there be? Would he have the will, or the courage, to step on that plane to Rome in August?

"Let me stay here and call some printers for estimates," he said.

Thinking that Nixie and Randall were still close behind, Pierre and Becky had walked to the corner of Temple and Trumbull. Now Pierre had doubled back in the wait and put his hand on Randall's shoulder just as he was opening the outer door.

"Musn't lose track of our Silas, hmmm?" he said in the whoosh of warm air.

"What do you mean?" said Randall.

"*Ah mon petit,* you know perfectly well what I mean."

Pierre removed his glasses, so Randall wouldn't misinterpet his warning from the land of dashed hopes.

To reach "Illyria Lady," Becky, Nixie, and Pierre had to cross what remained of fashionable New Haven. Walking down Bishop Street, they couldn't have guessed at the scene unfolding in a certain drafty side parlor.

"Are you my Valentine?" Nathaniel Gates asked Carolann. He had drawn his knees up on a sofa for warmth, so his genitals were leaking out the side of a pair of satin tap pants. His reddish-gray hair stood up on one side of his head like a hedge, and his lipstick was smeared.

Carolann's distracted yes did not mollify him. Although she stood in the light of a torchière, her fingers were too cold to untangle the knot in her lace-up corset. He repeated the question, and she shot him a no-non-sense-now look. "I have lots of Valentines," she said, provoking him with the truth. "This is the last time I let you tie the ribbon."

"If I do, then I get the brush," he said.

"Maybe, maybe not."

"Maybe not? If not the brush, then the wooden spoon?"

"Oh stop it, Nate. Just leave the ribbon alone. I don't want to have to be cut out of my underwear." She shivered and recalled the plush wall-to-wall in her bedroom in Wisconsin. "This house is like a meat locker."

"It makes your pointers hard," he said with dirty hopes.

"Yes it does, doesn't it," she said, absently pinching one to excite him. He wiggled with delight on the bath towel spread over the brocade. "Is that why you turn off the heat?"

Carolann had been withholding her satchel until Chairman Gates allowed her a house call. After Eleanor Gates had gone off to docent at the Historical Society, he had raised and lowered a window shade three times. Carolann rang the doorbell and introduced herself as a porcelain appraiser from the Hartford Atheneum. The eight-day wait, the slick of the lingerie on his legs, and her red wig, created a overpowering aphrodisiac. Nathaniel skipped the Cook's Tour and rushed Carolann into Eleanor's parlor to dilate upon her pointers, her boingers, her walinki, her bumble, her ogden, and her palouf. Anatomizing her in a private language was his strongest claim upon her. A younger feminist would have bridled at the objectification, but Carolann held all the props, and, as things turned out, the discourse was sometimes mightier than the sword.

"We keep the heat off so Eleanor doesn't thaw out," he giggled.

"Speaking of Valentines," she said, "I hope you're taking Eleanor out for a nice, romantic dinner on Valentine's Day."

Nathaniel Gates began to smooth down his hair. His pointers were blue and stiff. "You tease me about my wife because of the superfluity of your Valentines."

"I have Lou and Ronnie and Ricky. My boys are my Valentines."

"Then who was that I saw you with on Monday at Clark's Dairy?" While Carolann counted back the days, Nathaniel went on with righteous élan. "Late twenties, coarse features, tall, unshaven. An *ethnic*."

She laughed. "Oh him—that's my doughnut supplier."

"What is his name?"

"Are you following me, Nate? I won't stand for that, not from you, not from anyone. If you're following me, we can just stop what we're doing."

"Nonsense, my dear," he said, trying to conceal his panic. "I merely happened to be passing up Whitney Avenue on my way to a lecture in the Asian Studies Department and I saw the two of you having lunch."

Carolann let that whopper go by. For a Yankee like Nathaniel Gates, nothing in Asia was worth a listen.

"Your supplier looks as if he never went to any kind of a college," he said plaintively, and Carolann burst out laughing. Given the absurdity of her present situation with one of the world's most celebrated literary critics, she began to think that Luca's diploma from West Haven Vo-Tech was the secret to his success.

"What are you laughing at?" he thundered.

"You," she said, unable to stop.

From his purpling face and twitching hands, she perceived that no one was permitted to laugh at Nathaniel Gates. It was one thing to tease him, another to cause a stroke. Fortunately, Carolann had managed to untie the ribbon. She yanked open her corset as a peace offering. They winced in tandem as his knees missed the runner and hit the floor.

"Forgive me, Carolann, I—I—I'm so lonely. All I have are these hours with you. I saw you with that tradesman, and something died inside. Please be my Valentine. I don't have flowers, or candy, or a card. Might you—would you accept a picture of myself?"

"Of course, baby," she said, lifting him up to pet him. She held him close for a moment, trying to press some warmth into him.

"I know just the one. I'm in St. Tropez, just out of the army."

"You must have been dreamy." She watched him move to the piano and stifled a giggle. The tap pants were riding up his crack.

"It was the summer I began Proust. What is going on around here?"

"Is something wrong, Nate?"

Chairman Gates couldn't understand where all of the family photographs had gone to. Eleanor never rearranged things. Perhaps a Toby jug then, a less appealing likeness, but he needed something to give his first real Valentine in so many years. The Tobys were kept in the corner cupboard, but peering through the beveled glass, he was astonished to see only three of them. There used to be thirteen, no mistake. His son, Archie, had learned to count with the Tobys. Where on earth were the rest?

Silas removed his gloves and hung up his overcoat. He and Scott had come home to Hadley from another dreary Old French class. Mumbling something about "getting a jump on translation," Scott had followed him to his room. They had spent no time alone together since their last session. Of the mental hours Silas had devoted to contemplating the celibates downstairs it is better not to mention. For Peter Facciafinta to refuse Scott was criminal. Silas had tried to suppress the return of his one-sided obsession, but more stares from Scott during class had coaxed the genie out of the bottle.

"Let me see your thumbs," said Scott, still in his coat.

"My thumbs?"

"I have a thing about thumbs."

Scott motioned "give them here" from the bed. Silas thrust out his thumbs, à la Jack Horner, in front of Scott's face. In a lengthening silence that was neither quiet nor restful, Scott studied them, his only movement a moistening of his lips, his only sound a sharp exhalation that Silas felt on his knuckles.

Scott unzipped his bomber jacket, and the reveal of his chest raised the temperature in the room. He removed the jacket and spread his hands on his legs. Dusk was coming on, so Silas reached from his chair to turn on the desk lamp. The hot collar of light drew their focus inward. Their knees were almost touching as their eyes moved back and forth from their lips to their hands to their throats. They listened to their breathing. Silas picked up a book, then set it down immediately. They both knew it for a false gesture.

"I don't know what I'm going to do if I don't get to sleep with you soon."

The voice was so soft, Silas felt it might have slipped from himself, but when he read the hunger in Scott's eyes, the blood began to throb in his ears. He watched Scott swallow, watched his palms worry his knees. Silas decided to stall the narrative by locking into Scott's gaze. As long as he held his tongue, the possibility Scott was offering could exist in a suspended, infinite present. Words would set a cause in motion; the wherefores would be asked; action and reaction would replace dimensionless feeling, and Silas's old fantasy of Scott wrought from imperfect, pluperfect, conditional, and future tenses, would assume a shape and an eventual outcome. A physical answer was also wrong, so finally Silas decided to translate the one certainty he knew. To generate its syntax, he half-closed his eyes.

"If you're going to be unfaithful to Peter, please let it be with me."

Scott nodded. Released into liberty, on they looked. Each shifted to accommodate the swelling in his trousers, each invited the other to appraise the effect of his confession. Finally Scott got up and left the room, leaving Silas to tremble with the knowledge that it was going to happen.

Two hours later Scott was back. The fingers of his right hand were spread and curved like talons over the hard-on tenting his corduroys.

"This is so wrong," he said.

Silas stepped back. He decided to name the two syllables of his passion. "Scott Jencks," he said. " Scott Jencks, I have wanted you since the day in August I met you in the Co-Op. Holding Stendhal's *De l'Amour.* I wanted you before either of us said a word."

They stared at each other again, touching themselves in strings of gestures, like base coaches. "You defy fantasy," said Silas.

He wasn't quite clear as to the meaning of his sentence, but its force drew them together like magnets. They clasped each other's heads. They kissed, and only kissed, drawing hot, short breaths from the tiny cage of air held tightly about their faces with their hands.

When they broke apart, shuddering, Scott said, "He'll smell you on me."

"I can wait for as long as you can wait. No. I can wait longer."

Scott pointed to a pulse in his trousers. "This is what you do to me," he said. "I'm going to have to shower. I'm drenched."

"This is what you do to me," said Silas. He reached deep into his own jeans and rubbed scent on his fingertips. "I'm drenched too." He held them out, and Scott pressed them to his nose. He moaned, his knees buckling.

"Make sure you wash that off," said Silas, pulling his hand away.

"Oh God, please," said Scott.

"And come back for more," he ordered.

As for Becky Engelking's Valentine prospects, she had discarded La Cincha's "Who can ever really know what happens between two people?" in favor of "Venki is his own man." On Randall's suggestion, she had been reading scripture as a means to find forgiveness in her heart for Brent and Silas, so she approached her first dinner with Venkatesh as an opportunity to bring him to an awareness of Christ. But over a banquet of spiced vegetable matter at Memoun's Middle Eastern Café, Jesus hadn't come up, not even once. Venkatesh's wry observations of American customs kept her laughing and more importantly, made her consider global realities for the first time.

Heretofore Becky had viewed the world as a tiered network of opera houses to climb, but Venki made her see—sort of—that the Yale Corporation's investments in South Africa were helping to underwrite apartheid, and that the Pope's stance on abortion was mortgaging the Third World womb. To show that she kept current too, Becky mourned the recent death of Ethel Merman, but mostly she listened to her date with an appealing arsenal of moues and nods and tilts of the chin. Venki made her tingle every time he referred to her as "a white woman" and frightened her outright when, returning from Memoun's via High Street, he pointed out the "The Tomb," the gloomy Egypto-Doric home of the Skull and Bones Society. He told her that a century of international economic havoc, including the recent loss of all those family farms in Iowa—families that she, Becky, probably knew—had been cooked up by the predators who met Thursday and Sunday nights within its brownstone walls. Among their numbers was sitting Vice President Bush. A second Reagan term, if it happened, would be an invitation to apocalypse, and it would start in the Middle East.

They went out again, to an oboe recital, and then to a James Bond movie. Whatever Venki's intentions, the shift from farm girl to white woman had extended her tessitura half an octave. La Cincha, who had drawn her protégée back into the folds of her caftan after the Fladmo flameout, was pleased with her progress.

"Really, La Cincha, Venki is his own man," Becky sighed one afternoon at the conclusion of another fruitful lesson.

La Cincha didn't believe in leisurely unfoldings. "You must mold him to your will," she said, tightening a tortoise comb.

"I guess so," said Becky. "How do I do that?"

"The flesh will prompt you. You must obey its conscience," she said.

"The conscience...of the flesh...I must obey," said Becky, puzzling it out. "Are you sure? I mean, when you think about it, does the flesh have a conscience?"

"Do not contradict! And if *la voce* keeps spinning forward, who knows? Perhaps Donna…"

"Don't say it, La Cincha, I'll die!"

"I will say it, Beckità. Perhaps…Donna Elvira."

The Music School was presenting a studio production of *Don Giovanni*, and the voice teachers had begun lobbying for their favorites. If a deepening intimacy with Venki would help prepare her for Mozart, so be it, but Lakshmi, acting as duenna, cautioned Becky over late-night cocoa that an Indian man of his caste would have had no experience courting a white woman.

"Is it terribly taboo?" Becky asked.

"It would shame his mother, yes," said Lakshmi. "She would treat you as a prostitute. His father would secretly be proud."

"Well, it's not like we're dating or anything," said Becky, fishing. "I mean, really."

"You are dating, yes. He respects you, Becky."

Becky flared. "Oh that word again! Respect is a code word for 'homo.'"

"Venkatesh is not a homosexual."

"Does he respect me so much that that he doesn't want to make out with me?"

It really wasn't fair, she thought. Here it was almost March, Nixie Bolger was getting married in a matter of weeks, and she was back at square one, plotting kisses with a foreigner. "I mean, talk about taboo, Lakshmi. My parents had a fit when my sister asked a Methodist to Turnabout. They would drop dead if I were even contemplating dating someone who wasn't a Christian. Not to mention a man from another…" she hesitated, about to say "race," but she remembered Indians were Caucasians, technically.

"Hemisphere?" said Lakshmi, sparing her.

Becky nodded. "And gosh, he's practically a Communist."

Lakshmi started giggling. "What on earth would make you think that?"

Becky hesitated again, but Lakshmi had always been compassion itself. "Well, he uses words like "gulag." And "deregulation." He gave me pamphlets from the shantytown on Beinecke Plaza and told me to read the works of Karl—oh my goodness, did you hurt yourself?"

Lakshmi had flopped back on her bed and cracked her head on the wall. Now she was lying on her side, shaking with laughter, her hair covering her face like a ginkgo leaf.

Becky stood and yanked at both ends of her bathrobe belt. "What is so darn funny, Lakshmi?"

"Forgive me, dear Becky. I'm not laughing at you," she said, giving into another spasm.

"You're not, huh?"

Lakshmi took Becky's hand and pulled her back to the chair. "No, please stay. I will explain myself," she said, wiping the tears from her eyes. "I laugh because there are thirty house servants at Venkatesh's family compound. His father owns a petrol company. They keep a flat in London."

"You're joshing me."

"Venki says these things to you because this is the only moment of rebellion. He inveighs against capitalism now, but he will not bite the hand that feeds him."

"He sounds convincing to me," protested Becky, instantly sketching a new backdrop for her future. She was a white woman in Bombay with a flock of attendants and an American cook. An air-conditioned town car would ferry her through the teeming streets; water buffalos and rickshaws would part like reeds before a royal barge as they made their way to the stage door of the opera house. At night, with the moon rippling over the Ganges…

Lakshmi needed to get back to her reading. "I have it on authority that the desire for a snog is there."

"A what?"

"Snog is British for 'making out.' We snog, we are snogging, we snogged."

"Gross."

"What I'm saying is that Venki wants to snog."

"You're just saying that to make me feel better." Becky did feel better, much much better.

"I am the go-between. Always the go-between," said Lakshmi with mock self-pity.

Becky remembered Lakshmi's romantic bind. "Gosh, what about your fiancé?"

"Sharat is to be disappointed again. Let it be known to both families that I have completed my application to Rice Business School. He will not wait forever," she said.

"You're too pretty for business school," said Becky.

"I intend to study telecommunications," she said. "It is the coming thing."

"Tele-what?" asked Becky, not interested in the answer. These Indians knew everything.

Later that week, as their first snogging session wound down, Becky remembered Lakshmi's warning. Love was a two-way street, however, and theirs crossed hemispheres; Venki would have to get past *his* future mother-in-law too. Resetting the hem of her sweater around her hips, she turned *Don Giovanni* down on her stereo and went to fetch her Bible on the dresser. They could start with Song of Solomon. Venki's kisses were soft and grateful, and he smelled like cinnamon.

An unseasonably warm March heralded an early spring. The rush of melting snow in the gutters, the tender swellings on the forsythia branches, the sun bouncing off white clapboards, and the calls of swooping birds had put an uptick in everyone's gait. One particularly lovely afternoon, Nixie Bolger threw out welcoming arms to Jasmina Wha-Sab and dragged her into Room 319, which was as crowded as the inside of a gypsy peddler's wagon. Under the supervision of Pierre Humay, Nixie was having a final fitting of her vintage wedding gown. The bridal party—Becky, Lakshmi, and Debi—was on hand, as was Randall, designated worrywart.

Setting a Louis Vuitton cosmetics case next to Voltaire, Jasmina said she had come to, quote, "wring arms" for Nixie. Nixie and Lakshmi went off to Walt's room to put on the dress. Randall retrieved the legal pad from under Debi's behind and was ready to roll, but first Jasmina wanted to know whether the group thought Nixie was making a wise choice.

The question brought them up short. That Nixie's choice had accepted was the wisdom of it.

"But you see, I have never met Walt Stehlik," said Jasmina. "What is he like?"

"He's tall," said Debi.

"He's from Arkansas," said Randall.

"Handsome and brooding," said Becky.

"Well-endowed," said Debi. Becky made a gargling noise. "According to Nixie," Debi clarified.

"He can be moody, but that's his Slavic heritage; I sense that he feels the artist's sense of alienation in a—"

"Nixie is happy," said Randall, interrupting Pierre on his downbeat.

"They're great together. I mean, it's love all over!" said Becky. Everyone felt better to hear that, so they raised their cups of wine to toast to love all over.

"He *is* a farter," said Debi.

"He's a what?" said Jasmina.

"A farter. He toots all the time in rehearsal," said Debi.

"Don't say that," said Randall.

"He does?" said Jasmina, putting her hand over her mouth. "No!"

"Yes!" shrieked Becky, "like a motorboat!"

"Or a lawnmower," said Pierre.

"Or a tuba!" said Becky. "But Nixie doesn't know it."

"Or she pretends not to," said Debi, who blew a raspberry on her forearm.

Their collective release was the laughter of the insane. An understandable reaction under the circumstances—a stranger had challenged the mores of the community.

Then the door opened and there stood a war bride in ivory satin. Seed pearls formed a spray of lilies along the velvet bodice. The ruched three-quarter sleeves were trimmed at the ends in matching velvet. The skirt panels were embroidered petals, belling just below her waist. A lace net across the bosom, its scalloped edge just brushing her collarbone, lent Nixie an unfamiliar innocence.

Love was a miracle, wherever one found it. Becky teared up, and she held on to Debi, who had begun to dab her eyes. Afraid to muss perfection with his touch, Randall blew Nixie a kiss and asked her whether she felt as beautiful as she looked. Having submitted to the anthropology of the dress, she nodded with a dazed expression.

Tracking a tissue in her bag for Becky, Jasmina felt the cool outlines of a cloisonné cylinder. "Would anyone like a pick-me-up?" she asked. She popped its lid. The rest leaned in.

"It's blow," announced Debi, who began clearing a nest of bracelets from Nixie's mirrored dresser tray.

"Huh?" asked Nixie.

"Cocaine."

"Drugs!" gasped Randall. "No!"

All but Randall thought it safe to try cocaine under the supervision of a woman without a U.S. passport. Becky took the first snort through Debi's rolled-up ten-spot, but Lakshmi and Nixie and Pierre and Debi—and finally, Randall—held out for the silver spoon unstrung from Jasmina's neck.

Jasmina and Debi weren't letting on regarding what to expect, and the rest were feeling too sophisticated to compare notes. Whatever its hazards to the nervous system, cocaine got a lot done. Jasmina called her connections and haggled with a charming Lebanese ferocity. Rector Beale accepted a reduced fee for both the use of Dwight Chapel and the ceremony. The reception would be in the great hall of the Whitney Humanities Center. Jasmina then locked in a group rate at the Marriott for out-of-towners. Claiming to be the undersecretary of the deposed cultural attaché, she got an astounding deal from Yale Catering Services on the plates, stemware, flatware, tables, linen, and chairs. While Jasmina was staging the most for the least, the rest vibrated to the drug or her energy or both.

Becky Engelking, dramatic soprano, flew highest of all. "I am music," she quoted from one of her Swingletuner solos, "and I write the song."

"And for the ceremony you will sing what?" asked Jasmina.

Discussion was unnecessary. Becky began with Gounod's "Ave Maria," but, bored with the tempo, segued into the "habañera."

"L'amour est un oiseau rebelle, qui nul ne peut apprivoiser..."

Already twitching, Becky embellished Bizet's rebellious, untameable bird with some of the giddha tail feathers she'd learned from Lakshmi. She sang full out, rocking the gypsy wagon with such force that it felt as though the room might secede from the building. Everyone joined in fortissimo on *"l'amour, l'amour, l'amour, l'amour,"* an ecstatic septet appealing to love.

The familiar chorus, *"l'amour est/ enfant de/ Bohème,"* struck Randall like a bottle to the skull. Would he approach Bohemia in a pea green boat, or would he sail away, for a year and a day, to the land where the bong-tree grows? Were there bong-trees in Perugia? Would Owl stay in New Haven while Pussy painted the town with Scott Jencks? Randall's scalp tingled;

there were cicadas buzzing under his arms. His pressed his hands together to keep from screaming. What was going to happen to him? Everything would be all right, he thought, as long as Becky kept singing. As long as there was music, and not words, and he could stay in Nixie's room, he could keep it together. When the communal *l'amour*s came round again, Randall, the final love slave of Helen Hadley Hall, pressed his chains to his chest like a diva and wailed loudest of all.

Peter Facciafinta's wolf-whistle brought Becky's blues-tinged "O Promise Me" to a halt, but before she could take offense, Luca Lucchese, crowding in behind his nephew, said, "Hey, I like the way you sing, blondie. Maybe you know some Italian songs?"

"I do indeed," simpered Becky, fingertips at her collarbone. "My current repertory includes Verdi, Scarlatti…"

"No, more like 'Mambo Italiano,'" said Luca. "I'm just kidding you honey, you sing real nice."

The tiny room now held nine. Peter pulled out Nixie's makeup drawer and began blotting her face with a sponge. Debi, starting in on Nixie's fingernails, murmured to Randall, "Who's the hood by the window? His heinie looks like a double *challah*."

Even high as a kite, Randall hadn't needed anyone to tell him who that was. He had stroked the collar of Luca's jean jacket that fateful night he met Silas in the dining pen. "I think he's the caterer."

"Is everything under control for the big day?" Luca asked Jasmina.

"*Assolutamente, caro,*" she replied, handing him the Vuitton cosmetics case. "The invitations go to the printer tomorrow. We wait now for the flowers."

Luca put his hands in his back pockets, which accentuated his posterior accomplishments. "Nixie, honey," he said. "I'm just back from my cousin's in Providence. I got the dry ingredients for the big day, *imported* ziti, jars of peppers, a case of artichoke hearts, but I don't know where I'm gonna store it all. Is there a basement here?"

"There's a storage space across from the computer room, Uncle Lu," said Peter.

"*Uncle* Lu?" wondered Nixie, Lakshmi, Becky, Debi, Pierre, and Randall.

"Come, *ragazzino*. Show me."

Peter and Luca popped out, with the makeup bag and the Vuitton case, leaving Jasmina to unravel the Lucchese-Facciafinta family connection.

Then, with dramatic timing worthy of Feydeau, Silas entered, missing his nemesis by seconds. He wove a path to Nixie's feet, knelt, and paid homage to her beauty with a Verlaine sonnet. The tip of his slightly crooked nose and his ears were brick red. His lips were swollen. His hair, long enough now for Randall to interpret, stood straight up in front. The elbows of his sweater sagged. Silas finished the sonnet, found Randall, and conveyed with a glance that he and Scott had just "completed" their translation.

In unconscious imitation of the portrait of St. Sebastian in his *Picture Book of Saints*, Randall clasped his hands behind his back, thereby giving room for a dozen arrows to pierce his chest. He had called out *l'amour!* with the rest and the best. He had cut himself on Silas and needed to show the gashes, needed to be seen and heard. Should he stay in New Haven in the fall and bleed, to the death if necessary?

Chapter Ten

L et us pause to allow the tender new leaves to gather more thickly upon the branches, and the daffodils to replace the crocuses, and the first forsythia to bloom alizarin yellow, and the apartment rental notices, fringed with tearaway phone numbers, to sprout on the telephone poles so that the arrival of spring break might alarm one and all, not only with its precipitancy, but also with its ambiguous promise of summer freedom.

It has taken me all this while to spot a motif in my pages: Two in a cubicle; one on the bed, the other on a chair, seeking romantic advice. Variations have included two on chairs with an interposing metal grille; one in a chair, the other on the couch, with an interposing paperclip chain; one seated, the other standing, pouring a glass of Pernod. All that energy—so many millions of kilowatts and jules and calories—released, *spent,* in these cubicles in the hope of getting one and two into the bed, but the right two in the right bed, at the same time.

Many of you have doubtless noticed this before me, and I pray that what fascinates my eyes and ears has not wearied you. Yet, why should it be my post-organic fate to be most interested in observing four feet leave the floor in happy, lasting communion when I might have spent these decades listening to concerts at Woolsey Hall or attending lectures at the Asia Society? Is my voyeurism, if that is what to call it, the result of my own thwarted hopes? Or is it because I have hitched my wagon to the young?

Perhaps my stated attraction at the outset of my chronicle for Love and all its permutations might be emended to say that I am in love with the possibilities, suspended forever in the present tense, of the young in first flower. Sometimes I wonder how sympathetic, or more important, *helpful*, a listener I might have been to my love slaves that year. No one thought to approach my portrait with a direct question. Having never had the occasion to test my protoplasmic (such a silly word!) "limits," I cannot fathom what might have happened.

And so now, in all haste, it was spring break. Nixie flew home to stamp out fires in advance of the wedding. Walt, who might have wished to meet his future in-laws, remained in New Haven to work on a daring Cabaret remount of *Gammar Gurton's Needle*. Silas wouldn't budge from the prospect of epic fornications with Scott, and Randall wouldn't budge from Silas. The admissions offices at the various graduate schools had sent out acceptance letters, so Peter Facciafinta began taking long-distance calls from an anxious next crop of Danish, Pakistani, and Nebraskan Hadleyites. Brent Fladmo began climbing the worn slate stairs to the fifth-floor weight room at the Payne Whitney Gymnasium. Progress every which way, as it were.

Since Father Daley had implicitly warned Randall not to return to his confessional empty-handed, Randall resumed his search for solace elsewhere. Imagine my astonishment to locate him one afternoon seated at a heavy black table at Naples Pizza. Before him was a ramekin of rice pudding. Beyond that there was a sausage-and-pepper grinder, a basket of onion rings, a small Greek salad, a glass mug of birch beer, two slices of broccoli-and-mushroom pizza overlapping the edges of a round metal tray, a piece of chocolate layer cake wrapped in plastic, and a tidy stack of unused paper napkins. The last bite of crust from a third slice of pizza was held in the rolling grip of Dinah Chidsey's jaws.

"Why, if I may, do you ask for thirty cents?" said Randall.

Dinah Chidsey chewed each mouthful twenty-five times, so there was another patrician pause in their conversation. Year-round exposure to the elements had damaged her skin past repair, but Dinah's eyes were sharp, her brow wide and commanding, and, Randall was happy to learn, she kept a copy of Marcus Aurelius's *Meditations* in a skirt pocket.

"Thirty cents gives one pause, I think," she answered at last.

"I think so too."

Dinah dabbed her lips with a napkin from her lap. "Thirty cents is specific, non-threatening, and 'just right,' in a Goldilocks way. I have also learned, Randall, that if a potential donor doesn't have exact change, rather than stint me with a quarter, he'll always contribute more."

"That makes perfect sense," said Randall.

Heading from Hadley to Sterling Library, Randall had discovered the Thirty-Cent Lady in motion—a shock in itself—descending the steep marble steps of St. Mary's—a second shock. Her woolen fisherman's cap was a permanent accessory, but the warming weather had greatly reduced her layers of sweaters and leggings. Looking down Hillhouse Avenue as if she were summoning a hansom cab to ferry her to Knightsbridge, there was a twinkling, almost holiday, cast to her bearing. Randall was reminded of Mary Poppins, were she to carry a plastic Macy's bag along with her avian-headed umbrella. It was midday, and, given his own growling stomach, he couldn't help but consider her potential hunger. Rather than a bill or two, he offered her lunch. Flinns did that sort of thing; there was always room for a tenth around their dinner table, if noise didn't bother you.

The Thirty-Cent Lady suggested Naples Pizza. Her five courses left Randall with just enough money for his dessert, but he scarcely minded, for Dinah Chidsey, a Connecticut native, a graduate of Miss Porter's and Vassar College, who had begun a Yale dissertation on Livy's *Letters* in 1963, dispensed, like Mary Poppins, stern advice with warmth and humor.

Biography, I find, is a genre that readers take up in middle age. By that time, *nel mezzo del caminn*, one has developed a genuine curiosity as to what others have done with the raw materials of living. If Randall Flinn and Dinah Chidsey were to have their once-in-a-lifetime lunch today, I am certain that the fifty-something Randall would have insisted that Dinah break down the historical process whereby she came to be living at subsistence level on the streets of New Haven. Had there been a particular morning when she woke up and decided that this was the day to stop *trying*? Was it drugs? Unrequited love? A mental breakdown? Crime and violence? How had life happened to her? Where did she sleep?

But that April afternoon, Randall was in his first flower and acted his more selfish age of twenty-two. At Dinah Chidsey's express invitation, he catalogued the contents of his heart, from Debi Fleer's one-breasted Helga cootch down to the banana label scar under Silas Huth's chin. Two at a table, with an interposing feast. As on they talked, shifts of undergraduates ate and left, the sunlight through the stained glass traveled down their heavy wood table, and the stack of paper napkins dwindled one by one.

Life's challenges had given Dinah the long view. Her verdict for Randall? Positive intensities like his feelings for Silas were a treasure; on that point she would not give way. But rather than bleed to death in silence, the Owl must risk everything, take up his small guitar, and sing full out to the Pussy Cat. Monastic life was all well and good if this were the fifteenth century, and Randall was the third or fourth son, but Perugia was not the right way to go in 1984. Perugia was retreat and cowardice. God might have sent Silas as a test—had he thought of that?—but Randall would never know unless he revealed himself and allowed his friend a response. In other words, if God sends you a test, you take it. And think what might happen if Silas not only accepted his love, but returned it?

At this last point, Randall bridled, scoffed, flushed, tried to joke an escape with a quotation from *The Importance of Being Earnest* about "metaphysical speculation," but Dinah waited him out with her sympathetic gaze. He noticed how like Athena's were her eyes: gray, steady, trustworthy. Dinah, you see, was giving him permission, the kind of permission only total strangers and the most skilled therapists are capable of, to articulate his most secret wish.

Randall took a breath, clenched a phantom rosary in his right hand, and disclosed one image he deemed within the realm of possibility. An apartment to share in the fall in the Orange Street area.

Dinah didn't laugh. She asked a next question, easy to answer—"What floor?"—then speared a cucumber slice. The rhythm of her meal—a query, a bite, then twenty-five chews—coaxed Randall into elaboration. The apartment would be on the second floor of a Queen Anne house. Two bedrooms, a kitchen, and a living room-dining room-study. Two tables pushed together by a bay window to make a double desk, their chairs facing across, with books rising behind them to the ceiling via planks and cinderblocks. Two fountain pens and one bottle of ink. A map of the world plastic shower curtain. Two toothbrush glasses. A seldom-watched television set in the furthest corner. A set of signature china purloined from the Law School cafeteria. Walking across town to Pegnataro's to buy staples, walking down the street to DeRose's Market for splurges, spiking their receipts on a spindle next to the toaster oven.

Before they finished their session, Dinah shared a few practical pointers. If Randall stayed on in New Haven to pursue a doctorate—and after this lunch, it was looking mighty likely—he must be very careful picking his dissertation committee. She also predicted that Silas and Scott were not one for the time capsule; if Scott cheated on Peter, then he would cheat on Silas too some day, but Randall was *not* to point this out to Silas. And finally, Randall should help his friend solve the Katrinka mystery. Katrinka was not a good thing *at all*. Dinah's vehemence led Randall to wonder whether a portion of her pathology might not stem from a Katrinka of her own.

Finally it was time for both of them to earn a living. Stacking the dishes, Randall recalled Father Daley's penance.

"Dinah?"

"Yes, Randall?" Although they would continue on a first-name basis in subsequent street encounters, each knew they would never break bread again.

"How does a person forgive himself?"

Dinah Chidsey's trustful gray eyes filled with tears. With both hands she pressed the top of her woolen cap, as if the answer were in there, but must never ever come out. There was one napkin left on the table. They both reached for it.

We now cross state lines to peek in on Carolann and Luca attempting a late-morning siesta in a Motel 6 in Wanskuck, Rhode Island. Carolann was bushed. The night before, when Nathaniel Gates discovered that she wasn't going home to Wisconsin for break, but was heading east instead with her doughnut supplier, he'd torn into her business with a controlled, Anglican fury. He began by saying that her coffee tasted like gutter runoff and that doughnuts were proven carcinogens. Furthermore, he didn't believe in collegiality, not at Yale, not at Brown, not anywhere. He would shut down her franchises, charge her rent, make her pay taxes, unionize her sales force. He would have Luca Lucchese (Mrs. Bluder had done the research) barred from the campus. He would—

The rest of his tirade is lost to history, because Carolann had taken her striped satchel from the closet hook and made to pitch it out the window. Nathaniel lunged for it with an undignified shriek. She settled herself against her headboard, a swell of disgust lapping at the back of her throat, while he inventoried its contents with trembling hands. After she reminded him—*again*—that their relationship was based on respectful sexual sharing, and that jealousy was a negative, he asked her to marry him. Talking him down from that took three hours. Hence the late start with Luca on I-95 East.

After checking in to the motel, and coitus, they had stretched out on one of the double beds. Carolann's suitcase was on the other bed, its handle somewhat insulted by her consort's briefs, which had landed there in flight. A book and a yellow highlighter were sitting on the nightstand, but Carolann didn't expect to get very far into *La Vie de Marianne*.

Luca, his hair thrown back on the pillow like a pelt, dozed, but Carolann was restive. Another book was threatening their getaway weekend. She reminded herself that jealousy was a negative, but the volume of Lacan (!) she had spied underneath a canister of antiperspirant in Luca's gym bag kept her from slumber. Luca read *Sports Illustrated* and *TV Guide*. Period. What was Lacan doing in there?

Carolann drew up the shade, as if sunlight would help solve the puzzle. The chartreuse buds on the magnolia trees reminded her of the big cloth buttons on an Easter coat she had made back in the sixties. Before Lou got rich on rugs, she had sewn all of her clothes. Now, a month from forty, an adulteress twice over, she had been reflecting during the car ride to Rhode Island that the Chudeks' poorest years, which she associated with answering Lou's office phone with a spit-up rag on her shoulder and an infant sleeping in the stock room, had probably been their happiest. They had always wanted a baby girl, but had stopped trying at some point. Would a daughter, to cook with and make clothes for, have kept her from coming to Yale? Would having a little girl back home, to lead by example, have kept her out of Luca's truck or Nate's parlor?

She tiptoed over to Luca's gym bag. She crouched, rustled, read, and— oh, it was worse, much worse, than she could ever imagine. She ran to the nightstand and grabbed the plastic wrapper Luca had pulled off the water glass. Standing over him, she crinkled it near his right ear. When his eyes were open, she crossed her arms over her breasts and asked him how it happened that Runteleh Gidwitz had signed a copy of Lacan's *Écrits* with "For LuLu. Sweet dreams. Aunt RuRu."

Luca, instantly alert, worried a scab on his arm as a stall. "What are you talking about?"

"Don't play dumb. I know her handwriting. She calls you 'LuLu'? *LuLu?*"

"That was my nickname when I was a *bambino*."

"You *told* her that? You told Runteleh Gidwitz, of all people, about your childhood?"

"Hey, no skin off my nose," he said. "I'm not getting graded on it."

"Stop that!" she said, shaking his hand off the underside of her thigh. "How do you know her?"

"Hey, I know everybody in that shithole city. I did some wiring in her dining room."

Carolann felt nauseated. A woman like Professor Gidwitz shouldn't have a dining room. "You were at her *house*? And why is she 'Aunt RuRu'? And why would she tell you 'Sweet dr—?'"

She stopped, Luca flinched, and an ax cleaved her consciousness.

"You're not sleeping with her, are you?" she said. "That would—oh my God, if I thought you were sleeping with her, I'd kill you."

Luca jumped out of the bed. "I wouldn't touch Runteleh."

From the pillow in his hand Carolann knew he was lying. Immodest Luca had covered his nakedness at last.

"Meaning you would if you could," she said with mounting horror. "That woman is dangerous, Luca. She turned Silas Huth into a mental case. I'll bet she's a lousy cook. Not to mention she's a total lesbo!"

"She said that she was bi," said Luca. "And she's a decent cook."

"What has she made you to eat?"

"An omelet."

Carolann stood, speechless and sick. Runteleh Gidwitz had made her lover breakfast.

"Now shut up about her, okay? Please, Carolann, it hurts even to hear you say her name."

Had she heard right? If Luca Lucchese had actually said "*please*" and "*it hurts*," then his was the most advanced case of The Gidwitz

Effect known to mankind. Carolann took a deep breath and screamed, "RuRuRuRuRuRuRuRuRURURU!"

"Get a hold of yourself," he shouted over her, plucking his briefs from her bag and lifting a leg to put them on.

She ran into the gully between the beds and slapped his face. "I'll get that harpy turned out of the department faster than you can say 'Fugg your mudder!'"

"She has tenure," he replied.

"Ha! Don't forget I have the chair on my side. Nathaniel Gates asked me to marry him last night."

Luca stopped hiking up his underwear. "You're shitting me," he said.

The thought that she might never see that beautiful, enterprising penis again made her weak. "I told him no. I said I came to Yale to get an education." Pausing for breath, she saw the "Welcome to the Ocean State" brochure on top of the phone book on the nightstand and felt tears sting her eyes.

Luca's belt buckle tinkled as he zipped his fly. "Carolann, we've had a lot of good times together."

"No," she gasped, unwilling to consign him to the past. "I thought we were something special."

"Carolann," he said. "We've been using each other. You were the first to say so." She couldn't look at him. "Honey, you have everything you want now. You got your education. You got a business, room for expansion, Big Man Gates eating out of your bumble."

"Please don't use that word with me. I never should have told you those things." Carolann felt a stab of sympathy for the senior partner of their ludicrous triangle, quartet now if you included that omelet-making Oedipal banshee. Unable to force Luca into admitting he had a yen for his Aunt RuRu, she tried a nastier tack. "You'll screw anything that moves, won't you? Peter told me you used to have sex with men."

"Hey—anything that feels good is *abbondanza*. If a guy wants to suck my joint, it's no skin off my nose. Some guys are really good at it. Like that Silas fairy you know."

Another thunderbolt. How many could she endure? "*Silas?* You had sex with Silas Huth?"

"He took it between his legs, I know that much. If that counts as sex…" shrugged Luca, anticipating President Clinton's deposition to Kenneth Starr by fifteen years.

"When was this?"

"September."

"Where?"

"His dorm. Man, that egghead sure knows what he's doing."

His grunt of recollected pleasure prompted her to scream "Faggot!" and beat her fists against his chest.

Luca didn't hit women. Grabbing her forearms in self-defense, he struck with something harder. "Where are your boys, Carolann?" he sneered. "Where are Ricky and Ronnie?"

"They're at home safe," she said, trying to twist free.

"Safe, huh? With no mother watching out for them, they could be sucking joints all over town."

"Faggot!" she screamed again. Someone began pounding on the other side of the wall.

"They must hate your guts for walking out on them like that. Wisconsin's Mother of the Year, huh? They ought to take them away from you."

She cried for what seemed like hours. She cried through his shower, through his demands to pull herself together and meet his cousins. When he finally slammed the door, she cried through a long phone call to Rickie and Ronnie. She was having her own spring rain, she told them, and promised to catch the very next flight to Madison.

Lingering over coffee, Becky decided that what she needed was an assistant. It was sweet of Venki to wash her breakfast dishes, but opera stars had *staff*.

Grand notions were the due of the students cast in the studio production of *Don Giovanni*. The only penalty these happy few endured was the loss of their spring break. Becky thought she might miss the Ottumwa thaw, but it was too delicious, really, to saunter to rehearsals, the thick, creamy pages of Mozart's score weighing down her bag, too delicious to lower her sunglasses so that the guard posted at the side door of Sprague

Hall would recognize her as a member of the company and wave her through, too delicious to be cinched into her rehearsal skirt by the production assistant while she sipped tea from a mug with her name taped on it. By noon, the vocal coaches would have slipped into the mezzanine with scores to follow and scores to settle. La Cincha and Becky's Donna Elvira were presently locked in a struggle with Regina Pilbrow and the Donna Anna of Janda Rothman.

Mozart scholars might disagree, but Becky knew that Elvira was the better role, so Janda Rothman was far down the list of her concerns that morning. Most pressing was a letter from home. Dick Engelking, who never signed more than his name to a Christmas card, had sent his daughter a message in block-lettered brimstone. "Don't count on us to raise your brown bastards" was his least inflammatory statement.

Becky rinsed her coffee cup, wishing for human distraction, but the kitchen was empty. She trudged into the phone booth, its plaster walls adorned with the hopes, glyphs, and phone numbers of bygone love slaves, wiped the receiver with a tissue, and called Iowa collect. Her mother wouldn't accept the charges, so she fetched her coin purse from her room—an assistant could have done this too—and dialed direct.

"I didn't want your father to see the bill," said her mother.

"Mom, why did you tell Daddy about Venkatesh?"

"A Christian woman doesn't conceal things from her husband. She submits to him," her mother said. "You have wanted proof all your life that your father cares about you. Take this as proof."

"Daddy's letter was this crazy—racist—thing."

"Honor thy father, Rebecca."

"Which is worse, Mom, Venki's skin color, or his faith?" She listened to her mother set down something heavy. Wednesday was washday.

"You tell me, Rebecca. You tell me."

"You should be happy I am bringing Venki to Christ."

"I don't even want to know his name."

For the first time in her life, Becky hung up on her mother.

"Knowing who your people were," not just their kinship, but five generations of their struggles and values, was an obligation to an Engelking. Today Becky didn't know her people. This first rush of empty air where her parents' arms had always been upset her terribly. When you came right down to it, she thought, Venki and Lakshmi and Arup were the most Christ-like persons she had met in New Haven. To begin with, it was awfully Hindu of Venki, or Buddhist—or something peaceful and Eastern—to learn the Bible verses she assigned him. When she talked about Jesus' miracles, Venki didn't change the subject or distract her with caresses. Why couldn't she in fact be more like him: tolerant and thoughtful? Now she wouldn't be able to go home in the summer, maybe ever, unless she gave him up. Fastening her garnets around her throat, she pushed her father's letter from her thoughts and left for the Taft Apartments and her first appointment of the day.

Photography was a "special skill" on Debi Fleer's acting resumé, and Becky needed a head shot to hang in Sprague Hall for *Don Giovanni*. Before Debi had the chance to pose her in front of a square of black velvet taped to her closet door, Becky spoke her peace and announced that she wouldn't have sex with Venkatesh just to get back at her parents.

Loading film, Debi offered Becky a way out. She told her to set aside the Engelking Way; artists were her people, now and henceforward. "Becky, look at me." Debi's expression was grave and mischievous at once. "You don't have to be from Iowa anymore. Trust me, okay?"

Becky felt a lump in her throat. "How did you get to be so mature, Debi?"

From behind a tripod, Debi began clicking. "Child of divorce, indulgent parents, need for attention, the call of art, therapy, the whole nine yards. You look incredible, Becky. Blink. Again. Smile. Turn a bit to the left. Part your lips a little. The camera loves you."

"It does?"

"Now hum something. Give me some Mozart."

Becky began *"Ah! Fuggi il traditor!"*

Loading another roll, Debi said, "I thought you and Venki were doing it already."

Becky stopped humming. "Debi, really. Not everyone is doing it."

"Aren't you? You're his white woman."

"Not *his* white woman, *a* white woman." Becky bit a fingernail. "It's weird. I think I want to. He really wants to, but he says he'll wait until I'm ready. I don't know. Sometimes I wish he'd force himself on me and get it all over with."

"Hmm…rape fantasies, that's cool."

Becky stamped her foot. "That is *not* what I mean, Debi. We have done a lot of other things. Wonderful, meaningful things." Her reticence remained a mystery to herself. La Cincha was quite put out about it.

"Two virgins, that is tricky. Look left. Wasn't India part of the British Empire, like, for a very long time?"

"Yes, and it was called the *raj*," Becky replied with a lofty tone.

"So Venki's a Brit, basically. Wow Becky, that's going to be hard work. The Brits think sex is dirty. The summer I spent in London, I had this boyfriend Fletcher who would lose his erection every time I touched his butthole."

Becky screeched, but Debi kept clicking. "Have you seen Venki's penis?"

"I've felt it," Becky replied. "Not with my hands, though."

Debi stood up behind the camera and thrust out a hip. "Well, take it out and say hello." Becky screeched again. "You've got to start somewhere."

There were more screeches and a technical demonstration with a Phisohex bottle before Becky left Debi's apartment with a lighter heart. The switch on Rebecca Engelking's publicity machine had been flipped, so what better moment to change the tenses of her life? She *had been* from Iowa. She was once *from there*, but no more. Artists were her family now. Back at Hadley, Becky removed her jewels and picked up a folder. She had another errand before her fitting with Pierre Humay, who was making the bridesmaids' dresses. She turned the hallway corner and knocked on the sixth door down.

Brent Fladmo's nose and forehead were pink from sunbathing on the Hadley back patio. "Hi Becky," he said, carefully. "What's up?"

"The camera loves me," she sighed, apropos of nothing, and everything. "Nixie called from Louisville last night, and we decided on my song." She handed him her folder. "This will need transposing."

He studied her notations. "This will be fun."

"Let's look at it next week, shall we then?" she said briskly, as if to an assistant, but a valued one. "At your convenience, of course, Brent."

She wouldn't quite apologize, but they both knew she was sorry.

❦

"Work your body like a whore," the artist known as Prince counseled in *1999*, his platinum-selling double LP that advanced Hadleyites played on their stereo turntables that spring. The lyrics to "D.M.S.R" (Dance Music Sex Romance) gave Silas additional permission to go into hyperdrive with Scott. Their sex he likened to atom-smashing; each blasted against the other with an annihilating carnality that created new matter. And as the air warmed with the arrival of spring, Silas, haunching around campus, tumescent with thoughts of past days and nights to come, felt like a list of the *-id* adjectives. Fetid, squalid, humid, turbid, turgid, rabid, rancid, lurid.

One day he dragged Scott into a Sterling study carrel. From the halo of book titles above them, Silas guessed they were defiling the headspace of a German historian. Have I ever been so wanton, he wondered, pulling Scott by his knees further down on the desk? Scott was trying to spread his legs, but his boxers, pulled mid-thigh, prevented it. Without missing a stroke, Silas shucked Scott's sneakers with one hand, then yanked off his jeans and underwear. He felt Scott's hands in his hair and a foot investigating his crotch. Silas changed rhythm, and Scott groaned in a way Silas had come to recognize. Silas was close to release himself, but chose not to give way. How low can I go? he thought. Lower than blowing my love in the Sterling stacks? In a heartbeat—

Some books fell to the floor. Silas froze for a second, let go of Scott with his mouth, and turned to look. "Oh Jesus," gasped Scott and shot all over the left side of Silas's face.

Something shifted in the next aisle. "Who's there?" said Silas.

The sin of working his body like a whore with Peter Facciafinta's property, and a not-so-covert interest in being caught out had enlarged Silas's peripheral vision; for some time now he sensed he was being watched. The previous afternoon, while he was reading Mallarmé in the department lounge, a shadow had lingered several times in front of the door. Each time he turned, it melted away.

"Who's there?" he repeated, taking a step into the darkness. He swept Scott's semen from his cheek and temple into his hair. Arrayed thus with a wanton's pomade, he took three more steps. He stopped again to listen. He heard shallow breathing.

"I know you're there," he said.

Whoever was there retreated a step, then another. He would have to move fast.

"I think I know who you are," Silas crooned.

The other person took two more steps. Silas inhaled, then charged to the light switch at the end of the stack. Sixty feet of fluorescent tubing flickered on with the halting energy one associates with both the labor and equipment of university libraries.

Caught in a beam stretching through the tunnel of books was Runteleh Gidwitz. His adrenalin surged. He thought first of bludgeoning her in the stacks, but physical harm, he realized, would be inadequate. Gidwitz traded in derangement; slaying the Sphinx would require baiting her with a taste of what she sought.

"Pretty lady, why are you following me?"

Her body jerked at the sound of Katrinka's voice.

"I need to see you, Katrinka."

"You want to help me, don't you? Talk to you. Sit in your lap, don't you?" said the crafty little Dutch girl.

Runteleh Gidwitz swayed against the stacks. "I want to release you, Katrinka. Analyze you."

"You want to know all my secrets, don't you…Mommy?"

Being called "Mommy" for the first time made Runteleh gasp with pleasure. "I do, I do, oh I do."

"And I want to know all *your* secrets, Mommy."

"That would be so lovely, my precious little darling."

It was only then that Silas looked into the eyes of his prey. Her pupils were dark and deep. The cleft of her widow's peak was luring him into the tangled forest of her hair. He was staggered by what lay just within his reach. He could make her do anything he liked—he could make her pull up her skirt, take off her panties, bend over…

"In your fucking dreams, you crazy bitch!" he shouted.

Runteleh's head snapped forward, and her skirt belled out over her legs. "No, Katrinka! Don't go. Come back to Mommy!"

"Get out of here, Runty. If you ever come near me again, I'll bring you up on charges."

Gidwitz reached for a shelf to steady herself. "You have no authority."

"Maybe not," said Silas, "but I have an eyewitness." From the corner of his eye, he saw Scott, his legs now pulled onto the desk.

"You have killed Katrinka, Mr. Huth."

"No, I haven't," he said. "I can bring her back any time I want. Like I did just now."

Adjusting her shirt cuffs, straightening the pleats on her skirt, and sweeping her famous locks from her forehead, Professor Gidwitz had one last thing to say. "The authentic Katrinka has been destroyed. What is left is a simulacrum. Inferior material."

"But you were fooled, weren't you?"

"I wanted to believe," she admitted. She turned away. "What a career you might have had, Mr. Huth."

Although he was victorious, and felt as heroic as St. George to have called up Katrinka all on his own, Silas stood trembling in the orchard of books until Scott gripped him. "Baby, that was amazing," he murmured in Silas's ear as he began to undo his trousers from behind.

Confession he might momentarily forswear, but Randall Flinn would never skip a Holy Day of Obligation. On Good Friday afternoon he reappeared at St. Mary's for Stations of the Cross. In donning the black suit his father had gotten married in and a narrow tie and peridot cufflinks purchased on the Via Veneto, Randall was something of a pre-paschal peacock. A daring golf ball of mousse had removed the part in his hair.

Guided now by the positivist star of Dinah Chidsey, Randall progressed through the Passion of Christ with the prayer that Silas be given an opportunity to know of his love for him. In an ideal world, Silas would *guess*. Randall also prayed that whatever Silas's reaction, it would lead to peace in his own heart. He prayed for clarity. He prayed for family, for friends, for those in Purgatory, and for good weather on the day of Nixie and Walt's wedding.

Not among Randall's prayers was the wish to encounter Silas right then and there. Having finished the Stations close to the Communion rail, Randall faced the altar, crossed himself a final time and turned to leave. There was Silas in the back pew, his beauty a magnet for the paisley light streaming through the ogival stained-glass windows. A man was seated to his right. They were clearly sitting together. Moving down the nave, Randall saw that the stranger was wearing a clerical collar.

Randall paused in greeting, less than pleased. Silas, though, was happy to see his friend. "I figured you might be here, Randall. You look downright spiff."

The satisfaction that Randall might have derived from the compliment was mitigated by Silas's subsequent pat to the knee of the man beside him. Randall couldn't imagine that Silas would have annexed someone new, not when he'd been getting regular heaping doses of Scott.

"Randall Flinn, I'd like you to meet Brad…"

Brad looked to be in an advanced, and once Silas revealed his last name, understandable state of mortification. Randall withdrew his hand to hear it: Daley. The sibilant 's' in Brad Daley's "A pleasure to meet you, Randall" was—what? Insult to injury? The cherry on top? The icing on the cake? The bell on the cat? Whatever the cliché, the coincidence was as crushing to Randall as the LuLu RuRu rhyme had been to Carolann Chudek.

Father Daley had to maintain the privacy of the confessional, and Randall would not let on that they knew each other already. This left them to consider each other as physical entities while Silas caught Randall up on his day. Walking home from class, Silas had helped a man in a motorized wheelchair navigate the gimp ramp on the south wall of St. Mary's. Brad was on the other side of the parish door, and after wheeling the man to a nearby nun, he and Silas had gotten to talking.

Randall, already wroth to know Father Daley's given name, had never wondered how he looked. Just as Runteleh Gidwitz should own no omelet pan, Randall's intermediary to God should have no appearance. But if he did, it should be seamed with age and lacking in chin and jugged of ear and scaly of pate and weigh three hundred pounds. Brad Daley's altogether average looks infuriated Randall. He had a *mustache*. And sandy hair and brown eyes and snug ears and a tiny gap between his top front teeth.

Randall knew the drill. Silas, the Golden Calf of Brophy Prep, was behaving as if Father Daley was in the brotherhood of catamites. Scott Jencks could take the night off, rest up; what was one more clerical collar around Tumbleweed's bedpost if the moon was right? Randall's ire wasn't jealousy of the Fladmo sort. Silas was usurping his holy confessor. One false—or true—move in the direction of Silas on Father Daley's part would nullify the months of trust and absolution gained in the confessional.

It didn't take long. Brad Daley suggested dinner for three at the Whitney Winery, his treat. A priest dining out on Good Friday—heresy! No, thought Randall. It was the Huth Effect. You'd vacate your oldest beliefs, handcuff your relatives, renounce your orders if you found yourself wanting to make Silas like you, laugh with you, listen to you. It seemed preposterous that he should worship so utterly false an idol.

Randall's refusal was violent and guttural.

"What's wrong, Chet?" Silas asked, reaching over to touch a peridot cufflink.

Randall fled through the vestibule, draining the marble font of its holy water with the slap of his fingers. Once safe at Hadley, he ate fish sticks in his room. He watched MTV until his eyes hurt. He said a rosary, then another. He began, then abandoned, another letter to the Abbot of San Pietro. He didn't know whether he was staying, or leaving, coming or going.

We will leave him there to rejoin Silas and Father Daley. As with the Thirty-Cent Lady's appearance to Randall at St. Mary's, a Dominican locus of springtime miracles and narrative coincidence, Brad Daley had come along at the right time to help Silas work through some weighty matters. The fare was finer at the Whitney Winery, but throughout their meal Father Daley gently questioned Silas, rather than catechized, just as Dinah Chidsey had done with Randall at Naples Pizza.

Despite the academic and personal gains he had made second semester, Silas wished for a greater share of happiness. It was in his nature, as we know, to want it all. No longer satisfied with being the mistress, he wanted to be the wife. Sex with Scott was the best he had ever had, but Silas wanted commitment and fighting over the blankets too. Talk can hinder a passionate affair, but the lack of intimacy-spurring conversation had begun to depress Silas. When they did manage to talk, Scott never expressed dissatisfaction with Peter, or mentioned leaving him. Or what the summer might bring to the triangle, or who would live with whom in the fall. Silas, clever enough not to denigrate Peter, was left with the same maddening riddle with which he had begun the year: what hold could Peter Facciafinta possibly have over this blue-eyed epitome?

Then, in their odd moments of chat, Scott would bring up Silas's least favorite subject, Katrinka. How was it that the entire world seemed obsessed with this underage blonde? Silas took offense the time Scott wondered whether or not Katrinka was some "Indian versus Paleface" thing. This was an especially trying supposition insofar as Silas, when set in naked juxtaposition to Scott's Danish-Prussian milkiness, preferred to cast himself as a deposed prince of the Ottoman Empire. (Think Peter O'Toole and Omar Sharif in *Lawrence of Arabia*.)

"Who do you think Katrinka is?" asked Father Daley, framed in ferns.

It was a stale question, but instead of a sigh or a retort, Silas was able to consider her with more care than usual. Brad Daley, a man of the cloth, a bystander to boot, didn't need anything from Katrinka. Or me, thought Silas. Brad, he guessed, was queer but celibate, a sexual challenge for him at any other time, but not tonight.

"I can't tell whether she is an actual part of me, or whether she is something that happened to me."

"Or is a reaction to something that happened to you," said Brad, coaxing a littleneck clam from its shell. "Something traumatic."

Now Silas sighed. "Of course, but *what*? Bees, beehives, doughnuts, tulips, little Frankie Quigley, the AIDS trigger, I've gone round and round with this stuff but I never get anywhere."

"I see," said Father Daley, but his way of saying it was different from a Gidwitzian "Go on" or "Interesting." Those riled him up. Brad's was soothing.

Father Daley began a new angle of entry. "Did Frankie, or excuse me, does Frankie, have a sister?"

Silas set down his forkful of wild rice.

"Yes," he replied, suddenly conscious of two little girls at the next table, up past their bedtime. "There was a sister. But she died in a car accident with her mother."

"How old were you?"

"Not even five. They died right after I came to live with Nana Eagle Eye. I never met them. Only saw their coffins."

"What was her name?"

"I have no idea. It couldn't have been Katrinka, I'll tell you that much. Not in Bumfuck, Arizona."

The men laughed and ordered dessert. They talked of other things over their poached pears, but after the waitress had poured the last of the wine in their glasses, Father Daley asked him whether there was any way Silas could find out the first name of the poor Quigley child, whereupon Silas found himself bursting, not into flames of frustration or anger—habitual Katrinka reactions—but into a dazzling floral bouquet. Easter, that time of renewal and rebirth, had given him a new thread to pull.

Back at Hadley, Randall could endure his solitude no longer. Still dressed in his father's suit, he went out into a night saturated with the sullen perfume of lilacs. He rattled his chains for blocks on Whitney Avenue. He passed the antebellum backyard where Silas and Brent Fladmo had kissed in January. He said hello to strangers and dogs. He passed DeRose's Market and the Gates residence, greeted the mannequins in the Illyria Lady shop window. He sat on a band pavilion railing in a park on Water Street and watched a group of boys pop wheelies on the crosswalks. He wondered if among them there was one boy who cared desperately for another and had no way to confess. In other words, Randall was a monster of self-pity.

At the base of East Rock, Randall finally turned back. He avoided Hadley on his return through campus, which was filled with giddy undergraduates. He passed in front of the drama school and crossed Chapel Street at York. Two blocks east and six flights up was Debi's apartment at the Taft, but rather than have her jolly him out of his crisis, he looked down York Street instead. Apollo Adult Books, just past Oliver's Creamery and Thai Landing, was only a block from the art history building. It had been so close all this time.

Once inside, Randall got where he needed to go by striding past a rack of magazines and stepping through a portal hung with flyaway strips of cloudy plastic. Behind the curtained booths, he heard creaking stools and the sound of quarters finding, then falling into, slots, but he wasn't there for the peep shows. He was waiting for someone to look at him and see.

There was the sound of ball bearings rolling on a curtain rod, and a man emerged from a booth. Randall coughed to let him know he was there.

"Hey," the man said. He shifted a hand on his trousers, so Randall could see what he had in mind.

"Hey," Randall said.

It was about three in the morning when the man, given name Gary, dropped Randall off at Hadley. Before driving away, Gary was gallant enough to wait until Randall had cleared both sets of doors. Given the circumstances, Randall can be forgiven for taking what might seem an absurdly long shower. Afraid to grip the doorknob and reenter his room, afraid to see himself in his mirror, afraid to lie down and close his eyes, he paused in front of Room 328. Another door creaked open at the end of the corridor. Randall watched in horror as Peter Facciafinta backed out of Walt Stehlik's room wearing a tiny pink towel and nothing else.

Chapter Eleven

Randall's first impulse was flight. He would tie his sheets together and slide out the window, get home to Livonia somehow, and atone for one and all. The Flinns would not question his reappearance until he was ready to tell them.

A comforting fantasy, but in five short weeks Randall was to stand in front of a hundred guests and help sanctify the miracle of Nixie and Walt's love with a reading from Paul's First Letter to the Corinthians. "Why was I chosen to see, Lord?" he moaned over and over the next morning. When it struck him that being the eyewitness to Peter's strumpeting exit was his punishment for having gone home, *on Good Friday*, with the man named Gary, he knew what he had to do. He would shrive the other sinners.

Peter was bopping along with his Walkman at the front desk. Stacked in front of him were, of all things, my twelve Sèvres plates. Peter had just jimmied the lock on the cabinet to get at them. They had sat undisturbed for more than fifteen years, so I shivered at his touch upon them. It felt as if someone were gently blowing on my skin.

He shifted a headphone off one ear. "Hey, Randall, what can I do you for?"

There was no simple answer to that, so Randall wondered why my china was on parole.

"Pretty things need to be used, don't you think? I thought they could spruce up Nixie and Walt's rehearsal dinner."

Randall's stomach turned over at the mention of the groom. Peter bisected a shepherdess with a swipe of his finger and showed Randall an oval of greasy dust.

"They have all this gunk on them. See?"

Randall saw. He saw Peter in his Tom Tom Club T-shirt and skintight shorts, read the easy freedom in his movements, so happy to be alive with a fun, fresh idea for Nixie and Walt. There was nothing he could possibly say to him. Tempters tempt. That is what they are and that is what they do.

"What should I clean them with, Randall?"

"Vinegar."

"You think?"

Randall pushed the elevator button. "Vinegar and water."

Walt seemed disinclined to invite him in. The mess Randall spotted through the crook of his arm at his door induced unwholesome surmise. Had Walt been eating those waffles when Peter slid through in his towel? Had he pitched those bridal magazines to the floor so that Peter could sit down, or had they leaped directly onto the bed and ground out their lust?

"I'll pick up before Nixie gets back."

"You must miss her terribly."

"She's my girl. What can I do for you?"

Randall pushed away the image of Peter as Walt's girl. "Did you hear about the Hadley china?" I confess here to a flicker of egotism. Not since the opening of the dorm in 1958 had anyone drawn a direct connection between the china and me. Randall was such a dear.

"The what?" asked Walt.

"The yellow plates in the common room? By the portrait?"

Walt scratched his beard with both hands. "The shepherd girls?"

"That's right. Peter Facciafinta has them out right now."

Peter's name had produced no blush, blanch, start, or stammer. Randall ducked into the room. "Don't tell Nixie, but Peter wants to use the china for your rehearsal dinner."

Walt picked up his appointment book. He flipped some pages over and back with the stub end of a pencil, then passed some wind.

"I'm not sure what you mean, Randall. We're miming the dinner in Act Two."

"Not *Three Sisters*. The rehearsal dinner for your wedding."

"Oh," he said, thoughtfully cranking open the window. "Are we having one?"

"Yes. Here. At the dorm. It was Nixie's idea."

"Oh. Right."

Walt was an indifferent member of his own wedding. Randall learned in that moment that you can never be sure of other people, even when you've given yourself to them. The knowledge depressed him utterly, but he rallied for Nixie's sake. He closed the door and, without transition, began a chronicle of his own sexual confusion. He led Walt through his years of celibacy and prayer, then through Debi Fleer's blitzkrieg. He shifted to the alarming homosexual energy of the building, led by concierge Peter Facciafinta. He wove in Silas, Scott, Brent, Pierre Humay, Tómas Suovonemi, and all the lesser wayward saints. Walt's complete lack of reaction pushed Randall to reveal his furthest fall from grace. He had committed unpardonable acts *only the night before* with a man he had met at the adult bookstore across the street from the Yale Rep.

Stage managers are trained to deal with upsets, and Walt was compassionate. He pried the fork from the syrup on the plate of dead waffles.

"Wow, Randy. That's a lot to handle. Now don't take this wrong. I have nothing against gay guys. I wouldn't get very far in the theater if I did. It's just that I don't have any experience that way."

"You don't? Not ever?"

"I've been approached, but no, I'm not a homosexual."

"You're not."

He laughed. "I'm getting married, or didn't you hear?"

Walt was tall, bearded; there were beer cans in his trash and work boots in his closet; he could build things with tools; he kept Nixie satisfied; and he was a big, fat liar.

From her pillow, Becky nodded to the sentry of bouquets standing at attention. There were nasturtiums and irises on the dresser; early tulips and tiger lilies, yellow roses from Lakshmi, pink stock, peach sweet pea, and hyacinths on the windowsill. The more modest arrangements, the carnations and the daisies and the mixed bouquets, were grouped on her desk with the cards.

Lazing in bed the morning after *Don Giovanni* had finished its run, Becky knew she had exceeded the expectations of her public. So many had come, so many had waited at the stage door of Sprague Hall. Already she hungered to begin a next role. Fiordiligi? Manon? Butterfly? Especially satisfying had been the coaching with La Cincha between the performances. They discussed how to balance the competing musical and dramatic demands of the score, where to place a note, how to color a phrase, when to bank and when to blaze the fire. Theory had given way to theatre, and the push-and-pull between student and teacher as Becky defended her choices made her feel she had cleared another hurdle in the steeplechase to temperament.

She heard Venkatesh's quiet knock. After re-draping, she called for him to enter. He was holding something behind his back—another bouquet of violets, perhaps. They faded so quickly. She reached up and stroked his cheek. La Cincha had ordered them to stay apart for the sake of *la voce*, so Becky was quite ready to pull Venki into the bower of her achievement and snog until lunchtime.

"Do you have something for me, Venki?" she teased.

"Not really, no. Just a newspaper."

"Hmmm."

He bent over for a kiss, and she began playing with his bangs. "It is only the *New Haven Advocate* with a review of a recent production of *Don Giovanni*."

Becky smacked his chin with her head as she sat up. "What does it say?" she screamed. "Does it mention me?" Venki nodded. "What does it say? Is it good?"

"Here you are," he smiled, holding out the paper.

She saw a picture of herself with Don Giovanni and screamed into her hands. "No, you read it!"

"'Don Juan, the serial seducer, has inspired painters, poets, playwrights, and composers for centuries, and as such, remains an enduring'—"

"Skip the history, Venki!"

"...'Leporello is trying to warn his master to leave town, but Don Juan has other plans, for he has been charmed'—"

"I know the plot, Venki, stop this torture!"

He cleared his throat, and Becky fell back to prayer position.

"'Barnett Canfora's Don Giovanni shows promise; his baritone is reedy, but that'—"

"No! No! No! My performance!" The bed squeaked along with her screams.

Venki took another breath, and she held hers.

"'Rebecca Engelking's Dona Elvira is, in a word, *delicious*. Hers is an impressive portrait of yearning and revenge. For the purity of her vocal line, the unforced shimmer of her soprano, and the power of her acting, Engelking stands out among her classmates. The stage is most alive when she is on it.'"

Becky thought she'd died and gone to heaven. She heard Venkatesh fold the newspaper. Before she could give over to herself completely, she had a final question.

"What does he say about Dona Anna?"

"Nothing," he said.

"*Nothing*? How awful for Janda," she clucked. "Poor dear."

"Awful, yes."

She saw his wicked smile and threw her arms around his waist. She smothered the messenger's torso with kisses and bid him to reread her mention. Venki became aroused and, chivalrous to his core, disengaged. Becky filled her lungs with the scent of her tributes. The world of grand opera had given her a great big hello, she thought. It was time to say hello to this. She placed her hand on the placket of his zipper.

"No Becky," he said.

"I want to, Venki." She was a white woman, with unforced shimmer, and, in a word, delicious. "Please," she whispered.

He lay down with her on the bed, and she undid his trousers.

When Lakshmi's alarm clock next door started beeping, Venkatesh got up and bumped into every piece of furniture on his way out. Becky took a blemish pad out of her nightstand drawer and dabbed at the spots he'd left on her bedspread. Really, she thought, Debi was right; it wasn't that huge a deal. It couldn't compare, for example, with that rave in the *Advocate*. Reliving the thrill, she screamed once more and ran to the mirror.

Now that it was warm again, residents without portable fans were keeping their doors open for cross-ventilation. A cello, a clarinet, and a super ball bouncing on the linoleum could he heard one balmy night from Nixie's room. On top of her bookcase her peacock fan served as a hat block for her wedding veil. Using a student directory, Becky was jotting down the phone numbers of the drama students too artistic to RSVP, while Randall and Nixie checked response cards against the invitation list.

Nixie asked Randall why he and Silas were fighting.

"I wouldn't call it fighting," Randall said. Every day without him was an agony. They wouldn't look at each other in the kitchen or the hallways.

"He says you won't talk to him and you won't explain why. What happened?"

"I'm sure he's quite downhearted with the turn of events," Randall said. "Who are John and Clara Munsey?"

"Business associates of my parents," said Nixie. "Silas *is* downhearted. Why won't you talk to him?"

"Well, to quote my grandmother, Silas is too rich for my blood. His arrogance gets me down. Silas is arrogant."

"He sure is that," said Becky. "I suppose that's part of his charm."

This about-face was too much for Randall. "Did you just say *'charm,'* Becky? Two months ago you were sending him straight to hell."

Becky didn't quail before this judgment. "I'm not proud of that, Randall. I have searched my heart, and I realize I was too harsh."

"Did you consult your heart before or after his irises?"

"Silas loved my performance," said Becky, happy to recall it.

"God, the hypocrisy! The laxness!"

Becky and Nixie's exchange of glances were an additional irritant. They could trumpet their every change in temperature, but not him.

"People can change their minds, you know," said Becky.

"I do know! In my experience, that's all people do! There is no fixity of purpose, no fixity of intent, no rigor!" Randall thumped his hand on Nixie's bed. Silas would know exactly what he was talking about. He missed him so much.

Nixie ruffled Randall's hair. "Whatever happened with Silas, I know you're both too proud to kiss and make up. I'll do what I can to fix things."

Through clenched teeth Randall told her to do absolutely nothing.

Becky stood in the tension. "I might as well start calling these numbers now. I've got a roll of dimes in my room."

"Becky—don't be silly, use my phone," said Nixie.

"Thanks, but I don't know these drama people. I need to concentrate."

Randall gave Nixie a look not to challenge Becky's decision. In his wait to find the right moment to tell Nixie about Walt and Peter, days were passing. He brushed the crumbs off Becky's chair after she left. The last thing Nixie needed was ants.

Nixie poured herself some wine. "Silas and Brent hurt her," she said. "Silas didn't have to do what he did."

"Silas does just what he wants to do. He's a bad influence on everybody. I mean, how could Becky know, or anyone else, that Hadley would turn out to be the epicenter of the homosexual matrix?"

Nixie laughed. "You're so dramatic these days, Randall."

"Face it, Nixie, everybody turned out to be gay."

She waggled her ring finger, repressing the memory of her mother's offer over spring break to give her the diamond in her hi-fi needle, as it was bigger. "Not everybody, silly."

The moment had arrived. "More men than you would think."

Nixie blew the dust out of another glass, but Randall refused her red. She smoothed her knees as if clearing room for him on her lap.

"Randall, are you trying to tell me you're gay?"

"No," he said, surprised. "Why would you think that?"

"You know that stuff doesn't matter to me. You're my friend no matter what."

"I was with Debi Fleer, remember? Three times a night, remember?"

"So maybe you're bisexual."

"No! No! No! No!" Randall said, whipping his head from side to side like a simian guest on Johnny Carson.

"No what, Randall?"

Instead of shouting "No, *your fiancé* is bisexual," he scanned the room. He scooped some beads off the plaster hand and put them around his neck. Then he grabbed her cap and wedding veil off the peacock fan and put it on his head. Making no sense whatsoever, he was just reaching for an open lipstick on her dresser when she grabbed his hand and wedged him against it. They stood looking at their wide-eyed selves in the mirror.

"What is upsetting you, Randall?"

Not until they were breathing in unison did he dare to speak. "I'm worried about your wedding," he said slowly.

"What? What's wrong? Tell me what's wrong."

Randall felt her sag against him, her weight pulling the veil down over his face. How comforting life would be if all were veiled.

"Did you pick your flowers? Please have peonies for me," he babbled, "pink ones and white ones, they're a religion with me…since I was a little boy…I would take them to the nuns…the weight of their blossoms, and their fragrance, breaks my heart…but their beauty consoles me."

Try as he might, he just couldn't break her heart.

"Don't listen to me, Nixie. I'm nothing. I'm not anything at all."

Once he put his mind to it, the first facts were easy to uncover. Sterling Library had a microfiche run of *The Tucson Citizen*. Cathleen Virginia Quigley, age ten, had died, along with her mother Sandra, of internal injuries sustained in an automobile accident near Flagstaff on August 11, 1965. Sleuthing via Nana and her network of neighbors led Silas to Kathleen's younger brother, Frank, Jr., now twenty-five and living in a halfway house in New Mexico for psychiatric patients coping with addiction issues. Frankie's social worker wouldn't permit Silas to bring up upsetting events from the past, and most certainly not over the phone. Frankie's records were sealed, and there were, naturally, confidentiality statutes to uphold. The best the social worker could offer was a supervised visit sometime in the summer. Frankie's fate so depressed Silas, he made no attempt to bribe the social worker. Silas remembered Frankie as bright and athletic. Now he saw him as a drugged-out zombie brushing walls with his fingers wherever he walked. His discomforts with Katrinka were, by comparison, a stroll atop a dike.

Frank Quigley, Sr.'s voice was maybe the saddest Silas had ever heard. He remembered Silas as the genius papoose of Fruitland Acres. He was too unschooled a man to follow the psychological ramifications of what Silas was after, but he remained polite. Yes, he had always kept bees. No, he had never grown tulips. The name Katrinka didn't bring anyone or anything to mind. The only Dutch object in the double-wide trailer was a can of Old Dutch cleanser. Yes, his little Cathy had had blonde hair, like her mother. No, they never ate doughnuts. Not since the incident.

"What incident?" asked Silas.

There was a click and then a dial tone.

A child seeks help first from its mother. Why Silas hadn't taken his worries to Nana Eagle Eye after Katrinka's first appearance in November, I cannot say. Now he called her again and demanded to know about "the incident." At first she stonewalled. But because she was his mother, or the closest thing, he had no trouble bribing, threatening, and wheedling the facts from her. Such facts as there were to share had come to light in the critical care unit of St. Joseph's Hospital, where the six-year-old Silas was recovering from anaphylactic shock. He had been admitted to the emergency room wearing a dress and a clown wig of yellow yarn. When Nana showed up in the waiting room, little Frankie was sitting mute and glassy-eyed, leaving Frank, Sr. to relate what he had learned in the ambulance ride over. The boys played a game called "Dead Cathy." Silas would dress up as Frankie's sister and lay rigid on her old twin bed. Frankie would try to startle Silas into moving or opening his eyes. Silas's talent for playing dead would eventually upset Frankie. He would go from tickling Silas to pinching and punching him, from trying to make him laugh to screaming insults next to his ear.

The morning of the incident, Frank, Sr., had dug a hole in the backyard in which to sink a flagpole. He had gone off to the store to buy some cement, leaving the boys in the care of the next-door neighbor…

Silas relived the rest in a sickening burst of memory and completed the narrative for Nana. Frankie convinced Silas to play "Cathy" a new way that day. She would lie in the fresh hole in the backyard, and if Silas could stay buried underground until "Garfield Goose" came on TV, Frankie would let him have, for keeps, Cathy's *Picture Book of the World,* a global survey of boys and girls in native dress that Silas coveted more than anything else on earth.

The boys spread a blue tarp in the hole so as not to spoil Cathy's dress. Silas got into the hole, turned on his side, and tucked in his knees. The last thing he remembered before waking up in the hospital bed was the scrapey sound of the plywood board sliding into place above him.

Frankie had left two inches of open breathing room by Silas's head. It wasn't too long before the bees that lived and toiled in their boxes nearby found Cathy and woke her up.

"How dreadful knowledge of the truth can be/ When there's no help in truth," says Tiresias. Silas hung up the phone, relieved but also vaguely disappointed. The truth he had pieced together was more sad than dreadful. Once he set aside the matter of his complicity in playing such a macabre game, the other connections were almost too easy to decode. Impersonating Cathy Quigley, the first dead person he had heard of, connected to AIDS, the first mortal threat to his person. Frankie's rage at the loss of his sister and mother internalized in Katrinka. His body covered in bees. The Netherlands page—a girl and boy in front of a windmill—in Cathy's *Picture Book of the World.* Even his irritation at Carolann Chudek's "goosie boy" was explained away by "Garfield Goose."

Silas kept the knowledge to himself. Only Randall would understand his relief, and his disappointment, but they might never speak again. God, he missed him so much.

In the French Department lounge, Carolann Chudek was blotting her face with paper napkins and arguing with Jasmina Wha-Sab about the fate of All-Ivy Doughnuts. If Jasmina and Luca only knew how Carolann was pulled in so many directions, they might not persecute her so. If they had seen what her boys were eating for breakfast, lunch, and dinner. If they had seen how filthy the house was; if they had met the trashy girls calling Ricky every twenty minutes; if they had read their report cards, counted the empties in Lou's wastebasket, they would see where her priorities had to be. Let some other woman make breakfast for Connecticut. The Doughnut Lady was hanging up her apron.

"Accept this I cannot," said Jasmina. "You are Superwoman. You would not let your dynasty end."

"It's hardly a dynasty. It was a fun idea while it lasted. If there's one lesson I've learned, it's that even I have limits."

"I hope that Luca will not be...how do you say, unmanned, by this development," said Jasmina.

Carolann's eyes grew wide. "Don't you threaten me, Jasmina. Luca knows just where I stand. I can handle that hoodlum." Carolann heard footsteps clicking in the hallway. "Shhh!"

"There you are, Jasmina," said Scott, standing in the doorway.

"It is my shift, Scottie," said Jasmina, wiggling ciao fingers.

Behind Scott was an agitated Silas who, hoping for another quickie in the stacks, had come along on Scott's mission, which was a cocaine buy from Jasmina for Peter's birthday celebration. Scott's enthusiasm about the party was another sign that Silas's hold over him was only sexual. Silas had begun to imagine, and dread, a farewell fuck.

Jasmina went on with her argument. "What does Chairman Gates think of your plan?"

"Chairman Gates has nothing to do with this. It may be beyond your understanding, but I am putting my husband and children first."

Jasmina clucked her tongue. "Oh Carolann, I did not just fall off the truck of the, of the…" She turned to the source of the metaphor.

"Of the turnips," said Silas. "Fall off the turnip truck. *Le camion de navets.*"

Carolann was furious to see Silas, who not only had handled her hoodlum but also knew the French word for turnip. "You shut up, Silas!" She whirled back to Jasmina. "Who told you about—I'm going to kill Luca Lucchese for this."

"Luca Lucchese?" said Silas. "You know Luca?"

Jasmina made one of several internationally recognized gestures for sexual congress.

"You've been *doing* Luca Lucchese?"

Silas's incredulous tone was not flattering to hear. "That's right, Silas," said Carolann. "I have. And I've gotten more of him than you ever did. We had sex constantly. He just fucked your legs that one time. I got all of him. And he got all of me."

Silas scoffed. "You can have him, Carolann. That piece of trash was barely worth the once."

"You did Uncle Luca?" asked Scott. "And you didn't tell me?"

"As if you would care," said Silas. "*Uncle* Luca? Whose uncle?"

"Peter's."

Silas steeled himself to remain blasé at this piece of headline news. "Why am I not surprised? Peter and Luca are two peas in a pod."

"He is not trash, Silas," said Carolann. "Luca has gifts you aren't aware of."

"Like that hydraulic derrick of an ass," said Scott.

"You should see his thumbs, Scott," snarled Silas, the second dog in the manger; then he said to Carolann that he hoped Luca hadn't given her herpes, a notion that Jasmina found instantly hilarious.

Carolann snatched up a fistful of coffee stirrers. "What is so funny about that, Jasmina?"

"Oh—I am just imagining Chairman Gates waking up with a cold sore."

Carolann let fly with the stirrers. "Witch! Parasite!"

"Months now with him and you do not tell me, Carolann. I am hurt you do not tell me when I did my best to help."

Silas and Scott looked from Carolann's purple face to Jasmina's second globally legible hand gesture.

"You and Gates?" said Silas. "You've been cheating on your husband with Luca Lucchese and Nathaniel Gates both?"

Carolann's silence was a high, proud road. Silas's head began to spin with sick-making images. The commutative property of arithmetic was also coming into play. He had done Luca, and Luca had done Carolann, so he had done Carolann too. They were all rolling about in a sticky cage filled with doughnuts.

In a daze Silas dropped into the red leather chair and fit the last pieces into the puzzle. Doughnuts were the toll Frankie Quigley had had to pay Silas in order to get him to play "Dead Cathy." A plate of doughnuts had gone with him into the hole in the backyard. It was a plate of doughnuts that had drawn the swarm. And, finally, the various attentions from Frankie, the tickles, the pinches, the blowing onto Silas's face and into his ears, even the screaming insults and the punches, all to get his sister Cathy to rise from the dead, would give Silas erections that he prayed Frankie wouldn't notice and prayed Frankie would notice.

Carolann and Jasmina clawed on, but Silas, processing sex, death, sweets, and bees, heard them as a buzz through a keyhole. He was not yet wise enough or mature enough to hack a path through the Oedipal tangle of Carolann, Chairman Gates, Uncle Luca, Frankie and Cathy Quigley, and Katrinka. From his present experience as the mistress in his own adulterous triangle, he might have been able to show mercy to Carolann, but Silas wasn't terribly compassionate either. He was competitive and righteous, thwarted in love and unmercifully young, and so, as he emerged from his daze, he saw that Carolann had left the lounge. As he watched Jasmina transfer some white powder that wasn't sugar from a coffee can in the storage closet into a baggie that she then placed in Scott's hand, he was able to solve an easier puzzle, one he could act upon as soon as he found a campus phone box.

Just before ten that same night, Randall, who had hunkered down with MTV, answered a knock at the door. He had skipped Debi's *Three Sisters* opening for fear of finding Silas in the audience.

Becky was wearing sunglasses and a printed scarf around her curls. (The look, I believe, was Maria Callas on the tarmac.) "We must flee!" she said.

"Must we?"

"Venki is breathing fire."

She wouldn't elaborate unless Randall agreed to go out for a drink. Drizzle and a light fog enhanced the atmosphere of escape, but she refused the shelter of his umbrella, and with the sunglasses on, Randall was terrified she might trip and break her nose on a tree root.

Her predicament: La Cincha had placed her into a summer opera program in Tel Aviv—six weeks of private coaching, chorus in two mainstage operas, a role in a studio production of *Don Pasquale*, and an audition before European conductors. The School of Music would put her on scholarship, so the gig wouldn't cost a thing beyond airfare. Her arms were already around La Cincha when she remembered the ticket to Bombay Venki had offered her. Riding an elephant or a maestro cueing her from the pit? The fantasy that each destination held an equal claim upon her lasted an agonizing five seconds.

Becky had waited until Venki was smiling on her pillow to mention her change in plans. They would have another year at Yale, and India wasn't going anywhere. Things were settled, she thought, but then he had reached over and covered her lips with his finger.

"But I love you, Becky," he said.

A man had said it, had finally uttered those words to Rebecca Engelking. She had dreamed her whole life of hearing it, saying it right back, and meaning it. She reached over to pull some fuzz from his blue-black hair and did her best. "I care for you very very much, Venki. Very very much."

He pushed her down. "I will make you care more than that, Becky." He tore at her slip, pressed his fingers deep between her legs. "Let me love you," he pleaded. She flipped him off the bed and ordered him from the premises.

Becky fashioned the encounter as a near-rape, but Randall knew better. He told her that Venki wanted to love her *back*, to give her pleasure. He suggested that she could grow to love Venki, she just couldn't choose to love him right now.

She paused under a dogwood, its white blossoms a halo in the mist. "No, Randall. I chose something else today. Art."

"Doesn't that make you feel grown up?"

"Grown up, yes, but kinda sad."

Becky tried to look kinda sad, but the scales tilted again and she blurted out, "*Don Pasquale!*"

"Rosina?" Randall guessed.

"No, Norina! She's perfect for me. Here we are."

Randall looked at the neon sign above their heads. "Partners? *Partners?*"

She removed her scarf and shook her curls. The thump of a bass beat time on the roof of Randall's stomach, and the colored lights flickering through the glass bricks looked like the flames of a vengeful god.

"It's Peter Facciafinta's birthday," Becky said, placing a five-dollar bill into the door attendant's hand. "Two please."

"No, Becky."

"Party's upstairs," said the attendant, making change.

"There's more than one floor?" gasped Randall, as if this detail was an especial abomination. The attendant took his hand. "What are you doing?"

"Stamping your hand," he said.

Behind the attendant rose a staircase lined with silhouettes slouching against a mirrored wall. Becky bore left, towards a group of men in plaid shirts singing, "What Do the Simple Folk Do?" He recognized Brent Fladmo's squashy bum on the piano bench.

"Don't you dare, Becky," he shouted after her. "You'll damage *la voce*."

Without meaning to, Randall joined the floor of corpuscles pushing single file up the capillary of the stairs. On the second floor dozens were crammed into a dim L-shaped space. He could just make out a glue and glitter banner that read "Happy Birthday Peter" under the emergency exit sign. That was where he wanted to be, so he veered out of the line, which was now pooling at the fenced-off entrance to the dance floor.

Peter was sitting on a bar, taking slugs from a bottle of Peach Schnapps. "Well, this is a big surprise, Randy," said Peter, kissing what he could reach of Randall—his forehead.

Scott handed Randall a beer and Pierre Humay appeared, sopping wet from a spin on the floor. Peter wreathed Pierre's crown with paper napkins; they melted like cheese slices in the slick.

After another slug of Schnapps, Peter blew a disco whistle. He drew his finger across his throat to signal the deejay to cut the music. All over the room, ears rang in the silence and men gauged the dampness of their bodies, while Randall put a first foot onto the fire escape.

Peter gave his most dazzling smile. "Today is April 23, and something very important happened today."

"Show us your tits," someone shouted. Peter yanked up his T-shirt. Randall closed his eyes. He'd seen them prancing out of Walt's room.

"Now I want to get this name right," continued Peter. "Scotty?"

Scott handed Peter a slip of paper. Peter scootched down the bar to get under some light and began to read. "Health and Human Services Secretary Margaret Heckler held a press conference *today* in Washington to announce that they had discovered that AIDS is caused by a retrovirus they are calling HTLV-1."

"What's so great about that?" someone shouted.

"I'm getting there. She said they discovered it was a virus, and that a vaccine to prevent it will be available in two years!"

The cheers were long and lusty. Bottles clinked, lovers kissed, strangers high-fived and wrapped arms around one another. Twenty-four months for a cure? That was nothing. They could all hang on that long.

"Now everybody have sex on my birthday!" Peter screamed to the dance floor.

The deejay cued up Parliament's "Give Up the Funk." The lewdest dancers in the pack were grinding from behind, and some of their partners were leaning forward from the waist to give them a bigger wedge of pie. Randall might identify as homosexual for the sake of Silas but these were not his people. He was trying to unfasten his umbrella for a quick leap off the fire escape when someone said, "Bubi, thanks for the flowers!"

It was Debi—with Silas behind her, eyes averted.

"How was the opening? I'm coming tomorrow."

"I killed. Especially Act Four. When Chebutykin told me Tuzenbach was dead, I didn't just cry, Randall, I'm telling you there was *snot*."

She seized a mug from Scott's tray and blew foam everywhere. Then, taking two more beers, she dragged Silas and Randall to the corner of the dance floor furthest from the booming speakers.

"Did you hear the AIDS news?" said Silas.

"It's a virus," said Randall. "It will all be over in two years."

They clinked mugs to that and watched the dancers, rather than face each other.

"They're all stuck on themselves," Randall said, pointing to a man with slit eyes rubbing his crotch for the mirror.

"Occupational hazard," said Silas.

Debi gave Randall a "be nice" look and headed downstairs to duel Becky at the upright. Randall was setting his mug on the drink rail, so Silas said to his back, "I've missed you."

"You have? Really?"

Silas smacked Randall's arm. "Idiot. Of course I have. Don't be dense. Let's not fight anymore."

"We weren't exactly fighting," quibbled Randall, wanting to prolong their act of contrition when Silas needed to plow through it.

"You stopped talking to me on Good Friday. Why?"

Suddenly it was easy to tell the truth. "Your new best friend, Father Daley, is my confessor. *Was* my confessor. I freaked out to see you with him."

Silas, bless him, got it instantly. "Not my type, Randall. Gay, but not ever my type. The gap between the front teeth."

Silas had more to say, but found he couldn't.

"What? Silas?"

Afraid to ask, afraid to need, afraid to be turned down, Silas cooled his cheek on his mug. "Aw fuck, tell me you're not going to that monastery in August. Tell me you're going to stick around for a doctorate on the history of the marrow scoop."

Randall smiled. "Actually, I've been contemplating a *catalogue raisonné* of Second Empire ice cream forks."

"Ah—that would dovetail ever so nicely with my research on Balzacian typefaces."

Silas rubbed his nose and stuck out his jaw—more stalling. "And that being the case…"

"Yes?"

"I couldn't bear Hadley another year. What say you, Chester, to renting an apartment together?"

Randall, no stalling required, said that that was absolutely the best plan ever.

To pretend that something momentous hadn't just occurred, they declared thirst and started to push back to the bar. Randall froze at two paces. Standing at the top of the stairs was Gary, the pick-up from Apollo Books.

"Silas, I have to leave now. *Right now.*"

"What's the matter? Are you sick?"

"I'm going to be."

"What's wrong?"

"There's a man after me."

"What?" Silas yelped with surprise. "Who?"

"Top of the stairs. Striped polo. His name is Gary."

"Five-eight, five-nine, fleshy but not fat?"

"He sells office machines."

"How could he be 'after you'?"

A dash through a hundred bodies wasn't possible. Gary's position was blocking both the stairs and the passage to the fire escape. Randall's bowels had turned to flaming gruel. "I…I…I did him—he did me—we did it—that night, Good Friday, when you and I had that fight."

Silas was delighted. "You salty dog. What did you do?"

"I don't want to talk about it now."

Silas reviewed Gary through a new lens. "You could do a lot worse."

The lights throwing patterns on the gyre of dancing legs was intensifying Randall's nausea. "Stop looking at him!"

"Whatever you did, he liked it."

"Why do you say that?"

"Because he's coming back for more."

Gary was indeed bearing down on them. Randall lurched into Silas. "Help me, Silas, you have to help me." His head throbbed. He closed his eyes and pictured the two of them sitting safely together in their apartment. A double desk. Books. Sunshine, then snow. Tea. Life.

"Hey Randall, how's it going?" Gary's reedy tenor sent Randall straight back to a condo in Hamden, writhing with embarrassment on a sofa. He rushed through a "Hail Mary" before he could think of a reply.

"You shaved your mustache."

"You noticed," said Gary. "I thought about coming to your dorm and asking for you." Randall's eyes bugged. "To see if you were okay."

"That's a terrible thought," said Randall.

"Why?" asked Gary.

There were several answers, but none Randall could articulate once Silas's arm slid around his waist. "It's like this, Gary," said Silas, pressing his fingers into Randall's flank for good measure. "Randall met someone new." Silas placed his other hand on Randall's chest, leaned in, and kissed him slowly on the lips.

It was some rescue. "That's right," said Randall after Silas drew back.

Gary wiped his forehead, then didn't know where to blot the moisture on his hand.

"You don't waste any time," he said, backing away.

"Forgive me, Gary," said Randall. "Please forgive me." He started to shift direction too, but Silas held him in place. "Let's dance."

"Dance? *Us?*"

Before Randall knew what was happening, Silas was leading him by a belt loop onto the floor. The deejay had put on the last tune, a slow song, the final chance to come together. All around them men were hunching into one another, their hopes running especially high, what with a quick cure for the plague winging their way.

"You lead, Randall," Silas whispered into his ear.

"Me? But——"

"Gary needs more convincing."

Once Silas had crossed his hands at the wrists in the small of his back, and put his head on Randall's shoulder, Randall forgot all about Gary. He clasped a shoulder blade in each hand and led. For an instant he saw them slow dancing in the mirror. Then he shut his eyes to vanity and focused instead on the feeling of Silas's hair against his cheek, the pressure of his brow against his collarbone, the even puffs of breath against his throat.

They were managing nicely until Peter and Scott drifted close in their own embrace. To protect Silas, Randall spun away from them, but he felt a deep, miserable sigh against his breast. Silas lifted his head and murmured, "I love him, Randall."

"I know you do."

His eyes were shiny. "It's hopeless, it's wrong, I can't help it."

"Shhhhh," said Randall, rubbing a circle on his back. "I know."

Randall tucked Silas's head back under his chin and allowed his hand to stroke Silas's hair. They rocked in place some more.

"And now we've upset Gary," Silas said, choking down a sob.

He started to flap against Randall like a shutter in a storm. Soon they were laughing so hard they lost control and crashed into a standing speaker.

That very same hour, in the side parlor of a Greek Revival house in a more fashionable district of town, a pair of Yale security detectives, following a trail initiated that afternoon by an anonymous phone call, arrested French Department Chair Nathaniel Gates and one of his graduate students. They discovered Professor Gates, who was dressed in a schoolboy's blazer and rep tie, facedown on a coffee table, his hands and feet trussed to its four corners by loops of rope nailed inexpertly into each table leg. On the floor to his left was an old Harvard baseball cap and four books secured in a cracked leather strap. On the floor to his right was an open can of Crisco and a striped canvas satchel. Under his pelvis were bunched a pair of white short pants and a pair of boxers. They provided a clearer target, and a more comfortable angle, for the silicone penis loosely gripped in, and rhythmically propelled by, the left hand of a woman who had drawn, with an eyebrow pencil, a widow's peak in the center of her forehead just below the edge of a glistening black wig.

Simultaneous to the sodomy was a high-stakes argument between the pair about the merits of psychoanalytic literary theory. The detectives, who respected the precepts and traditions of the university, found themselves loath to interrupt such a spirited academic discussion, but interrupt they did.

Chapter Twelve

Thirty-six hours later, the headline in the *Yale Daily News* read "French Chair Fronts Coke Ring," followed later in the week by more careful reporting in the *New Haven Register* and the *Advocate*. A waggish editor ran a caricature of Nathaniel Gates snorting powder off a doughnut through a Silly Straw, the first of many distortions. These were the facts: coffee cans of uncut cocaine with an estimated street value of four-hundred thousand dollars, as well as a Vuitton cosmetic case containing ten Staffordshire Toby jugs, were seized at three points of purchase and a storage closet at Helen Hadley Hall. Local part-time electrician Luca Lucchese had disappeared. French student Jasmina Wha-Sab had left the country with an unspecified number of incompletes. Doughnut vendors in sixteen departments were deposed. Carolann Chudek maintained ignorance of all wrongdoing; the provisional loss of her Mellon Fellowship for a second year of funding could be regarded as a pre-conscious wish behind Silas Huth's whistleblowing.

In those innocent, more bipartisan times, the media cycle turned as quickly as a paddle wheel on the Mississippi; as a metaphor for educational dereliction—the tenure racket, the liberal bias of elite universities, the irrelevance of the humanities—the incident received brief national coverage, but since there was no proof that any cocaine had been sold to the student body, the furor died away.

Closer to home, the three weeks from the day after Randall and Silas's reunion at Partners until the close of the school year marked what Randall thought of, even while living them, as their honeymoon. Silas might shadow his Scott, and they both might dine in group settings, but for three weeks they were inseparable. They got fitted for tuxes, goofing and preening until the salesman asked which one was the bride. Silas's eggs Florentine led Randall to claim that Silas would be cook of their house. They got haircuts together, then taught each other how to use gel. Silas gave Randall a fragment of the Roman Forum for "continued eloquence," and Randall gave Silas a green cardigan that had belonged to his grandfather to go with his eyes. Randall met Nana Eagle Eye over the phone, and Silas flirted with a Flinn sister or two. They showed off for each other and fabulated their days and traded books and read each other's seminar papers and were self-congratulating and exclusive and possibly unbearable to others. Even the ugly moment when some townies leaned out of a truck cab and shouted "faggots" linked them in benediction.

They took walks along Orange Street, arguing their floral druthers as they took down phone numbers for apartment rentals. Silas was drawn to the houses collared with brilliant azaleas, but Randall was holding out for the promise of peonies. The merest edge of their colors—snow white, scarlet, icy pink—had begun to show in their marble-sized knots of green. Silas thought it was wrong for such beauty to flower all at once, and only once. They should be coaxed into repeating like a rosebush, but Randall said that their brief but glorious season was his favorite thing about them.

Randall would watch Silas drift from his door after hours of japing and feel almost ashamed of his happiness. He didn't care to overanalyze the change in their bond. Finding sex and love in the same vessel is a tall order for the young; Silas was siphoning to Randall the tenderness and attention he couldn't give to Scott.

The four-alarm fire was telling Nixie about Walt and Peter. When apprised, Silas felt that life was truly worth living if it could produce such a grotesque pairing. Yet he was invested only in exposing Walt, so entire dithering days passed. Silas would say, "We have to tell Nixie," and Randall would say, "You have to tell Scott," and Silas would say, "Don't be an idiot," and Randall would back down. Finally they got stinking drunk one afternoon and slalomed around two corners of the hallway with a fifth of bourbon. They heard the hum of an electric typewriter in Walt's room.

After a first belt, Nixie gushed about how great it was to see her boys together again. On the second, she and Silas caught up on department gossip; on the third, Randall began to fret. There are two ways to cook a lobster. Throw it into the boiling water; or bring it to a boil with the water. Watching Silas and Nixie get silly as they applied polish to their toenails, Randall was afraid he'd sober up long before the water got lukewarm.

Nixie showed them a black lace negligee that her Aunt Mae had sent ahead for the wedding night. The gift card read, "For Love's Mysteries Divine." Silas, laughing until the tears came to his eyes, begged her to model it. Nixie was tempted, but tossed him her wedding garter instead. Silas rolled it to a couple of inches below his khaki shorts. He adjusted the pink rosette to the left and struck flamenco poses. Recalling his own recent appearance in Nixie's beads and veil, Randall wondered what it was about the bride that encouraged cross-dressing. As if reading his mind, she said she hoped they would always be her handmaidens.

"Or eunuchs," said Randall. "We'll guard you. We'll dry you with our fans."

She laughed. "Promise to guard Walt too."

That nicked Silas at last. He stopped camping and asked her if she were happy, *really* happy.

"Of course I am. I'll breathe easier on May 27th, but I'm happy. Why?"

"How well do you know, *really* know, Walt?" asked Randall.

Edith Piaf might have scripted Nixie's reply: "He's my man. We sleep in that bed every night. I make his coffee. His underwear is in that pile of laundry. I know what he needs."

Her eunuchs saw his laundry, a stack of playscripts, a can of shaving cream, and a framed photo of his parents. Whatever else of Walt there was, was buried under Nixie.

"This isn't easy to say," Silas mumbled.

"Out with it," snapped our straight shooter.

They jumped, and Randall took over. "Sometimes I just wonder about...Walt's sexuality."

"His sexual identity," continued Silas, shifting in the chair to protect his viscera.

"He's been with men," she snapped again. "So what?"

"He told you?" asked Silas.

She drew a cigarette from a pack. "Of course he did, dumbbells. We know all about each other's pasts. He used to do stuff with his best man,

Eddie Bacino. It started when they were twelve. They kept it up some when he came home from college on vacations. It's a phase."

"Why didn't you tell us?" Randall asked.

"Because it's none of your business. Look, I found some dirty magazines under his bed right before Christmas. Men-with-men magazines."

"What did you do?"

She blew a smoke ring. "I asked him what they were doing there, and he told me it wasn't a big deal. He'd had them for a couple of years. He said it was another way to express himself. But he doesn't express himself that way anymore."

Silas attempted cross-examination. "What were the dates on the magazines?"

"I don't know, I pitched them out."

The slap of her hand on the desk dared them to produce more evidence. Randall took a breath, but with his eyes Silas said, "Stop."

"Nixie," said Randall, "Walt's been with a man in this dorm. Within the last month."

Silas looked away from the impact, but Randall saw her turn white and bite her lip to hold the questions inside her body. She resecured the hair on top of her head, not speaking until the last barrette was cinched.

"He told me about that too, Randall," she said. "He asked my forgiveness, and I forgave him, because when two people love each other as much as we do, they forgive each other. It's not going to happen again, because we're going to be together all the time. He did that because he wanted to be positive that he wanted only me. And he found that out. He wants only me."

She held out a hand for her garter, poured another slug, and pushed the bottle to the edge of the table. "Finish that, will you?" With a trip of the power switch on her typewriter she ended her trial. "We have great sex, boys, a lot of great sex. And he's man enough for me."

"I'm sorry Nixie—"

"We just wanted you to—"

"We care so much—"

"We want you to be happy—"

"I'm glad you came to me. And anyway, I've been kind of wanting to get this off my chest."

They drained the bottle, drinking to a lifetime of friendship and scholarship. If willing her man straight was her objective, Nixie would triumph again. Her boys stumbled into Temple Street in search of some starches to soak up the liquor. Silas pointed out that not only were all four of the male attendants gay, but half of them—Peter and Eddie—had had carnal knowledge of the groom. Randall leaned against a bicycle rack to process the fact and before he knew it, was vomiting into a patch of coleus. Silas went next.

Two weeks later, on a muggy Friday afternoon, all of Hadley was racing against the clock. The rehearsal dinner had snowballed from a potluck for the attendants and out-of-town guests into a dorm-wide expression of global pride. Casseroles and callaloos were cooking in and on every stove. Scott was frosting sheet cakes. Pierre Humay was making emergency alterations on Daddy Stehlik's tuxedo. In the common room Lakshmi and Becky were writing reception place cards by the piano, while Venki and Arup taped crepe paper swags to the ceiling. Before going to pick up the flowers in East Haven, Peter Facciafinta left Randall and Silas with 120 six-inch squares of mesh, a roll of blue ribbon, and ten pounds of Jordan almonds.

This shift in scale of the party was common sense to the students from cultures in which entire villages celebrated the transfer of chattel from one barn to another, but it ran counter to American ideas of order and good taste. Even if Nixie's Aunt Mae, who made much of my Sèvres plate, was seated next to a sixty-gallon trash can, and Pauline Bolger would always refer to it as "a parade of horribles," the outpouring of love and the culinary traditions honored and heaped on six folding tables were true to the Hadley spirit of international amity.

Between dinner and dessert a delegation of Indian students presented Nixie with a hot pink sari threaded with silver. She ran with Lakshmi into the TV room to change; when she re-emerged to an explosion of Instamatics, Walt answered the riddle of their honeymoon. They were going to spend six weeks in India, hosted by the families of the beaming Venkatesh and Arup. At the news, the crowd rushed the couple, as if their jet was already pulling away.

In America, the groom's family hosts the rehearsal dinner. Although Walt's father wasn't paying for the feast, he was aware that he must somehow leave his mark upon it. Today we live in a continual loop of public revelation, but not so in 1984. Mr. Stehlik's introduction of a tape recorder during dessert and subsequent invitation for personal witness seemed regrettably Baptist. Mr. Stehlik pushed the "record" and "play" buttons and held out the microphone.

Gene Bolger, hearty and game, strode forward. He took the mic and thanked everyone for coming to the shivaree. Then he told the story of how he and Pauline had felt like Abraham and Sarah, how they had prayed to the Lord to complete their lives with a child. He did not fail them. The Lord sent them the most precious hazel-eyed child in all creation. When Gene got to the moment of seeing their miracle bundle placed in his wife's arms for the first time, he broke down. Nixie led him to a quiet spot behind the piano, and no one could recall him speaking for the rest of the weekend.

Debi Fleer lifted the mood with impersonations of the bride and groom, and then relived the day she'd thrown a fit in rehearsal. If Nixie hadn't lured her out of the bathroom, Walt wouldn't have asked her out, and there would be no wedding, so put the blame on Debi. And she wouldn't have given her career-defining, avant-garde performance as Helga Two which had led to an even greater demonstration of her versatility, her recent realistic triumph as Irina in *Three Sisters*.

Becky stepped up next. After telling the Price Chopper Pampers story and thanking Nixie for being her role model, she cued Brent and sang a roof-raising medley of songs made famous by the late Ethel Merman. Making good on her New Year's resolution, she dedicated her performance to all the "fabulous and special gay guys" in the dorm, who had taught her so much about tolerance. Before closing out with "Ridin' High," she invited the room to hear her do a set at Partners Café, where she'd be headlining before she flew off to Tel Aviv to follow her truer musical muse.

On went the drinking and the witnessing; the mound of paper plates and plastic cups and foil pans climbed higher in the trash can next to Aunt Mae. Peter, giving time to the groom, embellished Walt's qualities in a way that made Randall squirm and Mrs. Bolger slit her eyes. Mr. Stehlik put a fresh tape in the cassette recorder. There were bawdy recollections from

Walt's Arkansas sisters, the Lord's Prayer led by Mrs. Stehlik, Chinese students practicing their English. Finally, Nixie took control. She kissed Mr.
Stehlik and turned off the machine. "Before we start the dancing, I want
to thank each and every one of you for making this the most amazing party I've ever been to. I only hope the wedding and the reception tomorrow
live up to it. Since we lost our original caterer to a brush with the law, I'd
like to especially thank Randall Flinn and Peter Facciafinta and Carolann
Chudek for working overtime to pull this off. Where are you guys? Take
a bow." Carolann and Peter blew kisses from the center of the room, but
Randall, who had too much to say to be able to say anything, stayed put
by my portrait.

In a last minute, possibly pre-conscious homage to Stavrolakis Heliotis, the man she'd left behind on the Feast of St. Clare, Queen Nixie
popped in a cassette of bouzouki music, and began to teach the syritaki to
her sozzled subjects.

Peter and best man Eddie Bacino skipped the dance lesson in order to
take a keg, a projector, and some stag films to the fifth-floor kitchen. There
was also a doll to inflate. Silas was next to leave, followed, after a discreet
interval, by Scott.

Scott found Silas waiting for him, naked, inside a stall in the women's
bathroom behind the ping-pong table. Scott hung his sport coat over Silas's clothes on the door hook. They had to be quick. Finding themselves
across from each other in the doubled buffet line, Scott had murmured "*Je
te veux*" and Silas murmured "*Toilette des dames.*" All through the taping,
they traded glances and writhed on their seats for each other, too wound
up to testify.

Scott fell to his knees and put one of Silas' balls in his mouth. Silas
tensed; this was not a favorite maneuver. When Scott went for its brother,
Silas pulled him up and unzipped his fly.

After stroking him to a fever, Silas crouched on the toilet seat, then
reached up and with each hand gripped a side of the top of the stall. He
hoisted his legs up and let his calves rest on Scott's shoulders. Scott surveyed the position with nasty appreciation.

"Are you sure?" he asked.

"Slick it up, baby."

When Scott was ready, Silas relaxed his arms, lowered his pelvis, and threaded his legs through Scott's armpits. Then he scissored them at the ankles. The cold metal of the stall door stung his bare feet. Scott gripped Silas's haunches and went in slowly, biting his tongue with concentration.

Scott started up, then stopped. "Hey, Silas, could you—could you—"

"Could I what?" said Silas, trembling with anticipation at Scott's first-ever request.

"Well." Scott closed his great blue eyes and zoomed in to bite his neck. "Could you...be..."

"Be what?"

"Be...Katrinka?"

On hearing her name, Silas's first impulse was to disengage, but then he understood that this was what Scott had wanted all along. "Be Katrinka what?"

"Could Katrinka talk to me? You know...cuss me out."

The whisper in his ear stirred Silas.

"You know...abuse me."

"If you call me Powerful Katrinka," she snarled.

Scott's head snapped back, and he gritted his teeth. They started up. Silas permitted Katrinka some filthy commandments, while Scott, heaving and stamping like the Minotaur, fought back with his own stream of obscenities. The greater part of Silas's consciousness was repeating the banal, but genuine, "*Je te veux.*"

It was the rut of their lives. As things neared the inevitable, Silas knew that they might never again be this close and decided it was time to lose control completely. When Scott shouted that he was climaxing, Silas released his arms from the top of the stall and let go. He could have split his head open on the toilet tank, killed himself, destroyed Katrinka—it didn't matter—if Scott cared for him, he'd keep him whole—but as he fell backward in his own orgasm, Silas arched up with his chest, and his hands caught Scott by the neck. They slammed once, twice, against the stall, but staggered together and held on.

They stared dumbly at each other, breathless, proud and slippery, until they emerged from the animal state.

"Oh baby, that was the best ever," said Scott.

"More, always always more," replied Silas, very close to tears.

"Christ," whooped Scott. "It smells like a swamp in here. Katrinka. Kee-rist."

Silas rapped Scott on the crown with his knuckles to remind him just whom he had been riding, and they began to laugh. Silas rubbed Scott's neck as he sucked up the semen on Silas's stomach. Silas stopped, rubbed a spot on Scott's neck, stopped, and rubbed more carefully. Just below and behind Scott's ears, his fingertips had found two short strands of pearls buried an inch beneath the skin.

"What are these?"

"Yeah, I know," said Scott, looking up with glistening lips. "I don't know what that's about."

A couple of hours later, a freshly laundered Silas couldn't figure out what he was doing in Scott's room. At the bachelor's party Peter had mentioned something about a tie. Whatever the lure, Silas drunkenly realized he had never once been in Room 209. It was a miniscule domain for two men as over-determined as Scott Jencks and Peter Facciafinta. The scholar was permitted three shelves of books and a Princeton pennant; the rest was given over to posters of male nudes, stuffed animals, and bright jars of candy.

"What am I doing here?" Silas wondered aloud.

"Showing me how to tie a bow tie," said Peter.

"Our tuxes came with clip-ons."

"I have to tie Scottie's tomorrow. God, I'm exhausted. I haven't stopped running all day." Peter jerked his polo out of his pants and shucked it over his head. It landed behind the bed.

"Where is Scott?"

"I don't know." Peter put the tie around his neck. His T-shirt was soaked.

"Why wasn't he at the bachelor's party?"

Peter stepped out of his shoes and kicked them away. "I don't know, Silas. You tell me."

The warning brushed against Silas's ears. He leaned into Peter and grasped the ends of the tie with clumsy fingers, only to have Peter kiss him. His breath was sweet and thick, like the inside of a cherry cordial.

Silas pulled back. "What are you doing?"

"What does it look like?" Peter braced himself against the closet door with a come-hither expression.

"I don't want to kiss you," said Silas.

"You don't." Peter started to massage his own chest as encouragement. "Why not?"

"Where is Scott?" Silas repeated.

"Far far away," said Peter, dropping his mouth open and rolling his eyes upward. He found his left nipple through the wet cloth and teased it with swift strokes from a forefinger, as if he were trying to get it to talk. "Maybe he's washing your smell off him, Silas."

Silas, staggered to have his mind read, tried to look perplexed.

"You're fucking my boyfriend, aren't you?" asked Peter.

"No I'm not."

"Yes you are."

"That's ridiculous. You two are a couple."

"You're fucking him, or he's fucking you."

"You've had too much to drink, Peter," said Silas carefully, as if proper enunciation was tantamount to innocence.

"Fuck yes we're a fucking couple, but you're fucking my Scottie too!"

"You really ought to discuss this with him."

Silas moved towards the door. Peter lunged, hands drawn like claws. Silas sidestepped, and Peter landed facedown on the bed. Dragging his legs up took the rest of the fight out of him. Silas, dreading what would happen if Scott came clean about their affair, wasn't paying attention to Peter until he noticed that his arms were twitching. He asked him if he were all right. Peter feebly kicked a leg.

Something was wrong. Silas moved to the bed. He turned him over by his shoulder. Peter's arm was cold. His hair was curled with perspiration, but his forehead was dry and chill. His lips were twisting and his tongue was moving, producing spittle and slurred, senseless curses. The cloying sweetness of his breath hung like a cloud over his darting eyes.

Once upon a time, Silas had taken chemistry, and he had a memory for unusual words. The word for what was happening to Peter was *ketosis*.

Down in the common room, while Lakshmi and Pierre bagged the remains of the potluck, Nixie turned the bouzouki mix over and over in the tape recorder until she was swaying all by her lonesome. Finally she slumped into the couch. Becky, keeping vigil as befits the maid of honor, took a half-bottle of red she'd held in reserve and wiggled it in front of her charge. Nixie woozily reached for it, but Becky took a step backward and wrenched the tape recorder cord out of the wall with a swift yank of her foot.

"Let's finish this in your room and put you to bed," said Becky.

In deference to tradition, the bride and groom were spending the night apart. Once in her room, Nixie peeled down her pantyhose and began to teeter. Becky held her shoulders until Nixie had freed her feet, then rewarded her with a glass of wine.

Nixie blinked with lachrymose appreciation. This was, after all, their final chance to weep as single sisters. "Aww, Becky, I wouldn't have made it through this year without you. But I promise you next year we'll only be two blocks away, so everything will stay exactly the same. I won't give up my booze hours. Everyone can come over for *apéritifs*, we can dance and drink, and nothing will change. I don't want anything to change." (I am told this last wish of Nixie's is commonly expressed on the eve of weddings, graduations, and foreign invasions.)

"Two blocks can feel like two miles," said Becky. Things would change, had already changed so much since that September afternoon when they'd first shared confidences.

"Did I ever tell you I think you sing like an angel?" said Nixie, spinning herself out of her sari. "I always wished I had a talent."

"You're a scholar, Nixie. Your talent is friendship."

Nixie drained her glass. Embarrassed by the compliment, she reverted to a traditional supportive saying. "You and Venki make such a cute couple."

"Not anymore. We broke up tonight, right before your party."

"Noooooo," said Nixie, shocked. Drink and the freight of the day had enlarged her reactions as much as they had Peter and Silas jousting one floor below.

"Oh Becky, after all your hard work. You must feel..."

Becky reached over to tidy the heap of silk. "I feel great. Venki and I will always be friends. My career is more important to me right now. Now let me hang up your sari."

"But you were going to see India, you were going to ride elephants and swim in the Ganges and get married like me and Walt."

Becky had to laugh. "Whatever gave you that idea?"

"You said you were you said you were you said you were..." Nixie interrupted her mantra with a mind-clearing belch.

"It didn't work out for us. But now you and Walt will ride the elephants instead of me. What a wonderful honeymoon you're going to have."

"I know. Why don't you come with us?"

By now Becky had had a glimpse of the girl Mrs. Bolger had found so challenging to raise. "Here, why don't you let me brush your hair? It's all tangled."

"Noooooo," said Nixie, sloshing wine on her slip.

"It feels good to have your hair brushed. It'll calm you down. My mother used to brush my hair whenever I was upset."

"My mother used to hit me with a hairbrush," moaned Nixie. "Oh my mother, my mother, my mother. Can tomorrow just be over already?"

"Now where is that hairbrush of yours?" asked Becky, looking around the messy room for the most likely surfaces.

"I use Walt's. It's in his room. We share it."

Nixie's hairbrush, which I spotted before Becky, had half-fallen behind the bust of Voltaire. Its oval back, heavy with so many long, luxurious chestnut strands, was more than ready to tip the handle behind the bookshelf and into several months' worth of dust bunnies on the floor.

With a sense of alarm verging on terror—quite unlike me—I saw that Becky was about to give up the chase. She was never going to locate Nixie Bolger's hairbrush and discover its power in the way that I suspected and wished and hoped and prayed she might, unless I, Helen Hadley, born in 1895 in Portsmouth, New Hampshire, reached across the great ectoplasmic divide and placed it myself into her hand. This would be my first and only physical intervention. I wasn't even sure I had the power to do it, or what the gesture might cost me. I only knew that Becky Engelking must absolutely grab hold of that hairbrush. And so, with all my powers of mesmeric concentration, I willed the brush in her direction. The intensity of my focus as I held to the strength in my past made the seconds stretch like minutes. Finally, the brush lifted itself over Voltaire's head, and began to float, handle first, across the room.

Becky, less than sober herself, didn't question how the hairbrush found her in the moonlight. First it was nowhere to be found, then it was suddenly in her grip. That's weird, she thought, as she began working a thick pad of hair out of the brush. She took Nixie's wineglass and told her to sit still.

Becky began with long, careful strokes. "You have such beautiful hair, Nixie. It's like a magic carpet." She began to hum the "habañera."

The brushing calmed Nixie down, but had the opposite effect on Becky. Before she knew what was happening, her body was flooded with overwhelming currents of sensation. Each pull of the brush, every touch to steady Nixie's neck, every flyaway hair that tickled her cheeks, was electrifying, stirring Becky's soul in the way that the nearness of Ada Bonner once stirred mine. When Nixie made a sudden turn, and one of her breasts shifted from her slip and grazed Becky's arm, Becky dropped the hairbrush and heard it hit the floor a hundred miles away.

Around the corner from Nixie's, Silas threw open Randall's door.

"Come quick! It's Peter. He's ketosing."

"He's what?"

"He's having a fit—low blood sugar, remember?"

Randall did remember. Flying down the stairs to the second floor, he pushed the words "diabetic coma" from his mind.

Peter was lying on his side, gurgling. Silas shook a shoulder and his head flopped back. His condition had deteriorated in the time it had taken to fetch Randall.

"Dead in twenty minutes, remember?" said Silas.

"Don't say that! That's not helpful."

"His brain will shut down, Randall. We have to save him."

Randall looked at Silas before he bent over Peter. He traced the chilled curve of Peter's cheek with his fingertips. Did they really have to save him? He filled his nostrils with the odor of rotting fruit. In a few hours, he wouldn't be Peter, Randall told himself. He would be a bowl of sodden peaches, a compote of bruised nectarines and oozing plums. Now he was an inconvenience, a person who stood in the way of what Silas wanted most. Soon he would be just a body. Only and merely a body. A sacrificial body. Randall looked again at Silas. He loved him. He would do whatever he could to make him happy. Randall stepped back from the body. Peter was a sacrifice Randall was willing to make.

"What?" whispered Silas.

Randall nodded to the door. "We could leave him for Scott to find."

"He'll die."

"I know. And you could have Scott."

"You would do this for me?"

Randall nodded.

"Why?"

Lacan says so it shall be spoken, so it shall be done. Dinah Chidsey said Randall's feelings were a treasure. He took his chances. He placed both hands on his heart. Then he let his hands fall open in Silas's direction. Silas blinked once, twice. From months of keeping watch, Randall knew how Silas's eyes fit to the twist of his lips and the slight turn of his neck. To keep him from speaking, Randall spoke himself and blessed the dying Peter beneath his fingers.

The Owl looked up to the stars above,
And sang to a small guitar,
'O lovely Pussy! O Pussy my love,
What a beautiful pussy you are,
You are,
You are!
What a beautiful Pussy you are!

And Silas took it up—*Pussy said to the Owl, 'You elegant fowl! How charmingly sweet you sing!*—and because they were thinking as one, giving life and giving death as lovers sometimes did, they finished in a whisper as the clock ran down.

Another groan from Peter woke Silas to his own discovery, which he delivered with shouts of terror.

"Scott doesn't want me! He wants Katrinka! Everyone wants Katrinka!"

"I don't want Katrinka. I want you."

"If Scott doesn't want *me*, he's not worth having."

"No, he's not. Of course he's not."

"If he cheats on Peter, he'll cheat on me!"

"Of course he will!" Randall shouted back. "Of course he will!"

Peter's eyes had bugged out. "Look Silas, his eyes are open!"

"We can save him," said Silas. "It's not too late."

"What do we do?"

"I DON'T KNOW!"

"There's candy on the bookshelves. Circus peanuts! Jelly beans!"

"He's too far gone to chew!"

"Sugar then, raw sugar!"

And then they were slamming the drawers and cabinets. Some sex toys popped out of a drawer in the violence. Randall found sugar packets with the coffee gear and ripped them open. Silas pulled open Peter's mouth, and they dumped some under his tongue. He started to choke, so they sat him between them and propped him up with their shoulders. Randall began the Lord's Prayer and Silas joined in.

With the right technology, recovery from blood sugar shock is miraculous. Within five minutes, Peter was pushing back. When he had recovered enough motor function to bat their hands away, Silas and Randall burned off their fear by jamming marshmallow circus peanuts down his throat. Finally he was strong enough to tell them to get the hell out. They told him he was lucky they were there to save his life.

"You should have just let me die," he said with unexpected self-pity.

"It crossed our minds"—Silas raised an eyebrow in Randall's direction—"but we didn't."

"Scottie is mine, bitch!" said Peter. He tried to throw a stuffed dinosaur, but he was still too weak. It slid off the bed.

"He's yours to try and keep," said Silas, high-hatting him.

Randall had his own two cents to spend. "And Walt is Nixie's, you tramp!" Peter's look of surprise was deliciously gratifying. "See you in church."

When they reached Randall's door, Silas went in first, taking his friend by the hand. He led him to the bed. He loved Randall, and he knew it. They unbuttoned and lay together, but as innocents, kissing and embracing and protecting what was best in each other until morning.

Ave Atque Vale

Sex is a momentary itch.
Love never lets you go.

—KINGSLEY AMIS

The day is cloudless and rather cool for late May. A light breeze rustles the lengths of silk and linen on the guests as they make their way into Dwight Chapel, the original home of the Yale University Library. At ten-thirty-five, the lawn surrounding this turreted stone fantasy holds a few Frisbee players and Dinah Chidsey, the Thirty-Cent Lady, who is holding a ten-spot and a tea rose from the bride.

Inside, the service has already begun. It is now time for Randall Flinn to place his hands on the lectern and glance at his text. Where newer Bibles translate the Greek concept of *agape* as *love*, the King James uses the word *charity*. ("*Charity* suffereth long and is kind; …and now abideth faith, hope, and *charity*," etcetera.) Nixie has chosen a modern translation of Paul's thoughts, but Randall was raised on King James and is acutely aware this particular morning of the connotative difference.

In the instant before Randall is to remind his friends of that place where love and charity meet, let us stop time to share his view from the pulpit. In the front pew Pauline Bolger, a rock tumbler in peach chiffon, is grimly wrestling with her rosary; her husband Gene's hand cups her shoulder in awkward comfort. Scott Jencks, who had come home in the wee hours to a vengeful consort and a floor gritty with spilled sugar, bears a blanched expression. Pierre Humay, fresh tint to his occiput, beams to think of his hand-stitched linings in Debi's, Becky's, and Lakshmi's frocks. A reflective Carolann Chudek has turned forty in the night. Her third pregnancy has just been confirmed. A blood test, should she seek it, will confirm paternity. She is hoping for a girl, a girl that she will name Natalie Louise. In the back pews, with the aisle between them, ushers Arup and Venkatesh sit like proud andirons, short and tall, in turquoise Nehru jackets.

Silas Huth, upstage with Peter Facciafinta and Eddie Bacino, is out of Randall's sight, yet from the warmth he feels on his own head Randall knows that Silas is held in strong, dazzling light. In the chapel dressing room before the service, they had put in each other's cufflinks and brushed each other's tuxedoes, but made no mention of their acts of devotion of the night before. In the days remaining to them in New Haven Silas will argue and plead and beg for more from Randall, for he has discovered to his perfect delight that he both loves *and* desires his best friend, but Randall will refuse Silas with increasing vigor and a perfect certainty. With the wisdom that a living God can grant to a soul such as his, Randall realized, even as his love slept beside him, that Silas, once given the opportunity, would go through him in a month. The Owl knows he would not survive the loss of the Pussycat. Despite Silas's desperate appeals, too heart-wrenching for me to relate, I believe Randall. They had flowered, once and fully, and had had their dance by the light of the moon.

Below and to the right are the bride and groom. Randall catches Nixie's eye, and she winks magnificently. He begins speaking, and Walt squares his shoulders. Randall will never reveal to Nixie the reason why her wedding had a late start. Five minutes before Brent Fladmo was to fire up the organ with the March from *Lohengrin*, the groomsmen realized that Walt had vanished. Willing to have Nixie call off her wedding, but not Walt, Silas and Randall split up to search the building, leaving Peter and Eddie Bacino to stall the celebrant.

Randall found Walt in a shadowy corner of the basement, rhythmically pulling at where his beard had been. Behind him was a wall covered with images of young men in fraternal organizations stretching back to the dawn of photography. One hundred and forty years of grooms, best men, organists, fathers, soldiers, athletes, preachers, scholars, statesmen, artists, and bachelors bore silent witness to the present drama, which was but one more flashbulb in a boundless continuum of human confusion. All eyes fail before Time's eye.

"Hey Walt, what are you doing?" Randall asked, pretending they had hours, not minutes.

"Thinking."

"Of course." Randall gave Walt an encouraging smile. "Big day, huh?" Walt flinched. "Do you love her?" Walt nodded. "That's important, Walt, because she loves you so much. She'll always love you, Walt, no matter what."

Walt let out a breath. Randall held out his hand, and Walt grasped it. "Let's go then," Walt said, as if it was he who had come to retrieve Randall from the darkness, and not the reverse.

Now, nearing the end of Paul's advice to the Corinthians, Randall turns away from the world to search inside himself. *"When I was a child, I spoke as a child, I understood as a child, I thought as a child; but when I became a man, I put away childish things."*

Was letting Peter Facciafinta die for the sake of Silas Huth—an act of love, an act of charity most perverse—the last act of a child or the first act of an adult?

Randall Flinn wonders still. His life today is one of contemplation and useful labor at the Monastery of San Perugia. Every spring, for several weeks, he has the consolation of peonies beneath his window, and now and again, a letter from Silas Huth. These letters, Randall has come to appreciate, continue their Hadley honeymoon. He hears his friend sounding through the years, as entitled, as mock-sour, and as hopeful for more, always always more, as when Randall first set eyes and ears upon him over thirty years ago. Whatever else its purchase, love had made Randall a better listener.

They never shared an apartment. Randall joined the Benedictines, and Silas quit the French Department after a third semester and began a lucrative career as performance artist Katrinka. No vaccine appeared in 1986. As the decade wore on, the Thirty-Cent Lady was joined on the streets of New Haven by a growing army of skeletal mendicants, and children were trained to fear doorknobs and toilet handles, and young people learned how to have sex in an epidemic, while major reversals in the tax treatment of business income swept across the land to replace sexual abandon with fiscal abandon, an equally morbid and global syndrome that goes untreated and unchecked to this day.

Silas Huth takes a regimen of pills but remains convinced that he cheated death by letting Peter Facciafinta live that night he discovered those lymphatic pearls in Scott Jencks' neck. Silas was spared, but others we have come to know—Scott Jencks, Brent Fladmo, Pierre Humay, Luca Lucchese, Brother Ted, Father Daley, and Peter Facciafinta—are gone. Their names are stitched on quilt squares, a more portable, but no less permanent, memorial than the marble rotunda guarded by a hoplite on Beinecke Plaza.

The anti-apartheid shantytown and the Soviet Union are gone too, dismantled long ago, but now there is China to worry over. Bisexuality remains a mystery to some and a nuisance to others. Helen Hadley Hall still stands on Temple Street, for a few more years, I hope, beckoning brilliant fools to come learn and unlearn lessons in the slipstream of their own sweet times.

For thirty years Randall has prayed that Silas never succumb to the virus. He prays with equal fervor to be forgiven for the mortal sacrifice he was once willing to make of another one of God's creatures. Silas insists in his letters Randall has been redeemed in full and that the time is nigh for him to forgive himself and rejoin the world.

We will leave that for Randall to decide and conclude with Becky Engelking. She steps from the bouquet of bridesmaids. She hands her tea roses and baby's breath, the ubiquitous nuptial arrangement of the era, to Debi Fleer. She adjusts her skirt at the podium, glances at her music, and nods to Brent. His introductory chords give her time enough to collect her thoughts and place her voice.

Earlier that morning she had been rinsing the egg from her plate in the kitchen when the bride walked in whistling. Becky turned crimson to feel strong arms embracing her from behind.

"Thanks for putting me to bed last night," said Nixie, so astonishingly, lovably, straight-shootingly matter-of-factly unaware when it counted most.

Becky set down her sponge. "Oh yes, Nixie. It was my pleasure," she replied, twisting her hands. Her rubber gloves scrunched dramatically. "The pleasure was completely mine."

She begins. As her voice connects to the lyrics and to the memory of the raptures she felt on Nixie's bed, Becky knows she has found the final, crowning jewel in her temperament, a power no one can ever take away from her. What she needs now is someone real to give it to. As she sings, an angel within insinuates that her proper destination awaits her in this very chapel. Yet before Becky can look for her—and let us look too—she sends a grateful farewell to Venkatesh, who bobs to her cadences from the back pew.

And so Becky, a lustrous, reverberant silver bell, calls for a partner through the song. Carolann is weeping at the sound of her music, but she's married and a mother. Risa Brandex is horrid, first to last. Faye Kringle is "in the lifestyle," but that worm had lain so long inside her.

But hold!

On the bride's side of the aisle, partway back, a woman has fixed her gaze upon her. She strips Becky to her birthday suit, causing her to recall the molten touch of Nixie's breast against her arm. Who is this forbidding woman with hands set like paws on the pew in front of her? And how does she know absolutely everything about Becky?

Brent Fladmo's feet paddle the stops. As the song nears its climax, Becky drags her focus away from the goddess with the widow's peak and turns to sing to Nixie and Walt and the wedding party.

And there, in radiant array among the maidens, is another face, a most familiar face.

...Follow ev'ry rainbow,
There you'll find your dream!

As the final chord from the organ rings, then fades into the stones and the stained glass and the gentling history of Dwight Chapel, Becky Engelking finds her dream. Sympathetic, brainy, tart, graceful, wise, wealthy, loyal, beautiful, warm, *sexy* Lakshmi Dawat. Her closest friend, her next-door neighbor, her truest heart, another color in the rainbow. Becky cannot wait to love her, and love her right.

Acknowledgments

Love Slaves of Helen Hadley Hall began on a train trip between Baltimore and New Haven in November 1996, so long ago I used pen and legal pad and there was no need for a quiet car.

I had no business attempting a novel, especially one with nineteen central characters, but I wouldn't know that for years. I'd therefore like to thank initial readers Jaan Whitehead, Peter Hagan, Lillian Groag, Pebble Kranz, Catherine Weidner, and David Pelizzari for their unfounded enthusiasm for the first draft. Also Kennie Pressman, who gave me the title. Much gratitude as well to the formidable Jean McGarry, then a new friend, whose notes on the manuscript in 2002 led to a drastic weight loss of 65,000 words.

Love Slaves languished in a box and on disk (remember those?) for years while I wrote my first short stories and published a different novel. A thank you to Amy Bloom, who reassured me in 2010 that it was no shame for a writer to return to a former obsession. Residencies and fellowships at the Virginia Center for the Creative Arts and the MacDowell Colony were critical to the resumption of my work. At the VCCA, a puff of Albuterol, a delirium-inducing asthma medication, in the early morning of 11.11.11, led me at last to my narrator: Helen Hadley, whose portrait had been hiding in plain sight on page one for fourteen years.

Closer to home, I'd like to thank Baltimore friends Kathy Flann, Christine Grillo, Jane Delury, and Elizabeth Hazen, who read a flurry of drafts over the last five years. Gifted writers all, they will read, diagnose, and mend sentences, pages, and chapters, with great skill and unstinting generosity. I am blessed to have them around.

This novel is so old, it predates my meeting my husband in 1998. A gentleman to his core, Steve Bolton claims to have forgotten the early, tantrum-filled years of my fiction apprenticeship. It was during our ten months together in Kampala, Uganda, in 2013, over the diurnal cacophony of distressed cocks and famished guard dogs at the kleptocrats next door, that I managed to finish *Love Slaves* once and for all.

As for the marketplace, let's just say that everyone always loved the title. It took Erin McKnight, a Scotswoman transplanted to Plano, Texas, who evidently shares my sense of humor, to risk publication. I cannot believe my good fortune to have found her and Queen's Ferry Press, and to have Lori Larusso design my cover.

I give belated thanks to the French Department at the Yale School of Graduate Studies for its misplaced generosity once upon a time, and to the Yale School of Drama for accepting my academic defection two years later.

Love Slaves of Helen Hadley Hall didn't begin life as historical fiction. Years and events have made it so. Part of me wishes I were still revising it; that way I'd never have to leave that dorm and that time and those people I loved, the living and the dead, who haunt these pages. By way of apology to them all, I hold fast to the maxim that there is no such thing as bad publicity, or a misspent youth.

JAMES MAGRUDER's fiction has appeared in *The Gettysburg Review*, *New England Review*, *Subtropics*, *Bloom*, *The Normal School*, *New Stories from the Midwest*, and elsewhere. His début novel, *Sugarless*, was a finalist for a Lambda Literary Award and shortlisted for the 2010 William Saroyan International Writing Prize. His collection of stories, *Let Me See It*, was published by TriQuarterly Books/Northwestern University Press in 2014. His adaptations of works by Molière, Marivaux, Lesage, Labiche, Gozzi, Dickens, Hofmannsthal, and Giraudoux have been staged on and off-Broadway, across the country, and in Germany and Japan. He is a four-time fellow of the MacDowell Colony and his writing has also been supported by the Kenyon Playwrights Conference and the Sewanee Writers' Conference, where he was a Walter E. Dakin Fellow in Fiction. He lives in Baltimore and teaches dramaturgy at Swarthmore College. Visit him at www.jamesmagruder.com.

CPSIA information can be obtained
at www.ICGtesting.com
Printed in the USA
FFOW03n1658160516
24130FF